POWER LUST

STEPHEN ROSS

BLACK PARROT BOOKS
San Diego, California

2016 Black Parrot Books Paperback Edition.

ISBN 978-0-9970876-2-8 (eBook)
ISBN 978-0-9970876-1-1 (paperback

Library of Congress Control Number: 2016903101

With love always to my kids,
Alexandra and Eliot

Special thanks to my friend Dennis Morrison for his editing assistance and to my sister Lou Ann Patterson for being my beta reader.

Nearly all men can withstand adversity, but if you want to test a man's character, give him power.

~ Abraham Lincoln

PROLOGUE

Beethoven's *Moonlight Sonata* flowed gently from the overhead speakers as the gurney carrying the small boy's body, head encased in bandages, was wheeled from the operating room.

Dr. Peter Lawrence carefully removed his surgical gloves, protective eyewear, face mask, cap, gown, and shoe covers before dabbing sweat from his forehead. It had been a grueling ten-hour surgery, and he was intently focused the whole time. It took a minute for his vision to adjust to distance and the absence of the surgical microscope. He could feel the fatigue winding its way through his body. His legs ached, his arms felt like dead weights hanging from his shoulders, and pain shot through the muscles at the back of his neck. The five hours of sleep he'd managed on the couch in his office before beginning the last surgery had worn off long ago. He kept going on adrenaline and the extreme concentration necessary to work on the human brain.

His world-renowned skill as a neurosurgeon had saved yet another life. The five-year-old boy had survived, although he probably would never regain full use of his right arm and leg. There was nothing Dr. Lawrence could do about that. The bullet had caused too much damage. The child was lucky to be alive. Another innocent victim of the senseless drive-by gang violence that too often rocked the neighborhoods of urban America.

Peter exited the operating room to the usual kudos from colleagues that always followed a successful procedure. "Great job, Peter." "That was incredible, Dr. Lawrence." "Way to go, buddy." He smiled and humbly acknowledged each of his admirers. For all his brilliance and prominence in the medical community, Peter was a genuinely humble man. He possessed a calm that comes from a true sense of self-confidence. His self-assurance never manifested as ego, and he was genuinely kind to, and interested in, everyone. He knew the first names of the nurses, surgical assistants, maintenance personnel, and hospital grounds keepers: people most of the other docs knew only as nameless cogs in the gears that kept the hospital operating.

Peter's office was on the fourth floor: one floor above the operating room he'd just left. When he got on the elevator, he pushed seven and silently rode to the floor where three of his patients were in various stages of recovery. Although he hadn't been home in thirty-six hours, Peter took a moment to check on each of them, offer encouragement, and see if there was anything they needed.

Assured his patients were OK, Peter returned to the office that doubled as his bedroom away from home. He switched on the desk lamp and collapsed on the couch, rubbing his temples and eyelids to relieve the tension brought on by the combination of surgery and sleep deprivation. He sat in the dimly lit silence and watched beads of water run down the window: the only sign the twenty percent chance of showers in yesterday's forecast had actually materialized. Rare in Southern California.

After ten minutes of solitude, the tension became fatigue. He was tempted to lie down on the couch and catch a few winks before heading home. But he hadn't seen his wife and kids for what seemed like days. The desire to be with his family and sleep in his own bed, with his wife by his side, provided the motivation he needed to endure the twenty-five-minute drive home. He reached for the phone on his desk and pushed the automatic dial button. The voice he loved to hear more than any other answered.

"Hello."

"Hi, honey, it's me."

"You sound tired, sweetie. When are you coming home?"

"Now. That is if I can get my tired bones off this couch and drag them to the car."

"Great. We've missed you."

"Are the kids still up?"

"They're just getting ready for bed, but I'm sure they'll want to wait up to see you. Meredith lost a tooth this morning, and she wants to read her Tooth Fairy letter to you. All evening she's been asking when you're coming home. And Greg got a hundred percent on his spelling, math, and geography tests. You know he'll want to share those with you."

"I'm on my way. Anything you need from the store?"

"I don't think so. Just get your bod home to me. I might even be able to keep you awake for a little while longer. That is, if you're in the mood for some raw sex."

"Oh, baby. I'm outta here."

"Peter."

"What, honey?"

"Be careful. It's raining."

"I will. I love you. See you soon."

"I love you too. Bye."

Peter hung up and looked out the window. The rain was coming down heavier now. Lights from the parking lot cast an eerie orange glow on the walls of his office. The mesmerizing effect of rain and soft light almost convinced him to lie down and make the drive in the morning. But with a burst of fading energy he got up, gathered his dirty laundry and a couple of files, and headed out the door.

The bright light in the corridor caused Peter to squint. He rode the elevator to the ground floor and exited into the cool night. The sudden spatter of rain against his face was refreshing. It revitalized him. Peter stood for a moment, face uplifted, taking in the stillness of the night: a stillness broken only by the gentle splashing of rain. A distant siren cut through the silence and brought Peter back to the moment.

A silver Porsche Boxster was parked in the space marked RESERVED FOR DR. LAWRENCE: one of the rewards for the long hours of medical school and demanding schedule he now maintained. Peter got behind the wheel and waved to the parking guard as he left the lot and settled in for the drive home.

Home was a six-thousand-square-foot Spanish-style mansion on two and a half wooded acres in the hills high above the lights of Los Angeles. It was built by a famous movie star in the 1940's and subsequently owned by a parade of *who's who* of the movie industry. Peter bought the estate from a film producer who decided the action of Aspen, Colorado, was more suited to his extravagant, cocaine-laced lifestyle. On a clear day, you could see Los Angeles and its various suburbs to the south, the San Fernando Valley to the north, and the San Gabriel mountains to the northeast. At night, the city lights were breathtaking. The grounds were home to over two hundred and fifty different forms of plant life: from rare ornamental trees to delicate flowers not found anywhere else in the United States. The pool was huge and shaped like a champagne glass. The original owner apparently had quite a fondness for the old bubbly.

Unaware of the passage of time, Peter found himself driving north on the 405 freeway about a mile from his exit. He fought to stay awake as waves of fatigue surged through his body. He felt as though he was staring into a tunnel as his peripheral vision narrowed to only what was directly in front of him.

Peter flipped on his right turn signal to head for the off-ramp. It was 9:05 p.m. He'd be home in less than ten minutes.

***

"Your Cheatin' Heart" blared from the jukebox in the dimly lit, smoke-hazed room. A thick, hairy hand squeezed Candy Murray's ass as she stumbled off the dance floor of Becky's Bourbon Barn: a haven for long distance truckers from across the country. Candy swatted at the hand but missed. Too many rum and cokes were having their way with her motor skills.

"*Sh*-stop that Wade," slurred Candy. "You gotta start treatin' me like a lady, dammit."

"Aw, come on, honey. Ya know you're my lady."

"Yeah, the one night a month you lay over in this godforsaken hole-of-a-town. I'll bet your wife don't know 'bout me."

"Course she don't. Do ya think I'm stupid? Shit, it ain't easy dealin' with her, especially now with the kid 'n' all. She'd take me for everything I got. Then where'd we be? Gimme time, baby. I'll work it out."

"You been sayin' that for two years now. Seein's believin'."

"You'll see. I promise. Hey, I got a hit the road in a few minutes. Let's get outta here."

Candy killed the last of her sixth rum and coke and checked herself out in the smoked glass wall behind the bar before heading out to the big rig with Wade.

The truck was parked, as usual, next to a row of tall trees at the far end of Becky's parking lot. The cab was bright red with a large chrome grille and blue lettering on the doors indicating it belonged to W. T. TRUCKING COMPANY. The *W. T.* stood for Wade Turner Sr.: Wade Turner Jr.'s father and employer. It was the newest rig in W. T.'s fleet of forty-plus long-haulers that were constantly on the move from one end of the US to the other, carrying everything from cows to cowboy hats. The best part of the eighteen-wheeler for Wade and Candy was the large sleeping compartment at the rear of the cab. It was always the last thing Candy saw before Wade finished with her and headed down the road to God knows where.

"Did ya bring the diaphragm?"

"Hell yes. Don't I always?"

The driver side door of the cab swung open, and Candy climbed up the steps of the motel on wheels. As she reached the last step, Wade noticed she wasn't wearing panties. She never did on these occasions per his instructions. He liked her for that. A firming sensation worked its way to his loins despite a lack of sleep and a beer-induced fog. He reached up and cupped a round, white cheek in each hand. Candy swatted at the hands and missed again, almost falling in the process. Wade steadied her and guided her into the seat behind the steering wheel.

"Come on, Candy. Get your butt in the back. Ya know I ain't got much time."

"When did you ever need any time, Mr. Slam-Bam-Thank-Ya-Ma'am? The last time you took more 'n fifteen minutes was about our second roll in the hay. When was that anyway, Wade? About two hours after we first met?"

"Jus' get in 'n' shut up. I don't need no crap to carry with me down the road."

Candy crawled through the opening that led into the sleeper berth of the cab. She wondered how many other lucky ladies had made the same journey for a special fifteen minutes of Wade's bumping and grunting. It really didn't make any difference though. She knew she'd tame him down once a ring was on her finger. And after all, he'd talked about a wedding ring the last time he passed through town. She just had to be patient like he said.

Candy was half undressed by the time Wade found his way to her side. He unhooked her bra and planted kisses on the back of her neck. She felt goose bumps rise up on her arms and legs. His mustache tickled as his tongue moved from one shoulder to the other. In spite of his crass, tough-guy exterior, Wade possessed a gentle side Candy loved. It was the part of Wade that attracted her to him and made her feel special. Not many men in her life had expressed their gentle side—assuming they had one—in her presence.

Wade moved Candy onto her back as his hands explored her body. The compartment was dark except for a small beam of light that found its way through the slightly ajar door. She could just make out the naked bodies in the girlie magazine photographs that adorned the interior of the mobile bedroom. Candy wondered what Wade did in there when he was alone on his long cross-country drives. She thought it was ridiculous for a thirty-five-year-old man to be so obsessed with those magazines. Maybe all men were like that. She hoped not.

Just as Candy was beginning to feel aroused, Wade's movement stopped amid an eruption of groans and short blasts of air from his lungs. Her breasts were covered with his sweat and a few chest hairs. God it was hot in there.

Candy held her watch up to the thin shaft of light. Six and a half minutes had passed since she entered the sex den—less than half his usual time. She felt cheated and pushed Wade off her as she flicked on the small, wall-mounted fan. Wade didn't say anything. He just laid on his side, totally spent, trying to regain enough strength to get dressed and back on the road.

Candy pulled the cotton dress over her head, checked her makeup in the cracked mirror of her compact, and crawled over Wade to the door. She looked back as she got into the driver's seat, but Wade was fast asleep. She reached to wake him but pulled her hand back. It would serve him right to oversleep and be late for his San Diego drop off. That would teach him to be so selfish in bed. Besides, he probably needed to catch up on his sleep and let some of the beer wear off before getting behind the wheel. Candy slid to the ground and quietly closed the door behind her.

An hour later, the air horn blast from a passing semi jolted Wade out of a deep sleep. He bolted upright, pushing the compartment door open in the process. It was getting dark. *Damn.* Wade squinted to see his watch. It was 8:00 p.m. *Dammit.* He'd have to really hustle to stay on schedule. One more screw up and the old man would boot him out of the business. He was already responsible for the loss of two big accounts. Another one would get him tossed for sure.

Wade yanked up his jeans and buttoned his shirt. *Why the hell did Candy leave me here asleep? She knows I'm on a tight schedule. Shit.* A major headache started to bang its way into the center of his forehead. Just what he needed.

Wade slid into the driver's seat and cranked her up. The big diesel began to rumble. The vibration stirred his sleeping bladder to the realization he had to pee—bad.

He kicked open the cab door and stood on the step. Another truck had pulled in next to him, blocking the view of the bar and highway. He pulled out his member, and for some strange reason found himself trying to write the name Candy in the dirt below.

With his bladder back in control, Wade eased the big Kenworth out onto the highway. His head was now pounding. He prayed there was still a beer in the cooler he kept hidden under the seat. That would relieve the migraine. The same hand that was filled with Candy's large, firm breast a little more than an hour ago flipped the latch to the cooler. It was Wade's lucky day. There was not just one beer, but three. That would definitely get rid of the pain.

He popped the transmission into high gear with his right hand at the same time he popped the tab to beer number one with his left. The cold golden liquid filled his mouth and found its way to his belly. The pain in his head began to dissolve. He wouldn't be able to speed with an open beer in the truck, but at least he'd feel no pain. Wade lowered the windows of the cab to blow out the smell of beer in case he got pulled over. If traffic held up OK, he'd be in San Diego by 11:30 p.m., unloaded by 1:00 a.m., and headed back home shortly after.

It was a cool night with a few scattered clouds that thickened to the south. The weather report indicated he'd be hitting rain in the L.A. area. Wade reached for beer number two. He'd be in L.A. in about forty-five minutes. Even with rain, the traffic shouldn't be too bad at that time of night.

He lowered the windows some more to let in the cool air. It helped him beat back the oppressive fatigue that was again coursing through his body. The oncoming headlights and endless red taillights seemed to blur out of focus. Wade promised himself he'd catch some sleep in San Diego before starting the trip home.

What was he going to do about Candy? He liked her well enough, but the thought of another divorce and not being there to watch his kid grow up was not pleasant. Hell, he'd not be any different with Candy anyway. Once out on the open road, every available skirt would still end up in the back of the cab. What was the use in changing wives? The one he had was pretty, good in bed, and always there when he pulled up after a long stretch on the road. Wade guessed he had it about as good as it would ever get. No, he'd just continue to string Candy along as long as she'd go for it, and when she started bitchin' too much, he'd find a new spot to stretch his legs in that part of the country.

The radio was blaring a Clint Black number as Wade reached for beer number three: the last one until after his San Diego drop. He was on the 101 freeway and just making the turn onto the 405 freeway to San Diego. Up over the rise that divides L.A. from the San Fernando Valley, down into the

L.A. basin, past Long Beach, through Camp Pendleton, and on to San Diego at last. It was 9:03 p.m., and the waves of weariness were relentless. As he reached the top of the rise, the car in front of Wade tapped its brakes. The sudden glow of the red taillights startled him, and he hit the brakes—hard. The remains of beer number three spilled in his lap. As he grabbed for the can, Wade lost control of the truck. He could feel the heavy trailer shift to the side as he fought to regain control. Tires squealed as smoke from the burning rubber blinded drivers to the rear. The cab lurched, and Wade found himself sliding across traffic lanes at a forty-five-degree angle, headed for the center divider. It was 9:05 p.m.

As the truck was catapulted over the concrete divider, Wade caught a glimpse of what looked like a new silver Porsche Boxster coming directly at him with its right turn signal flashing. The Kenworth landed on top of the Porsche with an explosion that resounded throughout the nearby hills.

1

The words rang out strong and clear: inspiring, challenging, praising, and inviting those gathered to celebrate their achievement and launch themselves into the practice of law. No one could have guessed how someone with ties to their school would abuse the responsibility and power conferred by the degree they were about to receive.

Archbishop Tomlinson had just finished blessing those gathered and admonishing the graduates of their responsibility to themselves, future clients, and above all, the Higher Power through whom all things were possible.

California State Senator Maxwell "Max" Johnson was expounding on the importance of our legal system to a free society, and how this group of young lawyers would help shape the political, economic, social, moral, and ethical future for generations to come. No matter what people thought about his politics, Max was a great motivational speaker.

Everyone knew Max Johnson was the fourth choice among the students and faculty to deliver the commencement address. The Speaker of the U.S. House of Representatives, California's governor, and Bill Gates had all respectfully declined the invitation. It was no secret Max Johnson was out of favor with many voters for supporting legislation that encouraged illegal immigration, and sponsoring bills that made it more difficult for California's small business owners to succeed: both important issues for Californians, especially those Max represented in the more affluent 39th Senate district. When the Dean of the University of San Diego School of Law called, the Senator jumped at the opportunity to get on the soap box. He had his staff call all the local television stations, radio stations, newspapers, and specialty rags in hopes of generating favorable press. The election was less than six months away, and he needed all the votes he could muster.

"Dare to dream. Dream big. Find an area of practice you enjoy and excel at it. Find time in your busy career to help the little guy, the less fortunate, the poor. Be moral. Be ethical. Do not let greed and the lure of power deter you from using the degree you receive today to truly benefit humanity. There is more to our existence than amassing wealth and following the well-traveled path." Senator Johnson paused to acknowledge the applause.

The sun beat down causing small beads of sweat to form on his forehead. Max looked at the youthful faces before him and recalled the day when he sat on this same field to receive his juris doctorate degree. That was thirty-two years ago. He was valedictorian of his law school class and had used the very lectern before him to address his classmates. He knew it was the same one because the initials he'd scratched in small letters on the lower right-hand edge were still visible.

The innocent eagerness of this year's crop of new lawyers reminded him of his graduation-day enthusiasm. Where had it gone? Too many court-room battles as a high-powered lawyer. Too many closed-door deals during the past three and a half years as one of California's most controversial senators.

Power mattered to Max. He would never admit that to another living soul, but it was the one thing that kept him motivated, enthusiastic, alive. Sex—at least with his wife—ceased being exciting years ago: a fact known only to himself and Mrs. Johnson. Their interaction at public functions left one with the impression they were as romantically linked as newlyweds. In truth, Max's infrequent sexual encounters over the past many years were both clandestine and pricey.

Was he going to be able to keep his power for a second senate term, and after that as San Diego's mayor or California's governor? He was fifteen points behind his opponent according to recent polls. For the first time in his political career, Max's opposition seemed to have struck a chord with the voters. His less-than-stellar participation in last week's televised debate at a San Diego high school didn't help his ratings: the result of one-too-many martinis the night before, and the night before that, and the many nights before that. Another fact known only to his closest inner circle.

Max was still a handsome man. However, the effects of job pressure, sleepless nights, and booze were beginning to take their toll. Sagging skin under the eyes, often accompanied by dark circles, was nature's way of telling him to slow down, relax.

To make matters worse, his rival was outspending him three-to-one. His fundraising efforts so far had produced thirty percent less than was raised by the same time in the last election. Max no longer had the financial wherewithal that had come in so handy during his first run for office. His family's wealth took a severe beating in the last economic downturn. The result of too many high-risk investments and an inexperienced money manager: a bad combination. Johnson and Associates, the law firm still bearing his name, was not generating the revenue it did when the economy was strong, and Max was the official rainmaker and litigator. His son, Brad Johnson, had run the firm since Max entered politics. Brad was handsome, intelligent, and competent but lacked the drive for greatness.

After winning his first election, Max structured the practice so he would receive seventy-five percent of the net profit, and Brad would receive twenty-five percent. Gross revenues had averaged a million dollars a year for the past four or five years. With a forty percent net profit, Max's annual income from the firm was around three hundred thousand. California taxpayers added an additional $90,000, plus perks. Not bad for most people: but not enough to keep up his affluent lifestyle.

Max thought about all the cash it takes to keep afloat. Given the ungodly alimony payments to Brad's mom, a brain-injured daughter requiring round-the-clock care, and the outrageous spending habits of his not-to-be-outdone wife, Max needed at least twice his current income.

A hot breeze brushed his face and alerted Max to the fact the applause had died.

2

Brad Johnson was staring at the computer Solitaire game he was playing when he heard a knock at his door. A whispered "Damn" escaped his lips. He'd won four of the last five games. He couldn't stop now. He was on a roll. Red three on the black four. *Click*. Another ace. Drag and drop. *Click*. Two of clubs on the ace of clubs. *Click*. There was another knock. Brad clicked on the screensaver so it would give the appearance he was working. "Come in."

Jan Bennett opened the door and entered. She was, to say the least, beautiful. Shoulder-length, dark-brown hair, big smile, high cheek bones, and a perfect figure. Best of all, she was friendly, smart, and not the least bit conceited. Male lawyers endured otherwise boring depositions just to sit across the table from her. Women always checked her out, wondering what they could do to be more like her.

"Hey Brad, have you got a minute? I need to talk to you."

"Sure, Jan. What is it?"

"I'm giving my notice."

"What? How come?" Brad seemed surprised, although no one stayed with the firm long. They soon tired of doing all the grunt work while Brad took up space.

"It's nothing personal," Jan fudged. "You've been good to me. I really appreciate how much you've done. I've gained an incredible amount of legal experience the past two years. You gave me a level of responsibility most beginning lawyers don't get for many years, if then."

Brad asked, "What are you going to do?"

"Start my own practice. My dad has agreed to help me until the cash flow gets going."

"Wow. Is there any way I can get you to change your mind? You're a real asset around here."

"Thanks, but I don't think so. This is something I need to do for myself."

"I can appreciate that. So, when are you planning to leave?"

"There's no big hurry. I've got a lease on some space starting next month. I'll be glad to help get someone up to speed on my cases."

"Jeez, do you know anyone who might be interested?"

"Not off the top of my head, but I'll keep my eyes and ears open."

"Great. I'd appreciate that. Good luck, Jan. Let me know if there is anything I can do to help you get started."

"Thanks, Brad. I will."

Jan left Brad's office and closed the door behind her. Thank God that was over. She'd dreaded telling him ever since she made the decision to move on. At least now she'd be able to put a hundred percent of the profits, if there were any, in *her* bank account. That would beat working her tail off to make money for someone else. Especially when that someone wasn't willing to pull his own weight.

Brad stared at the clock on his credenza. He had to find a replacement soon or be stuck making tedious court appearances and handling what seemed like never-ending discovery. That just couldn't happen. It would have too great an impact on his leisure time—which was most of the time.

He tapped the mouse. Exit screen saver. Hello, Solitaire. Black ten on the red jack. *Click*. Who could he get to replace Jan? He couldn't cut back on his favorite computer game and office pastime. Red five on the black six. He clicked again as the phone rang. *Damn*. Another interruption. Brad answered the phone with an edge to his voice and said, "Yes, Barb."

"Sorry to bother you, sir. There's an Adrian Fitch for you."

"Who?"

"Adrian Fitch. Should I put him through?"

"Yeah, sure."

Barb said, "Here you go," and forwarded the call.

"Hello, Brad here. Yes, sir. That's right. He's giving the commencement speech at his old alma mater. OK. Spell your name for me. A-D-R-I-A-N-F-I-T-C-H. I'll tell him. Thanks for calling." Brad hung up.

Adrian Fitch. The name didn't ring a bell.

3

Tom Davidson watched the breeze push around palm trees in the canyon where he was sitting. A group of caps and gowns clustered around Senator Johnson, eager to speak with him. Tom thought it interesting how people were attracted to power, even when that power was fourth on the list of potential keynote speakers.

Tom was tall, built, with a youthful face. He had an easy way about him. His mellifluous voice retained the slightest hint of a Southern upbringing. A likeable guy.

He completed law school a semester early and took the California bar exam in February. Although certain he'd failed, Tom received the word several weeks ago he was a full-fledged lawyer. It was bittersweet news because his beloved mother died two weeks before the results were published. She fought the cancer for two years so she could attend his graduation, but the seat he'd saved next to him was empty. Sometimes things just don't work out the way we plan in spite of our efforts. It wasn't fair. His mom had raised him since his father died in a car accident when Tom was six months old. She was the source of his motivation and would be forever missed.

The shouts of joy and general chatter of graduates and their families moved Tom from his thoughts. The crowd was thinning as people headed to restaurants, parks, and homes to continue their celebration.

"Congratulations, young man." Tom turned in the direction of the voice. It was Senator Johnson making his way off the field.

"Thank you, sir." Tom rose to shake the hand thrust in his direction.

"I'm Max Johnson. What's your name?"

"Tom. Tom Davidson." A group of flapping, black gowns rushed by, almost pushing the Senator into Tom.

"It must feel pretty good to have this all behind you. I remember how excited I was when I walked off this field a hundred years ago, ready to take on the world."

"Well, I don't know about taking on the world, but yes sir, it does feel good."

"I'm sure. What are your plans?"

"I hope to get a job here in town. I graduated early and luckily passed the February bar. No job yet, just clerking at Benson and Reilly."

"That's a great start. They're a good firm. Bill Benson graduated from USD. He was a year behind me and is a really smart guy. Let me know if I can ever be of help to you."

"Thanks, I will."

Max turned and walked away. He liked the young man he'd just met. Something about his quick smile and engaging manner. Max had a feeling he'd run into him again.

Tom watched the Senator grasp palms, slap backs, smile, and small-talk his way through the remaining crowd. It appeared campaigning was a full-time job for Max. Tom recalled considering the possibility of running for public office someday, but he cherished his privacy and more introverted nature. The thought of giving that up turned his interest away from politics. There's no way he wanted to spend his life attending fund raisers and being hounded by special-interest lobbyists. Besides, it had to be difficult talking out of both sides of your mouth at the same time. No, not for Tom. He wanted to make a difference with his life—without excessive compromise.

Benjamin Harrison Patterson III—Ben to his friends—shook Senator Johnson's hand, then waved to Tom. Ben and Tom were best friends in law school. They took lots of classes together and spent countless hours quizzing one another for exams. In many respects, they seemed to confirm the axiom that opposites attract. Ben was as short and round as Tom was tall and trim. Ben's family was wealthy, whereas Tom grew up in a lower middle-class neighborhood. They did, however, share some significant life experiences. Each lost his father at an early age. Both had an involved, supportive mom.

Ben had clerked for Brown, Backus and Ford during his last year of law school. It was the largest insurance defense firm in San Diego, employing forty-three lawyers and sixty-two support staff, not including the ten clerks that were law students recruited from local schools. It was the latter who did most of the tedious research, document review, and brief and motion writing.

The work could be grueling. His first day on the job, Ben was asked by one of the senior attorneys to prepare a demurrer to a complaint and a motion-in-limine. The former was a method of attacking the plaintiff's pleadings, and the latter an attempt to limit issues at trial.

The completed documents were to be on the attorney's desk by 7:00 a.m. the next morning, with Ben available to make any requested revisions. Ben had thought he was going to have a coronary. He'd never done research for a real firm before. He was just beginning to get the hang of Westlaw on-line legal research and had no idea how the documents he was to prepare were to be organized. The ten-minute briefing by the attorney as he was walking out the door for lunch was of little help. Thank God the firm had an extensive computerized form file comprised of all kinds of legal documents prepared by clerks over the years. Whenever a clerk completed a project, a copy was saved to the form file. That way they didn't have to reinvent the wheel for every new assignment. Fortunately, Ben found an exemplar for each paper he was to prepare. Some of the law cited in those documents was still good and could be inserted into his work.

The experience was a real eye-opener into the world of law. Ben pulled an all-nighter, but he got the documents on the attorney's desk by 7:00 a.m. Of course, the attorney didn't arrive until 8:00 a.m. Ben was lucky no revisions were requested because he had a constitutional law class at 9:00 a.m. that he couldn't afford to miss.

Insurance defense work was, without a doubt, trial by fire. But Ben survived his initiation. He'd worked twenty hours a week the entire school year and still graduated number four out of the one hundred thirty-one students in his class. At twelve dollars an hour, the two hundred and forty dollars a week gave him spending money, and as his mom liked to say, helped build character. He now felt like he could handle just about anything the law could throw at him.

"Hey, bud, congratulations," said Tom, as he extended his arms to give his friend a congratulatory hug. His robe clung to the damp front of Ben's shirt. The slightest heat caused Ben's skin to leak like a sieve.

"Thanks. You too," said Ben, embarrassed by the wet mark on Tom's robe. "What've you been up to? I never see you anymore now that you're a hotshot lawyer."

"They keep me real busy: mostly research, motions, opposition papers, briefs. You know the drill. Sometimes I wonder if name partners ever work."

"Me too. I'm quitting in two weeks so I can prep for the bar. Gave my notice yesterday."

"Good idea. Man, am I glad that's over."

Ben said, "I heard the bar pass rate dropped a couple of points the last exam. Just my luck. They're probably trying to drive more lawyers out of California to reduce competition."

"Don't worry about it. If I passed it, so can you. I think the key is to not make it such a big deal.

Look at it as another law school exam—only long-er."

"Easy for you to say." Then, tipping his head in Senator Johnson's direction, Ben asked, "What did you think of his talk?"

"It was OK. Motivating. But I got the feeling he was trying to create good sound bites for the news."

"You're probably right. Have you ever met his son, Brad?"

"No."

"Nice guy, but I hear he's lazy. I interviewed with him for a clerk job about a year ago. A friend of mine said it's a good place to get experience."

"Are you going anywhere to celebrate tonight?" said Tom.

"Yeah, I thought about going to O'Connor's for one last fling. You wanna go?"

"Sounds good. Shall we meet there about seven thirty?"

"Sure. Hey, maybe we'll get laid. Haha. I've heard most women fantasize about making it with handsome, rotund guys."

Tom gave Ben's shoulder a light push and said, "Get outta here. I'll see you tonight."

Ben watched Tom walk off the field—square shoulders, tall—maybe someday he *would* work out and lose weight. He pulled at the front of his shirt. The wet cloth reluctantly separated from his stom-ach.

4

Tom inserted the key into the driver's door of his light-blue, rust-spotted '69 VW Bug. He twisted it left, then right—nothing. He repeated the procedure several more times before the lock turned and the door creaked open. The duct-taped seat reflected sunbeams in his eyes as he got behind the wheel. Cracked dash, no air, broken radio—he couldn't wait to earn enough money to buy a real car. Twelve dollars an hour as a part-time law clerk didn't provide for any extravagance.

It was 12:15 p.m. by his watch. The grumbling in his stomach reminded Tom he hadn't eaten since lunch the previous day. Regular meals would be another advantage of greater income.

Tom turned the ignition key and the engine popped to life, sounding more like a go-kart than a car. He pulled out of the USD parking lot and headed down Linda Vista Road to Ocean Beach and his favorite eatery, Dum Sum, an all-you-can-eat Chinese buffet, where for three dollars and ninety-nine cents you could gorge yourself on greasy egg rolls, sweet and sour pork covered with a questionable red sauce, tempura shrimp—so read the sign—and a host of other items passed off as food. It was perfect for a law student living on below poverty-level finances. Many was the time Tom and a bunch of friends would descend on Dum Sum for lunch, pig out, and make that the only meal of the day. The place was usually filled with ravenous students trying to save enough on their food budget to afford a six-pack of beer for those rare occasions when they weren't face down in a book.

Tom turned off Sunset Cliffs Boulevard onto Newport Avenue. Dum Sum was a block and a half down on the right. He slowed the car as he looked for a parking spot. It was difficult finding parking on Newport during busy times of the day. As he was approaching Dum Sum, backup lights of an older model Honda Accord flicked on. What luck. Parking right in front. It must be a sign his career was about to take off. Tom eased in and killed the engine.

The usual O.B.—short for Ocean Beach—activity filled the streets. A legless, shirtless Vietnam vet whizzed past on a skateboard: his dirty, gray hair trailing behind in the breeze. Tom wondered what it would be like pushing yourself around on concrete with bare hands. *Did the guy ever fall off?*

As he got out of the car, two bikini-clad sun goddesses strolled by, silicone implants bulging out of tiny fabric patches and pointing the way to the beach. Deep brown, obviously past life's prime, soft pouches of wrinkled skin hung over the front of their thong bottoms. Mother Nature wasn't fooled by the bleached blond hair.

Tom faced the restaurant. Dum Sum had needed a face lift twenty years ago. A gray-black tinted film, replete with alligator cracking, covered the front window. Several holes were present in the brick facade that extended from the sidewalk to a height of about two feet: the names of long-ago lovers were scratched in the bricks. The front door was dirty with remnants of what must have been white paint.

As Tom entered, Johnny Wong threw him a smile from the far corner where he was busy making small talk with a table of regulars. Johnny bought Dum Sum thirty years ago from an uncle who returned to the homeland to be with family and has been a slave to the place ever since. He and his wife, Su Lee, cook, set up, buss tables, and wash dishes seven days a week. Help comes from a never-ending stream of relatives and friends eager to grasp a bigger chunk of the American dream. A dream that never seems to materialize.

Tom headed to the steam tables lining the west wall. The heavy scent of cooked food, sweet and sour sauce, soy, and grease filled the room. After piling his plate with the usual: steamed rice, beef with vegetables, sweet and sour pork, and fried shrimp, he arrived at the cash register. Water was the drink of choice since all beverages, except beer, were a dollar twenty-five. Beer was two fifty. Tom guessed liquid refreshment contributed the most to Dum Sum's profit: that is, if there was any.

A new face appeared from behind the cash register framed by short, curly black hair, dotted with pimples, and flashing buckteeth separated by a space large enough to accommodate a number two pencil. Change was slowly counted. Tom sensed from the way she said, "Thank you," the young cashier was more than willing to accompany him to a movie, for a walk on the beach, or whatever. Although she had a cute personality, Tom decided she was not for him, thanked her, and headed for the only empty table.

He pulled out a well-worn wooden chair and sat down. Bits of rice and traces of sauce dotted the table. Tom used one of his napkins to brush the food from under his tray: a small price to pay for a three ninety-nine all-you-can-eat meal.

Johnny approached, smiling with his hand out-stretched and said, "Tom, my friend. Where you been? I not see you since yesterday. I think you get rich and go someplace else to eat."

"No way, Johnny. I'll be coming here forever," Tom laughed.

Tom and Johnny had become friends over the past three years. Tom even filled in a few times during peak hours when the help didn't show for some reason. It was a great way to get a free meal or two, and Johnny really appreciated it.

Johnny always seemed so happy. Tom admired that. It couldn't be easy spending most of your waking hours working for a modest income and raising a family. He wondered how many of his law school buddies could keep up Johnny's pace and still be smiling.

Dum Sum was a Mecca, and Johnny a saint, to the many street people of O.B. Every evening at 7:00 p.m., an ever-growing number of those less fortunate lined up in the alley behind Johnny's place. The back door would open, and paper plates piled with all the food that could no longer be saved were passed to dirty, wrinkled, sunburned hands. A few near-by business owners and residents had complained to Johnny that his generosity was polluting the neighborhood: but no formal complaints had been filed.

"How's it going, Johnny? Busy today?" asked Tom.

"Yes. It going good. Probably slow down a little now your school out, but summer tourists already start to come." Johnny's English was broken. His strong Cantonese accent demanded greater-than-usual attention from listeners.

"That's good."

"Hey, Tom, congratulations. Your big day today." Johnny reached into his shirt pocket and pulled out a small, rectangular package wrapped in last year's Christmas paper and adorned with a red bow. He handed the gift to Tom.

"Thanks, Johnny. You didn't have to get me anything."

"Sure I do. You my friend. You come through for me many times." Pointing to the package, Johnny said, "Go ahead. You open."

Tom put down his chopsticks and unwrapped the box. Inside was a gold Sheaffer pen. Beaming, Johnny said, "You important lawyer now. Need pen to sign papers."

"Thank you, Johnny. I'll always keep this at my desk."

"You don't forget your friend Johnny when you a big hot shot, OK?"

"Never," Tom replied.

"You find lawyer job yet?" asked Johnny.

"Not yet. I've sent out a bunch of resumes but haven't gotten any positive responses. The job market's pretty tight right now: lots of big firms are consolidating or closing their doors, but I'm sure something'll come along."

"You good man, Tom. You deserve good job. Hey, you know Johnson firm?"

"I don't think so," said Tom. "Where is it?"

"I not exactly sure. Someplace by downtown."

"What kind of work do they do?"

"I don't know, but have you heard of Senator Max Johnson?"

"Sure. He spoke at graduation today. Why?"

"It was his firm. I hear he still involved somehow. His boy, Brad Johnson, in charge, I think. He here a lot. He eat here today. I hear him say something about needing new lawyer. You should check out."

"Thanks, Johnny. I'll do that."

A loud crash near the steam table sent Johnny scurrying away. A boy with the face of a ten-year old was bending over a large pile of rice he'd just spilled. Customers were taking a wide path around the still-steaming mess. Tom could not understand the stream of staccato Cantonese pouring from Johnny's mouth, but his displeasure was obvious. The boy lowered his eyes and rapidly scooped the white mass back into the pan. Johnny headed to the kitchen for a mop.

Tom picked up the chopsticks, pulled them apart, and rubbed the sticks together several times to smooth away wood splinters. By this time his food was lukewarm, but he was so hungry it didn't really matter. Besides, it was always good to talk with Johnny.

He finished the last piece of broccoli from plate number one and headed back to the buffet line for more shrimp and beef with vegetables. The second serving took longer to devour than the first. As his stomach filled, the desire for food dropped lower on Tom's hierarchy of needs. His thoughts began to turn to his desire for fun: something he had not had much of the past few months. An evening at O'Connor's sounded good. He was certain lots of his law school buddies would be there. It would probably be the last time he'd see some of them, at least the ones who were heading upstate or to jobs in other parts of the country.

Tom picked up his plate, chopsticks, napkin, and glass and carried them to the buss tub at the back—something others rarely did. He was considerate that way.

As he reached the sidewalk, the distinct smell of salt water and seaweed turned him west toward the ocean. He'd spent many hours studying on the beach and watching the vast array of humanity parade by. With an afternoon to kill, it was a great time to catch up on one of his favorite pastimes.

5

Max pulled the sleek gray Mercedes into the driveway of his residence. He pressed a remote-control button, causing the large wrought iron gate to open. Resting lions, eyes staring straight ahead, sat atop stone columns on each side of the gate: a practice popular with those in power since Cleopatra's reign. Although the lions could do nothing to deter anyone intending harm, they gave Max a sense of security.

The brick-inlaid drive curved past the front of the house and exited again on the other side of the property: pygmy palms lined the way. A well-manicured, deep green lawn swept from the driveway to the street where a tall, equally well-manicured hedge provided privacy. At the top of the arc, a tile-lined fountain sprayed water while silently laughing mermaids assumed playful poses. The grounds provided a sense of peace. A great place to escape the pressures of politics.

Max set the parking brake and got out of the car. He wondered how much longer he'd be able to hang on to his paradise. By the time he reached the portico, the front door opened, revealing a smiling Sanford Toddman dressed in his usual white from head to toe. Sanford had been the Johnson's butler and all-purpose help for the past twenty years. He defined loyalty.

"Afternoon, Senator."

"Hi, Sandy. How's it going?"

"Pretty well, sir. You?"

"I'm OK. Wish I could get those polls to turn around though."

"I wouldn't worry much about that, sir. You always come out on top in the end. People know you're their friend. Would you like a drink?"

"No thanks, Sandy. I've got work to do in my office. Maybe later."

"Yes, sir. Just give a call if you need me." Sandy disappeared in the direction of the kitchen.

Max picked up mail off the ornate entry table: a ten-thousand-dollar Louis XIV piece the current Mrs. Johnson insisted she could not live without. Bills. More bills. He wondered if they'd ever stop.

"How ya doin', honey?"

Max turned to see his wife, still wearing her long white-satin robe from the evening before, with shoulder-length hair unbrushed and matted to her head.

"You've been drinking again," Max said, disgusted.

"You betcha, babe. How else's a girl supposed to get through all those lonely hours without her big politician? Huh?" Claire slurred.

"You really should get dressed. It's almost mid-afternoon."

"I s'pose. I was hoping ya might be feelin' frisky when you got home. You know, all pumped up from a big speech 'n' all."

Max looked at his wife. At forty she was still in great shape. Her body was one of the main reasons he'd been attracted to her in the first place. Her youthful breasts peeked out from the top of her gown giving her a rather sleazy look Max found arousing.

Claire pressed against him. She looked into his eyes. An impish smile formed on her lips. Max took her in his arms and gave her a long, passionate kiss. It was the first time they'd been so impulsive and spontaneous in months. Claire sensed she was about to be carried up the stairs to the master suite for an afternoon of wild sex. To her disappointment, the press of business, finances, and the polls killed Max's desire as fast as it had been stirred. He let go of her and backed away.

"You bastard." Her right hand struck Max's cheek.

"Claire, I'm sorry. I've got things I have to do."

It was too late. She was already through the door, headed for the liquor cabinet in the family room and another scotch and water on the rocks.

Max touched his cheek. He couldn't blame her for the smack. He deserved it. After all, he hadn't spent any quality time with Claire for weeks— months. Always a call to return, some proposed legislation to read, a plane to catch, a speech to give. Max wondered if being Senator was worth the many sacrifices required of the job. He answered the question as it was forming. *Yes.* He loved the power, the respect, the way people often seemed nervous in his presence. He was shaping the future of the State on a daily basis. What was not to like? Claire would have to learn to deal with the life he provided her.

Max walked down the hall, into his study, and closed the door.

The study was his sanctuary. No one disturbed Max when the door was closed: no one except Sandy. And only to deliver occasional refreshment and urgent messages.

He crossed the room, opened the wood shutters, and for a moment, took in the beauty. The view of his rose garden was spectacular. A landscape architect friend designed it to provide a breath-taking panorama from every corner of the study.

Max was an amateur horticulturist: a love instilled by parents who were ardent gardeners. Roses were his specialty. In fact, he'd developed a new variety that was named after him; an accomplishment he considered right up there with winning a senate seat.

Each day, Sandy placed vases of fresh roses throughout the house. A radiant bouquet graced the table at the center of the study: red, orange, yellow, pink, lavender, and white. Colors blending together. A still life waiting for canvas.

Max dragged his fingers along the corner of his custom-made rosewood desk, then sat down to begin work. The deerskin-covered seat crackled under his weight.

Tomorrow morning, he was scheduled to speak to a group of teachers at the Balboa Park Organ Pavilion. He'd been working on the speech for the past week, but it was only half finished. The concentration just wasn't there. Besides, he was confident of receiving support from educators. They'd been there for him during the first election, and he'd done nothing to offend them. It was the pro-business types he needed to win over. They were pressing hard to unseat him: the result of his support for a measure that increased taxes on companies conducting inter-state business. It wasn't that Max was anti-business at all. He merely compromised his true pro-business beliefs a little in order to gain the support needed to pass his environmental legislation. Always a trade-off. He wondered if it was possible to succeed in politics and stay true to the vision that was the catalyst for seeking public office in the first place. He guessed not.

Public service. What a misnomer. Serving the public had little to do with getting and keeping a Senate seat, or any other elected position for that matter. Compromise. That was the ticket. Do or say whatever was necessary at the moment to get the votes required to win. Steal from Peter to pay Paul. Bend statistics to achieve the desired result. Divide and conquer. Pit various political, ethnic, religious, and socioeconomic groups against one another. Muddy the water, and in the confusion, turn some special interest group's greed into law.

Max knew the general public would be appalled, sickened, and ready to revolt if they knew how big government was run. He wished he could change the system, but his desire was not strong enough to tempt fate and push for real reform.

Reaching for his legal pad, Max noticed the message light flashing on his private line. He pressed the speaker phone button and dialed the message retrieval code. Six new messages: Two from his secretary in Sacramento to confirm speaking dates. One from his long-time friend and closest ally, Senator Braxton, wanting to set a golf outing. Two were hang-ups. And the last one was from Brad wanting to discuss business and, "Oh yes, an Adrian Fitch called, wants you to call him right away." Brad repeated the number Fitch had given him.

Reviewing the completed portion of the education speech, Max pressed the auto-dial button to his secretary. After one ring, she answered with, "Good afternoon, Senator Johnson's office, this is Miriam, may I help you?"

"Miriam, it's Max."

"Hi, Senator."

"I'm just returning your calls about the speaking dates. Go ahead and set those. I'll need a plane out of San Diego for the Berkeley date. See if my buddy Dave Schroeder is up for a house guest that night. If not, book me into the Hilton, same deal as last time. And Miriam, get hold of Braxton and see what he has in mind for a golf trip."

"I'll get on it, sir. How're things in San Diego?"

"Where?"

"San Diego. How's it going? You know, the district you represent."

"Oh, San Diego. I almost forgot—just kidding. Things are fine. I should be back in Sacramento Monday afternoon. Any fires I should know about?"

"Nothing I can't handle."

"That's what I love about you, Miriam. You keep me out of trouble."

"Just doing my job, sir. Glad to help anyway I can."

"I appreciate that. I'll see you in a couple days."

"Sounds good. Good luck with the speech tomorrow. Have a nice flight back."

Max disconnected and pressed the button for Brad's office.

"Johnson and Associates, this is Barb, how may I direct your call?"

"Barb, it's Max, is Brad in?"

"Oh, hello, sir. No, sir, he's out of the office. May I take a message?"

"Do you know where he is?"

"I'm sorry, sir. I don't. He said something about researching a case."

"Just tell him I returned his call. He can reach me at home, or I'll see him at dinner tonight."

"Yes, sir. I'll give him the message."

"Thanks, Barb. How're you doing? I haven't seen you in a while."

"Me? I'm fine. Thanks for asking."

"How's your little girl? Is it Chandra?"

"Yes, sir, Chandra. She's doing great. Starts preschool in the fall."

"My, they sure grow up fast."

"Yes, sir, they do."

"Barb. Brad left a message for me to call an Adrian Fitch. Do you know what that's about?"

"No, sir, I don't know who that is. Wait, a gentleman by that name did call this morning and asked for Brad. I don't know what he wanted, though."

"OK, thanks again. Take care."

"I will. You too. Bye."

Max guessed Brad was either surfing or playing tennis at the San Diego Tennis and Racquet Club. It would not be the first time he'd been told Brad was out doing something on a case only to track him down later on the beach or on the court.

If he could just, somehow, get Brad motivated, focused. They'd both be in a lot better shape financially. What to do? He'd discussed the art of rain making with Brad over and over. He'd taken him to numerous political functions, introduced him to countless people who could send him business, and encouraged him to run for a county bar office. Nothing worked. The firm's gross income was going south, while the cost of staying afloat was headed north. Something had to be done—soon.

6

Wearing shorts and a T-shirt under his graduation robe proved to be a great idea. It not only kept him cooler during the ceremony, but Tom was now appropriately dressed for the beach.

He picked a spot on the sea wall and sat down. The mix of people was incredible.

The beach babes he saw strutting past Dum Sum earlier were now basking in the sun: their beach chairs set at the perfect angle to maximize the effects of the rays. Designer water bottles were stuck in the armrest depressions created for that purpose. One was reading *Glamour* while the other meticulously applied garish-red polish to talon-like nails. Both were trying to appear oblivious to the parade of stares from passing studs. Bimbos in the true sense of the word.

"Got a quarter?" The voice was deep, raspy.

Tom turned.

Before him stood a gaunt man in heated discussion with invisible demons. Arms flailing the air, feet jerking from side to side, dirt encrusted dreadlocks whipping his face with each turn of the head.

"Eat it. You did not. Bastard. I seen it with my own eyes. Git 'im, Jerry. Hahaha. Shithead."

The frenzy stopped. Crazy bloodshot eyes stared deep into Tom. Amused, saddened, and shocked,

Tom reached for his wallet and took out a dollar. A bruised, hairy hand shot out and snatched the bill before it was offered.

The deranged soul moved on. One pant leg missing from above the knee. No shirt. No shoes. The demons were back. A yuppie family passed him, neatly dressed, obvious tourists. The kids stared opened-mouthed and startled while mom and dad tried to herd them to safety.

God. This place was something.

Tom got off the wall and headed down the beach toward the tide pools. There were fewer people at that end: Some kids walking with their parents. A black lab chasing waves. And an elderly couple collecting shells with pants rolled to the knees. It looked peaceful.

Tom found a broad expanse of dry sand, built a sand pillow, and got comfortable. A perfect place for a snooze.

7

The office was quiet except for the occasional closing of a file drawer or the *click click click* of Barb's heels as she walked in the kitchen or file room: the only two rooms without carpet.

It was after 3:00 p.m., and Brad was still not back from lunch. Not an unusual occurrence, especially on Fridays. Jan was sure he was gone for the day. Brad would be too relaxed to bother with work after tennis and a couple of beers. Besides, it was well-known around the firm that one of the bored wives at the club had taken an interest in him. Jan hoped, for the sake of his family, he would give up his philandering behavior.

The paralegal had gone home early to care for her sick child and left Jan and Barb to run the show: not that there was much of a show to run these days. The case load was at the lowest it had been since Jan started with the firm. Thirty-five cases, total. She figured the firm's gross income for the year-to-date was about twenty percent below what it had been at the same time last year. Her estimate was probably pretty accurate since she did the vast majority of the work on all the cases. She was glad to be leaving. Clinging to a sinking ship was not her idea of fun.

Jan was a conscientious lawyer. She communicated with each of her clients at least once every thirty days, even when there was nothing new to report. Her practice of staying in touch with clients was not motivated by a desire to avoid malpractice. Unlike some lawyers, Jan was truly concerned about the people she served and wanted to do her best for each of them. She'd been involved in a fender bender during law school and knew firsthand how frustrating it was to be kept in the dark by your own lawyer. After that experience, she promised herself never to take clients for granted.

Each morning, Barb searched the computer case list for files that had not been reviewed during the past thirty days. Those files were then pulled and placed on Jan's desk for review and a status letter to the client. It was tedious work but critical to maintaining good client relations.

Three files were neatly stacked at the corner of her desk. Jan hoped to complete her review of the files, correct the rough draft of her opposition to a summary judgment motion, and get out of the office by 5:00 p.m. Working all last weekend on a project for Brad had taken its toll. She needed a break.

Jan picked up the top file. It was the Eleanor Davis case. Ms. Davis was one of her favorite clients. A sweet little old lady of eighty-six years, sharp as a Buck knife, never complaining, and always so happy to talk with Jan. Whenever she came to the office, Ms. Davis brought a dozen, just-out-of-the-oven, chocolate chip cookies. She'd learned of Jan's chocolate addiction at their initial meeting. Since none of her own family was still living, Jan was her excuse to bake.

Eleanor Davis had been struck by a car as she walked through a Vons parking lot on her way into the store to buy groceries. The driver of the car backed out of a parking stall without checking to see if anyone was behind her. A broken hip and brain concussion kept Ms. Davis in the hospital for nineteen days: followed by many weeks of physical therapy.

She had tried unsuccessfully to resolve the matter herself and contacted Johnson and Associates the day before the statute of limitations ran out on her case. Because a complaint had to be filed immediately to protect her rights, there was no time to negotiate a settlement with the driver's insurance carrier prior to formally commencing suit.

Not bothering to see if a settlement was possible, the insurance carrier transferred its file to a local insurance defense firm that was notorious for milking cases. There was no way her case would settle before the defense lawyers racked up a few thousand dollars in billable hours doing discovery, much of which was unnecessary.

That's how the insurance defense business worked. The name partners of a firm hire a bunch of green lawyers to churn files at an hourly rate less than most other lawyers charge for similar work. Volume is the key. The result: one or more top lawyers make a lot of money at the expense of the grunts who do the boring, day-to-day practice of law.

Once the defense vultures got hold of a case, you could plan on being in it for the long haul, most likely until just before the date set for trial. Defense lawyers almost always settled before trial. That gave them plenty of billable time without having to do the intense work involved in trying a case.

After a quick review of the file, Jan called Ms. Davis.

"Ms. Davis, hi. It's Jan Bennett. How are you?"

"Just fine, dear. It's so good to hear from you."

"Well, we finally got defendant's interrogatory responses. Nothing new. Pretty much substantiates your description of the accident."

"Oh, good."

"I received interrogatories from defense counsel today for you to answer. I'll review them and get them in the mail to you on Monday. You can call me if you don't understand any of the questions or have any difficulty responding to them."

"OK, I'll do that, honey. Thank you so much for everything you do for me. I couldn't get through this without you."

"It's my pleasure, Ms. Davis."

"How's everything outside work? Any lucky boy caught your fancy?"

Jan laughed. "Not yet. Lots of frogs out there. Of course, a busy career doesn't help."

"I remember how it was. You just keep lookin', deary. Kiss the right frog, and you might get a prince. That's what happened with my Walter, bless him. He wasn't much to look at, but the sweetest man you ever met."

"He was a lucky man to have you. I haven't given up. Mom always says it'll happen when you least expect it."

"She's right."

"Oh, Ms. Davis, I should tell you. I'll be leaving the firm as soon as my replacement is found."

"Oh no." Ms. Davis was clearly upset. "Whatever will you do, dear?"

"I'm opening my own practice. My dad's going to help me out."

"Well, I want you to be my lawyer. I'll be your first client."

"That would be great Ms. Davis, but your agreement is with Johnson and Associates."

"I don't care. You've done all the work on my case. Nobody else knows it, and I think you're a great lawyer. I trust you."

"Thank you, Ms. Davis, but—"

"I won't take no for an answer. You let me know what I have to do to make it official."

"Alright. I'll talk to Mr. Johnson and see what he says. I'm sure we can work something out if that's how you feel."

"It is. You let me know what to do."

"OK, I will. You have a great weekend. I'll call you next week."

"You too. Bye."

Jan hung up the phone. Ms. Davis was the fifth client who had asked her to take their file with her when she left. Brad was not going to be happy about that. But, what could he do? A person has the right to choose their own lawyer. Besides, the Johnson and Associates' contract gave the client the right to terminate the attorney-client relationship at any time upon written notice to the firm. Brad would want to be reimbursed for any costs he'd incurred on the files, and he'd probably want a portion of any fee recovered.

That was fair. Jan could live with that. A part of the fee was better than nothing at all. Every dollar would get her that much closer to independence. Of course, the client would have to approve any fee-splitting arrangement in writing. Maybe she'd get her dad paid back sooner than planned. He could use it. He'd done well as a small-town plumber but helping get her started would pinch him financially. She'd talk to Brad on Monday.

Her phone rang as she reached for the next file. "Jan Bennett, may I help you?"

"Jan, it's Chrissy."

"Hey, girl. How are ya?"

"Up to my eyeballs in contracts. I swear, putting deals together for these people is like walking on loose sand that's always shifting. It's driving me crazy."

Chrissy Patterson and Jan had been best friends since grade school. They grew up in the same small Nebraska town, went off to college together, and decided to become lawyers.

The decision to work in San Diego was mutually agreed upon in high school. Chrissy and her parents had spent Christmas vacation in San Diego during senior year. The die was cast after she told Jan about walking on the beach on New Year's Day in shorts and a summer blouse. Of course, the stories about all the gorgeous guys roller blading shirtless on the boardwalk were factored into the decision.

Chrissy was hired by a big local developer to help its only attorney run the legal department. The so-called legal department was in shambles. Project files were all mixed together: Some were kept at the National City office. Others were stored in San Diego. Portions of some contracts were missing, and others couldn't be located at all. Chrissy often wondered how such a large, successful corporation could stay in business with the records it kept—or didn't keep.

After she'd been on the job about six months, the senior lawyer of five years accepted a more lucrative position in San Francisco. Chrissy was left holding the bag. She'd done a great job getting the business organized, was a shrewd negotiator, very meticulous, and was promoted to head of legal during her first year on the job. Not bad for a kid from the country.

"Well, I did it," said Jan, her voice cautiously excited. "I gave my notice today."

"Good for you, Jan. That's great. How did Brad take it?"

"He seemed to be OK with it. I'm sure he's concerned he may have to do some work if a replacement isn't found."

Chrissy knew Brad, and said, "It would do him good to get involved with the day-to-day firm activity. Who knows, it might motivate him."

"I doubt it."

"Does he even know who's on the client list these days?"

"Not without looking at it."

"Jeez, I swear, if he hadn't been handed that firm, he'd be walking the streets and eating out of garbage cans."

"He's not a bad guy. Just had too much given to him all his life. Takes the drive out of some people. We get along OK. He said to let him know if there was anything he could do to help me get started."

"At least now you'll be able to run the show the way you want. You might as well keep all the profits yourself since you do most of the work anyway."

"I agree."

"Hey, it's Friday. Do you feel like celebrating your new venture? Maybe grab some dinner, drinks, go dancing?"

"Yeah, that'd be great. I should be out of here by five. What's your schedule like?"

"I'm flexible. I was hoping to leave early since it was such a killer week. Why don't I call you later, and we'll work out the details?"

"You're on. Talk soon."

"OK. See ya."

8

Max paced back and forth in his study while rehearsing his speech on improving California's education system. An antique mirror, strategically placed in one corner, allowed him to observe his mannerisms and facial expressions while speaking. No detail was too small when it came to Max's public appearance. Claire often accused him of being obsessive about his image. He would repeat lines over and over again until he found just the right smile or hand gesture to emphasize the point he intended to make.

Sanford was often pulled from his household duties to critique Max's performance. Sanford, in loyal-servant fashion, kept his observations and opinions of his employer to himself. But Max had insisted he drop the servant mentality when it came to acting as speech critic. He was to put himself in the shoes of the average Joe and provide Max with his gut reaction to both the opinions being expressed and the manner of delivery.

Max finished the second complete run-through of his talk and was on his way to the door to summon Sanford when the phone rang. He altered his course and answered the call.

"Max Johnson."

"Senator, it's Barb again. Sorry to bother you at home."

"You're never a bother."

"That guy you asked me about earlier, Adrian Fitch, just called for the second time and said it was urgent that he speak with you."

"Who is this guy?"

"He's apparently with California Affiliated Insurance Network. You know, that insurance company with all the corny late-night TV ads?"

"Yeah, I've heard of them. They write a big chunk of the California auto insurance business. You know, now that I think about it, I believe I met that guy about a year ago at an insurance convention I addressed in San Francisco. I think he owns C.A.I.N. What does he want?"

"I don't know. He just said it was important, and he needs to talk with you. I have his number if you want it."

"OK, shoot."

Barb repeated the number she'd been given.

"Thanks, Barb."

"You're welcome, sir. Bye."

Max pressed the disconnect button but held the phone in his hand. He wondered what favor Fitch was after. There had to be something. It seemed nobody called anymore unless they wanted him to use *his* position for *their* benefit.

Although Max really wasn't in the mood to talk with anyone, Fitch, if he was the guy Max thought he was, had a lot of power in the California insurance community. Max hit the talk button and got a dial tone. He punched in the number Barb had given him.

"Fitch here."

"Mr. Fitch. Max Johnson. I understand you've been trying to contact me."

"Senator. Good of you to call. We actually met about a year ago up in San Francisco."

"Yes, I remember. It was after my speech at the automobile insurers' luncheon."

"I'm flattered you remember."

"What can I do for you?"

The voice at the other end of the line changed from its initial cordial tone to one that was all business.

"Let me get right to the point, Senator. I don't have to tell you you're considerably behind in the polls, and the election isn't that far away."

"Thank you for reminding me."

"I think that problem can be corrected, if you're interested."

"What's your idea?" asked Max, with obvious interest.

"I would prefer to discuss it face-to-face. I don't trust the ability of telephones to keep matters private. I'll be in San Diego tomorrow on business; perhaps we could meet after your speech to the teachers."

"And how did you know about that?"

"Let's just say I'm interested in your career and would like to see you stay in office."

"Well, I appreciate that, Mr. Fitch."

"I'll be staying at the Marriott downtown. Let's plan to meet there at one thirty, but I think it best we not be seen together in public."

"Really? And why is that?" asked Max.

"I'd rather not discuss it on the phone. I'm sure you'll understand when you hear my plan."

"I'm not sure I like the sound of this, Mr. Fitch."

"You will, Senator. Trust me. I'll be in room 2204. Why don't we meet there?"

Max's instinct told him not to trust Fitch. He didn't really know the man. Something in Fitch's voice revealed a dark side, but Max's campaign desperately needed fresh ideas, and he believed Fitch might possibly have the clout and financial wherewithal to help.

"I'll hear what you have to say, Mr. Fitch," said Max, his curiosity gaining the upper hand over his reservations.

"Good," said Fitch. "I'll see you tomorrow."

The click in the receiver told Max that Fitch had hung up. He looked out at his garden and wondered what the man had up his sleeve. As was typical with most plaintiff lawyers, Max didn't care much for the insurance industry. He hated the way adjusters often tried to push accident victims to settle their claims fast and cheap before knowing the full extent of their injuries. But he was a politician now, and those sentiments would not stand in the way of accepting campaign assistance from an industry he once openly loathed.

Max headed out the door of his study to find Sanford.

9

The staccato barking of a long-haired Chihuahua jolted Tom from his sleep. The dog was no more than three feet from his face, and each blast from the little beast went off like a high-pitched bomb. Tom was upright in an instant, but his mind was still trying to find its way back to consciousness. The dog's owner stood looking down at Tom: his Buddha belly pushing its way out from under a too-tight T-shirt emblazoned with a Grateful Dead logo.

"Sorry. You musta scared Muffy," said the dog's human in a high-pitched, rather bitchy voice.

Tom put a sandy hand above his eyes to block out the late afternoon sun and get a better look at the body behind the voice. Dog and owner were already headed down the beach. Tom noticed the satin bow around the dog's neck and its owner's tight black pants that were set off by hot-pink sandals with colorful feathers dancing from the toe straps. Not a pretty sight.

Tom glanced at his watch. It was 4:15 p.m. He'd been asleep over two and a half hours. The back of his body was caked with sand. His T-shirt and shorts were damp from extended contact with the beach. He stretched his neck and low back to work out the stiffness caused by prolonged inactivity. A warm breeze blew off the water as Tom got to his feet to head back home and get ready for a night of celebration.

He needed a drink—bad. His lips were chapped, and his skin felt dry from the combination of sun and wind. He guessed he must be red as a lobster, or soon would be. He stepped from the sand onto the sidewalk and headed back up Newport to his car. As he approached Dum Sum, Johnny came out. One look at Johnny's face confirmed Tom's sun burn suspicion.

"Tom, what happen? You fall asleep on beach? You look like red rose, only maybe not so pretty," said Johnny, a grin spreading from ear to ear.

"Yeah, I did. Guess I needed it. It sure felt good."

"I think you need a drink my friend," said Johnny, as if he could read Tom's mind. "What your pleasure? Lemonade? Diet Coke? Iced tea? You name it. It on me, Mr. Lawyer."

"You are too kind, Johnny. I'd love an iced tea."

"You got it, my friend. Come in, help yourself."

Tom entered Dum Sum, got his drink, thanked Johnny, and drove home.

10

Jan finished typing her final client status letter for the week. She was as caught up with work as a lawyer could expect to be and ready for a weekend. She retrieved the watering can from under her desk, added a pinch of Miracle-Gro, filled it with water, and gave each plant in her office its weekly drink. Although her thumb was not particularly green, the plants had been thriving for two years. Thank God for plant food and the small window in the south wall of her office.

Jan grabbed her brief case and flicked off the light as she headed for freedom. Barb was still at her desk inputting client billing information and filing the pleadings, discovery, and correspondence received in the day's mail.

"What's up for the weekend, Barb?"

"Not much. Chandra's going to her daddy's tonight. I'm picking her up at noon tomorrow, and we'll probably go to the zoo. I won two free tickets a couple weeks ago from KGON when I was the first caller to guess the year the Beatles first appeared on The Ed Sullivan Show."

"Gads, how did you ever know that? It happened way back in the sixties, I think."

"February 1964 to be exact. I only knew it because my dad recently mentioned it during one of his memory strolls down rock and roll lane. He does that all the time. To listen to him, you'd think the only good rock happened in the fifties and sixties."

"Well, you have to admit, some pretty good music did come out of that era."

"That's true."

"Congrats on the tickets. That's pretty cool."

"Thanks. What's up with you this weekend?"

"Chrissy and I are going out tonight, probably dinner and drinks, maybe dancing."

"Sounds fun. Have a good one. I'll see you Monday."

"You too, Barb. Lock the door after me. You're here alone."

"OK. See ya."

"Bye."

Jan caught herself smiling as she walked across the parking lot to her car. She felt a sense of relief now that her notice was official. The drive home was filled with thoughts of decorating her new office, computers, printers, fax machines, and the legal software she'd need to get her office up and running. Exciting thoughts.

Ten minutes after leaving work, Jan pulled her Camry into the garage of her condo located in the Point Loma area of San Diego. It was about five miles from work and an easy commute. Thanks to down payment help from her dad, Jan was able to buy the one-bedroom unit she'd called home since starting work as a lawyer. It was perfect. A rustic ten-unit building on a Jacaranda-lined street one block from a secluded beach as yet undiscovered by tourists. Jan inhaled the briny scent of the sea as she unlocked the door to her home.

Chrissy's voice could be heard on the answering machine as Jan entered the living room. She ran toward the phone, but the message ended before she'd taken her third step. Kicking off her heels, Jan hit the speed-dial button that connected her to her friend.

Chrissy answered. "Hey, buddy. I just left you a message."

"I know. I caught the end of it when I walked in. What's up?"

"What do you think about grabbing some wine and dinner at O'Connor's for old time's sake? I haven't been there since we graduated. We could check out the latest batch of law school studs, if you're so inclined. The Verigolds are playing there tonight. I've heard they're an awesome indie rock band."

"Sounds great. But I don't know about checking out the studs. I'm really not into that."

"Yeah, right. And the Pope isn't Catholic."

"Alright. Alright. You win. Maybe I'll look, just a little. What time works for you?"

"Why don't we meet there at seven thirty?"

"Super. That'll give me time to take a bath and relax a bit. What are you going to wear?

"Something casual. I've dressed up enough this week. O'Connor's dress code is shorts and a T-shirt. Anything more and you're overdressed."

"You got it. See you there."

"OK, bye."

Jan hung up and headed to the bathroom, executing a perfect pirouette on the way. The ceramic tile floor felt cool against her bare feet. A hot soak was the quintessential elixir for stress. She turned on the tub faucet, added a generous dose of jasmine-scented bath crystals, and adjusted the water temperature to just on the tolerable side of hot. As the tub filled, Jan slipped out of her suit, lit a candle, grabbed the latest copy of *Architectural Digest*, and let her body slide slowly under the steamy surface of the water.

11

Tom's apartment building was located on the side of a hill below the University of San Diego campus. It was a nondescript two-story structure with a view across Mission Valley to Presidio Hill: the site where Father Junipero Serra and a group of Spanish soldiers established California's first mission and presidio. Each unit had a bedroom and bathroom with a small combination kitchen, dining room, and living room. The furnishings were cheap. Tom's carpet was worn thin and separating at the seams. It was the least expensive housing he could find when he started law school three years ago. On the upside, its proximity to the school meant Tom could walk to classes. The money saved had been used to buy books and food.

Dorothy "Dot" Harmon managed the Vista Isle apartments. It was a job she had performed since the building opened twenty-one years ago. It was Dot who reviewed the first rental application, performed the credit check, and accepted the deposit and first month's rent checks from a first-year law student whose name had long ago faded into the depths of her memory. Dot preferred renting to law students. She figured they were too busy with book learning to cause her much trouble. She was probably right. Over the years, most of the late-night parties and San Diego PD visits had involved the few undergrads to whom she'd made the mistake of renting.

Dot liked Tom from the moment he knocked on her door in response to the FOR RENT sign she'd propped in her window. He was polite, always willing to help with odd jobs around the place, and his looks were pretty easy on her eyes too. Not that she could do anything about it. She was old enough to be his grandmother. The years of smoking, too much sun, and an abusive husband had long ago erased the fairness of her youth. She was left with thinning, gray hair, a weathered face, and a jagged front tooth. The latter a testament to her now-deceased husband's drunken rages. Nevertheless, when it came to Tom, she still enjoyed an occasional mental dalliance.

Tom waved as he pulled into the parking space next to the building entrance where Dot was sweeping. She leaned on her broom as Tom got out of the car.

"Dot, you work too hard."

"Don't I know it? How was graduation?"

"Hot. I'm glad it's over. All I need now is a real job so I can get on with my life."

"Any prospects out there?"

"Nope. Although a friend of mine mentioned a firm he thought might be hiring. Ever heard of the Johnson law firm?"

"Can't say I have. That don't mean nothing though. I don't run with the lawyer crowd."

"I'll keep you posted on my progress. See ya later, Dot," said Tom, as he patted her shoulder and headed to his apartment.

Tom opened all the windows to get the air circulating and blow out the odors that seeped from the carpet and drapes. The condition of the apartment confirmed his bachelor status and the absence of a female in his life. The off-white walls were bare except for an unframed poster of an old woody that hung off-center above a drab-brown sofa. Tom found the poster in a dumpster behind his building the day he moved in. It reminded him of the beach and his dream of learning to surf. He'd meant to get more art for the walls, but the demands of law school and a tight budget resulted in his austere decor. Numerous books lined the wood shelves opposite the sofa. A small television with its antennas extended was wedged between the books. It received four or five local channels: enough to catch the news or a mindless sitcom on those occasions when he was too burned out to study. Cable TV was a luxury he hoped to acquire as soon as he landed a real job. The kitchen sink, as usual, was stacked with dishes waiting to be washed. A dishwasher may have alleviated the problem, but Tom doubted it. He had been plagued since childhood with a condition his mother diagnosed early on as *dishphobia*. He knew of no cure and was in no hurry to find one.

Tom pulled off his T-shirt as he headed to the shower, pausing long enough to open an almost-empty jar of peanut butter and spoon out a mouthful. It had been his primary source of protein for the past three years. He took a long, hot shower that was momentarily interrupted when the tenant above turned on her water to draw a bath. She was a beautiful and brilliant second year law student. Tom had talked to her a couple of times in the parking lot but never asked her out. As he waited for another burst of hot water, Tom gazed at the ceiling and wondered what she must look like sitting directly above him, naked.

Tom stepped out of the shower, toweled off, pulled on his shorts, and plopped down on the bed to review a file he'd brought home from work. He usually left work at the office, preferring to keep business separate from other aspects of his life. But the managing partner had handed him the file as he was getting on the elevator to leave and requested a status report by 9:00 a.m. Monday morning. The file had slipped through the cracks, and the adjuster handling the case was demanding an update. Slipped through the cracks meant other matters were heating up so that this case—and probably many others—had been relegated to the back burner. It was vital to get the report out without further delay. The carrier involved represented nearly thirty percent of the firm's entire book of business. Lose that carrier, and there would be attorneys and support staff looking for jobs.

Tom was familiar with the file spread out on the bed next to him. It alleged defects in the construction of a one hundred-forty unit condominium development. The complaint listed numerous problems with the construction, including improperly installed drywall. The firm's client was a small drywall subcontractor who had hung drywall in five of the units. The builder's attorney refused to dismiss the action against the client even though no drywall problem had been identified in those five units. Tom found that typical of construction litigation. The plaintiffs' lawyer would sue the builder, who would in turn sue everyone who had any involvement in the project. Once entrapped in the web of litigation, a party didn't get out of the case until settlement money was squeezed from its insurance carrier. The lawyers knew it boiled down to economics. Resolving a lawsuit became a business decision. It was usually less expensive for a defendant to pay something to get out of a case than to incur the legal fees and costs of vindication through trial. The latter could be very costly. The expense, combined with the possibility of an erratic jury ignoring the evidence and finding for your opponent, or an ill-prepared lawyer blowing your case, resulted in approximately ninety-eight percent of all cases being resolved short of trial. One of Tom's professors used to say we have a legal system, not a justice system. In other words, our system of laws was designed to resolve conflicts. Sometimes justice was served in the process: sometimes not.

12

Tom was surprised by the number of people waiting to get into O'Connor's as his Bug sputtered to a stop with a shotgun-like backfire. He reached down to the passenger's side floor as though searching for something and waited for a ten count to give the crowd time to resume chatter and stop staring his way. Sensing he was no longer the center of attention, Tom sat up and pushed the door open to get out. As he stood, the window crank fell off and into the dirt. Thankful no one noticed, he picked it up, pushed it back into place, and headed toward the mass of Friday-night revelers.

Tom saw a hand waving above the sea of heads and recognized Ben standing near the back of the line. He changed course and joined his friend, grateful for the jump-start to the club entrance.

"How long have you been here?"

"About ten minutes. I came a little early because I thought it might be crowded tonight."

"Good move. I don't think I've ever seen the place this packed."

As Tom surveyed the crowd, his gaze was stopped by the profile of the girl standing directly in front of him. He knew that face: the bright blue eyes, full lips, and perfect smile. It was Jan Bennett. She was the first person he saw when he entered the law school building at the start of his first year. The moment was indelibly etched in his mind. He'd glanced to his left as he walked through the front door and saw her standing about half way up the curved stairs to the second floor. She'd looked in Tom's direction long enough for their eyes to meet and to flash her incredible smile before disappearing from view. Although they spoke a few times during the year, Tom never asked her out or made any move to advance the relationship. In addition to being busy with school, Tom was a little intimidated by the fact he was a first-year student, and Jan was in her third year. When the school year ended, Jan graduated and disappeared into the world of work.

Now there she was again, standing two feet in front of him. She looked so beautiful. He'd heard from a friend that Jan was still in San Diego but had no idea where she lived, worked, or her relationship status. Tom had only dated two significant girl-friends. One during his senior year in high school that ended when she left to attend Syracuse University. The other in his junior year at college that he broke off when he found out she was seeing her philosophy professor on the side.

Tom felt his pulse quicken as he watched Jan talking to the girl next to her.

"Tom, you OK?"

Ben's voice brought Tom back to the moment.

"Yeah, fine," Tom replied, as he tipped his head in Jan's direction.

"Oh, got it," whispered Ben.

Just then, Jan turned toward Tom, and their eyes met. A moment's pause, then recognition as she flashed that gorgeous smile, her blue eyes sparkling. "Tom, it's so good to see you. How are you?"

She remembered his name. Tom wasn't sure she ever knew his name. "I'm great. It's good to see you too. What are you up to?"

"Mostly work since graduation. What about you?" said Jan, her gaze still fixed on Tom.

"I finished early, took the bar in February, and have been clerking while waiting for the results. I passed, and now I'm looking for a real job."

Remembering she was with Chrissy, Jan said, "Oh, Tom, this is my friend, Chrissy."

"Hey, Chrissy. I remember you. You guys were in the same class." Putting his hand on Ben's shoulder, Tom said, "This is my good friend Ben. We were in the same class together too."

Jan said, "Hi, Ben," as she reached to shake his hand. "I remember seeing you guys hanging out together in the first-floor lounge."

"Yeah, we did that a lot first year," said Ben.

Chrissy said, "Good to see you again, Ben."

Ben shook Chrissy's hand and said, "You too."

The evening was warm, and a gentle breeze moved inland off the Pacific. The sinking sun painted the sky a brilliant reddish-gold as far as the eye could see. A few billowy clouds added drama to a scene as perfect as any nature had ever created. The scent of jasmine filled the air from a hedge surrounding the parking lot: punctuated by designer perfume.

Tom was about to ask Jan and Chrissy if they came to O'Connor's often, when the doorman walked down the queue and stopped about ten people in front of them. He said the place was full, and no more people would be let in until those inside left. He estimated it would be about thirty minutes before the next group could enter. A simultaneous groan arose from the crowd.

"Aw, man, I'm hungry," said Tom, in response to the news. Jan, Chrissy, and Ben concurred. Tom continued, "I don't know if I want to wait. I've heard the band is really good, so it's possible most people will stay, in which case, we may not get in at all."

"I have an idea," said Jan. "How spontaneous are you guys?"

Everyone indicated they could do spontaneity.

Hearing a unanimous response, Jan said, "I gave notice at my job today and am opening my own practice. So, in celebration, if you're all up for it, I'll pick up some fire wood, a couple bottles of wine, and Kentucky Fried Chicken. We can eat on the beach around a fire. My treat."

"Let's do it," said Chrissy.

"I'm in," replied Ben.

Tom responded with, "Me too."

"Why don't you all leave your cars here? I'll drive and bring you back later," said Jan.

With that, they all walked to Jan's car, got in, and headed for the grocery store and a KFC.

13

The distinctive aroma of the Colonel's eleven herbs and spices permeated the car as Jan pulled into the parking lot near the small Shelter Island beach. It was the closest beach where fires were allowed, and fire rings provided. Dusk painted the sky as the lights of the city and Coronado Bridge punched holes in the dark.

They were in luck. The far-right fire ring was open. A group of teenagers danced and chased one another around a huge blaze in the far-left fire ring. About two dozen people were gathered next to the ring near the teenagers. It looked like a religious meeting of some sort. As they stood facing the water with heads bowed, a man in a baggy white shirt and drawstring pants was speaking: his arms upraised, palms open, and face to the sky. The rest of the group repeated some unintelligible phrase in response to their leader's words. Two small groups of what appeared to be close family members and friends were enjoying a fire and potluck dinner around the remaining fire rings. It was nice to have the family groups separating them from the teenagers and religious folks.

"This is really cool," said Ben, as he got out of the car. "I never made it to Shelter Island the whole time I've been in San Diego. I heard about it but just never got here."

"I found it a couple of years ago after I moved to Point Loma. It's a great place to run and clear your head after a long day at work," said Jan.

Tom said, "I read an article about Shelter Island in the *Reader* a couple months ago. It's not an island at all. It's connected to the mainland by a narrow strip of land that was a sand bank in San Diego Bay. It was built up into dry land around 1934 with sediment dredged from the bay, and developed in the 1950s with the hotels, restaurants, marinas, and public park that are here now."

"My, aren't you a wealth of San Diego knowledge," teased Chrissy.

"Not really. I happened to read the article. For some reason I remembered it."

Tom grabbed the two bundles of firewood, Ben picked up the bags of KFC, and they headed down the bank to the beach. Chrissy retrieved the wine, opener, and plastic cups from Jan's trunk while Jan shook out the old blanket she kept in her car for just such an occasion.

"Gads, Tom is cute," whispered Chrissy, "I saw the sparks between you two back at O'Connor's. This could prove to be a more eventful evening than we planned."

"Yeah. And the best part is, he's a nice guy," said Jan, as she closed the trunk.

They joined the boys and began spreading out the blanket near the fire ring. Tom had opened one of the bundles of wood and stacked several pieces in the center. He turned to the girls and asked if either had a lighter and something to start the fire.

"Darn." said Jan. "Wait. I think I have an old newspaper in my trunk. I'll check."

"And a lighter?" asked Tom.

"No, no lighter. But I bet we can get some matches from Humphreys across the street," said Jan, as she headed to the car for the paper.

"I'll run over to Humphreys and see what I can find," said Tom.

"Hold up," said Ben, "I'll come with you."

Tom sprinted up the bank as Ben did his best to keep up. The knowledge that two gorgeous girls might be watching him seemed to help propel Ben up the bank with less than normal effort. They walked through the parking lot, across the street, and into Humphreys.

Humphreys was a hotel, restaurant, bar, and for many years, one of San Diego's top music venues. Ringo Starr, Stevie Wonder, America, and many others performed there during the summer concert series.

Two young girls greeted them as they approached the front desk. Music blared from inside the bar as a local rock 'n' roll band did it's best to wow the after-happy-hour crowd. Tom explained their dilemma to the girls, and he and Ben were each handed a small box of matches with the Humphreys logo emblazoned across the top. They thanked the girls, worked their way through a small crowd that had gathered inside the lobby, and headed out the door.

The bucket of chicken, box of biscuits, and containers of coleslaw and mashed potatoes were open and placed in the middle of the blanket when Tom and Ben returned. The girls had opened a bottle of Merlot and were sitting on the blanket sipping wine and reminiscing about their law school days. A harbor cruise boat inched its way out of the harbor toward the tip of Point Loma while passengers milled about the decks taking in the city lights. A harbor seal could be heard barking in the distance: complaining because another seal had stolen its spot on one of the buoys that marked the channel. Tom lit the paper Jan had placed under the fire logs. He and Ben each grabbed a corner of the blanket and poured themselves a glass of wine.

"Tom, you said you're looking for a job, right?" asked Jan, as she reached for a piece of chicken.

"Yeah, I am. Why?"

"Any interest in litigation?"

"Sure. That's what I was hoping to find."

Jan continued, "I told you I gave notice today. Well, my boss wants to find a replacement—fast. It's not the greatest pay, but you'll get to handle cases from intake through trial. A lot more freedom to manage your own cases than most beginning lawyers get at the big firms. You'll get to do more than research, prepare motions, propound discovery, and take depositions."

"Sounds interesting. What's the name of the firm?"

"Johnson and Associates."

"Is that Senator Johnson's firm?" asked Tom.

"Yeah. He started the firm, but his son, Brad, has run it since the Senator entered politics. Why, do you know it?"

"It must be an omen," said Tom, as he reached for another piece of chicken. "The Senator spoke at graduation today and told me to let him know if he could ever be of help. Then, the owner of the restaurant where I had lunch told me he heard Brad Johnson say he needed to find a new lawyer. Now you."

"If you want, I'd be happy to put in a good word for you with Brad. I'm almost sure he'll hire you if you want the job."

"Thanks. That would be great."

Jan handed Tom her card and said, "Why don't you call me Monday morning and I'll see what I can do?"

"You're on. Thanks again."

The four of them spent the rest of the evening in idle conversation with topics ranging from favorite books, to childhood memories, to law school professors, to work, and favorite pastimes. The religious crowd left after an hour. The teenagers got louder as they consumed more alcohol. The family groups settled in on blankets and beach chairs. A few people walking dogs, and an occasional jogger, passed by on the sidewalk above the beach. A white barn owl swooped low over the beach in search of a meal. Chrissy remembered that she'd read where some people believe aliens appear in the form of a white owl.

Tom liked Jan and sensed the feeling was mutual. He hoped so. They downed the last of the wine as the fire settled into quiet, glowing embers.

After they discarded the trash and loaded the car, Jan drove everyone back to O'Connor's. It had been a good night.

14

As expected, the speech before San Diego's teachers was well received: interrupted by applause, cheers, and banner waving. It ended with the crowd chanting, "Reelect Max. Reelect Max. Reelect Max." Mass adoration was a heady experience, and Max had been addicted to it since first running for office. As the momentary euphoria died, Max wondered if he would have been greeted with the same enthusiasm by a group of small business owners. Not everyone believed a shorter work week, the expansion of already generous benefits packages, and ever-escalating business taxes was the way to expand California's economic base, improve its infrastructure, and regain its status as a leader in education. In fact, polls showed most business leaders and small business owners believed just the opposite. Max was inclined to agree with the pro-business group, but California was a left-leaning state, and his reelection chances dimmed substantially without support from the liberals.

Max walked to his car in the company of several board of education members and an old law school buddy who had come to say hi. After promising to look into some local school district concerns and saying his goodbyes, Max got in his car and drove out of the park, onto Laurel Street, and to his meeting with Adrian Fitch. The day was warm and sunny, and the tree-lined canyons were so inviting that he was tempted to pull over and spend the rest of the day wandering the vast expanse of Balboa Park. How long had it been since he'd done something that spontaneous? The press of business, however, and the lure of Fitch's reelection insinuation kept Max driving in the direction of the Marriott.

As he pulled up to the harbor-side hotel, Max was greeted by several young, smiling faces eager to park his car and collect a small ransom when he returned to retrieve it. A handsome surfer-looking kid opened his door and handed him the claim ticket needed to get the car back. The valet must have recognized him because he said, "Welcome to the Marriott, Senator," as Max got out of the car and grabbed his suit coat.

Max entered the hotel and didn't recognize anyone as he walked to the elevator. After a few seconds, the elevator doors opened, and an attractive couple in their mid-fifties emerged wearing swimsuits. They looked like tourists. Max stepped inside and pressed the button marked twenty-two. The ride up was fast. Max's curiosity increased as he knocked on the door to room 2204.

As he raised his hand to knock again, the door opened, revealing a large man in white tennis shorts and shirt. He was tamping sweat from his forehead with a hotel towel while clenching a fat cigar between his teeth.

In a voice raspier than Max remembered from the telephone conversation, Fitch said, "Senator, good of you to come. Please, come in and have a seat. Can I get you a drink? I'm gonna have a martini, dry."

As he sat down on a sofa facing the vast Pacific, Max replied, "No. Thank you. I can't stay long."

Fitch proceeded to mix his drink while Max sat in silence. With his back still to Max, Fitch said, "Please understand that anything we discuss here is strictly between you and me. I've not shared my idea with anyone and don't plan to."

Max said, "Sounds clandestine."

"It is." The tone in Fitch's voice was serious and cold. The smile dropped from Max's face as his hand tensed on the arm of the sofa.

"You may have heard about an accident that happened up in L.A. on the 405 about two months ago. A prominent surgeon was on his way home to his wife and kids when a semi jumped the center divider and landed on his Porsche. The poor guy lived in intensive care for three weeks then died with his family at his bedside. The hospital bill alone was over two hundred thousand dollars, and the decedent was one of the highest paid neurosurgeons in the country."

"That's a shame. But what does that accident have to do with me?"

"Nothing. Absolutely nothing. But it could make the difference in your winning or losing the election," said Fitch, his voice deep and gravelly.

"Really?" said Max, a tinge of sarcasm in his voice. "And how's that, Mr. Fitch?"

"Please, drop the Mr. Fitch. Call me Adrian."

"Fine, Adrian. Please enlighten me."

"Remember, Senator, what I'm about to tell you is only between you and me. Should anyone suggest I ever did anything improper, the headlines would not be good for your campaign."

"Are you threatening me, Fitch?"

"Not at all, Senator. I just want to make myself clear. Our conversation is not to be shared with anyone outside this room."

"Get on with it, Fitch. You've got thirty seconds."

"Let's not get testy, Senator. I truly am interested in helping your reelection effort." The voice remained calm, clearly not intimidated by Max's political clout. "Now, about that accident. The truck that killed the good doctor was owned by an outfit out of Fresno. The driver of the truck, Wade Turner, is the son of the owner. Mr. Turner had a .18 blood alcohol level at the time he lost control of his rig."

"Get to the point, Mr. Fitch," said Max, his irritation level rising.

"It so happens, Senator, my company provides liability coverage to that trucking company to the tune of twenty-two million dollars."

"So what?" snapped Max.

"There's more. I also happen to live next door to the doctor's widow and two lovely children. She and my wife are good friends. We sometimes have dinner together, play tennis, that sort of thing."

"If you've got a point to make, make it," said Max, his patience strained. He hated people who wasted his time. He had thought Fitch might be one of those people, and yet, something about his directness—his I'll take shit from no one attitude—

appealed to Max. Besides, Fitch did say something about the accident making or breaking Max's reelection bid. That was enough to hold his ear.

"I had a little chat with the grieving widow the other day. You know, neighborly stuff over the garden wall. She mentioned she was looking for a lawyer to handle her wrongful death case and asked me if I had any suggestions. I guess she's not aware of the connection between the trucker and me. She made an initial inquiry with Braden and Welker up in L.A. They're a big PI firm out in the valley, mostly assholes. Anyway, I thought your firm might be able to use the business. A third of the potential settlement money could buy a lot of reelection sound bites." Fitch paused.

There was a strained silence as Max stared out the window, focusing on the white dot of a sailboat working its way toward the safety of the harbor. Fitch imagined the wheels whirring in Max's head. He could almost feel the flex of Max's jaw as he clenched his teeth while calculating that his cut could be well into seven figures. That kind of money would go a long way toward making up for the decrease in campaign contributions. It might even be enough to fund an ad blitz just before the election and give Max the numbers he needed to retain power.

"So what's in this for you, Fitch?" Max asked, knowing full well an offer like that was not going to be presented without a catch.

"You, Senator. Just you."

"And what's that supposed to mean?"

"It means you use your influence as chair of the Senate Standing Committee on Insurance to pave the way for legislation beneficial to companies like mine. Very simple."

"Bribery's a felony. Do you know that, Fitch? You could spend several years in the slammer for what you've just suggested."

"Bribery? What bribery? We're simply discussing a business proposition. I don't believe there's anything illegal about that now, do you, Senator?" Fitch sounded sure of himself. He was obviously comfortable operating in the shadows. The result of years of under-the-table business dealings.

Max wondered how many times and in how many ways Fitch had screwed his insureds and employees. One thing was certain: Fitch was a big risk taker and a dangerous man. Max's gaze returned to the sailboat with its white sails racing the wind. It looked so peaceful, innocent, and carefree. He noticed the light-gray silhouette of a Navy destroyer that was rapidly bearing down on the tiny boat. Max, an analogical thinker by nature, envisioned himself as the sailboat and the destroyer as the upcoming election. Would he be sunk or take the action necessary to avoid disaster and retain his power?

Turning his attention to Fitch, Max asked, "So, just how does this plan of yours work?

"It's not complicated. I convince the aggrieved widow, Jillian Lawrence, that Johnson and Associates is the best firm to handle her case. Your son, Brad, receives a call from her inquiring about representation and gets her to sign a contingency fee agreement. The agreement provides for a forty percent attorney's fee if a lawsuit is filed. Brad does some basic written discovery: medical records, police report, income documents. That sort of thing. He makes a policy limits settlement demand which is rejected and then files a complaint. My company's in-house legal will handle the defense, with me supervising. Brad takes the depositions of Mrs. Lawrence and the truck driver before pressing for settlement again. This time, the policy limits are offered and the case settles. It's a win-win for everyone. Mrs. Lawrence gets her money, Brad makes more than he ever dreamed possible, and you wind up with several million dollars a few weeks before the election. That kind of money will help you win the election and solve your financial troubles." Catching Max's quick glance in his direction, Fitch continued, "Yes, Senator, I'm aware of your fiscal woes. No one will ever know what happened behind the scenes. It'll look like another wrongful death case where the insurer made an economic decision to settle rather than face the risks of trial and a potential bad faith claim."

"And you?"

"And me? Oh, I have you sponsoring bills and flexing your muscle as chair of the Senate Standing Committee on Insurance: ensuring the passage of legislation favorable to California's insurance industry, and my company in particular."

"You're crazy, Fitch. Why would I do something that could jeopardize my entire political career?"

"Because without it you may not have a political career. You know as well as I do the election laws allow me to personally contribute a maximum of forty-one hundred dollars toward your campaign. And a PAC isn't going to do much better. What good is that? Besides, it's a great plan, and you won't get caught. Cases like that settle every day. No one will ever suspect your efforts to aid the insurance industry are at my direction."

"I take direction from no one." shouted Max.

"OK, calm down. With my assistance then," said Fitch, his voice calm.

Max knew Fitch was right about him possibly not having a political career without the infusion of substantial capital into his campaign. Could he actually be considering taking Fitch up on his insidious plan? Maybe. He was slipping in the polls. Campaign contributions were way down with no sign of picking up, and Max was fresh out of fund-raising ideas. He didn't want to lose this election and return to the humdrum practice of law. Regaining his composure, Max looked Fitch in the eye and said, "I'll think about it."

"Good. But I suggest you let me know by this time tomorrow. I told Mrs. Lawrence I'd make some inquiries and get back to her before Monday. We wouldn't want her to find someone else, now would we, Senator?"

Max stood and buttoned his suit coat. He opened his mouth to speak, paused, and exhaled as he left the room.

15

Max awoke at 5:00 a.m. Sunday morning after a restless night's sleep. He was unable to go back to sleep and couldn't get the conversation with Fitch out of his mind. His conversation had been forced during dinner with Brad and family Saturday evening—unusual for Max. Everyone had commented on his reticence, but he passed it off as being fatigued. The evening was made worse by Brad's announcement that Jan Bennett was leaving the firm to start her own practice. Max knew Jan was a smart woman, a hard worker, and the glue that had held the firm together for the past two years. Her replacement would have to be found as soon as possible.

It was dark outside, so Max slipped out of bed, grabbed his robe, and went to the kitchen to make coffee. The house was quiet, and the lack of distraction kept Fitch's offer playing over and over again in his mind. As the coffee brewed, Max caught his reflection in the kitchen window above the sink. The darkness outside contrasted with the soft light of the kitchen, making the window mirror-like. He stared, transfixed by the image he saw. It seemed he had become more wrinkled and grayer overnight. He looked down at the back of his hands and the age spots that now dotted once flawless skin. *Am I really considering Fitch's offer? Do prestige and power mean that much to me? What if I get caught?*

The *beep beep beep* of the coffee maker broke Max's train of thought. It took his mind off his dilemma for a moment: long enough to pour a cup of coffee and head to his favorite lounge chair on the patio.

Fitch was right when he said personal injury cases were settled every day when the insurance carrier believed it was in its best interest to do so. There's nothing wrong with that. It's good business to weigh the risks and make an economic decision based on those risks.

Max took a sip of coffee. But there was more to it in this case than a settlement based on sound economic judgment. This was a scheme to get around the political contribution rules and give Max a large sum of money to dump on advertising the last few weeks before the general election. It would allow him to get around California's Political Reform Act which required political candidates to prepare campaign disclosure statements itemizing contributions received. He'd still have to fill out the form, but he wouldn't have to list the settlement money as a political contribution.

In his first election, Max had abided by the voluntary spending limits requested of California's political candidates. This time he'd have to make an exception. He was desperate and hoped the increased spending wouldn't be brought to the voter's attention.

Max worried about getting caught. He could be charged with all kinds of things: insurance fraud, violation of the campaign contributions law, conspiracy, bribery, and on and on. His political career would be over, and if convicted of a serious crime, his bar license would be revoked so he couldn't practice law. Prison? He'd never survive the humiliation: let alone being shower buddies with a gorilla named Bubba.

Max felt like he was going to vomit. His stomach was in knots and his hand shook as he raised the coffee mug to his lips. The rush of caffeine wasn't helping—not a good coffee morning. It was 5:30 a.m., but he needed something to calm his nerves and distract his mind. A Bloody Mary sounded like the perfect remedy. Alcohol, but in a form suitable for breakfast. He dumped the last of the coffee into a planter next to his chair and went inside.

Max opened the liquor cabinet beneath the bar separating the kitchen from the family room. He was in luck. There was three-quarters of a bottle of vodka he'd brought back from his trip to Poland with Claire. He prided himself on his bartending skills and thought he made a particularly good Bloody Mary. Now, did he have the rest of the ingredients? Tomato juice, check. Fresh lemons, check. Worcestershire sauce, check. Tabasco, check. Celery sticks, check. Things were looking up.

A person could convince themselves a Bloody Mary qualified as a semi-healthy breakfast, given the tomato juice, fresh lemon, and celery. Max was certain Claire had rationalized as much on many occasions.

He retrieved the shaker from the cabinet and removed the cap that doubled as a measuring cup for the vodka. He poured one and a half ounces of vodka into the shaker, followed by one half cup of tomato juice. He picked out a large lemon from the mini fridge, cut it in half, and squeezed three teaspoons of the juice into the mix. The recipe called for two, but Max liked extra lemon. Next, five drops of Worcestershire sauce, five drops of Tabasco sauce, a dash of salt and pepper, and a handful of ice cubes. He shook the concoction for ten seconds and strained it into a tall glass filled with ice cubes. He grabbed a celery stick left over from the prior evening's dinner with Brad and dropped it into the mixture. After sticking a lemon wedge onto the lip of the glass, Max raised his masterpiece in a toast to its perfection and headed back to the patio to enjoy some liquid courage.

A mockingbird, high up in the neighbor's tree, began welcoming the first light of morning by belting out every bird sound it had ever heard. Max wondered if its vast repertoire included non-bird sounds as well. He was certain he heard barking thrown in every few seconds. God those birds can be annoying when inspiration strikes at 3:00 a.m., and they're perched outside your bedroom window.

The shrill singing proved to be a great distraction for Max. He finished Bloody Mary number one as the mockingbird flew away and allowed stillness to once again overtake the morning. The alcohol was working its magic: Max felt much calmer, more courageous, and sure of himself. Alcohol was good that way. He began to feel confident Fitch's plan could work. He'd be able to hold onto his political power, and he wouldn't have to shower with Bubba. Reassured, Max walked to the kitchen to concoct libation number two.

Morning turned into afternoon, and afternoon into mid-afternoon, with Max having spent most of the day alone, alternating between the back patio, his study, and the family room. He'd kept the booze flowing enough to stay numb without losing control. Sandy spent most of the day reading in his room, and Claire had slept until 9:30 a.m. She left to meet a girlfriend for tennis, lunch, and an afternoon getting sloshed. He hoped she'd maintain sufficient decorum to not raise eyebrows at the club and get more people talking about the Senator's lush of a wife. He didn't need any negative publicity, although most people at the club were well aware of Claire and her habits. Max had always tried to keep his drinking more private: at home, with close friends, and at his office after the staff had gone home.

It was 3:02 p.m. by his study clock, and time to make the call to Fitch if he intended to accept his nefarious offer. Max reached for the vodka tonic he'd poured, took a big swig, and dialed the number Fitch had given him. He knew it was now, or after the vodka wore off, never.

The phone rang three times and was answered with, "This is Adrian."

"Fitch, it's Max."

"Max, good to hear from you. I knew you'd call."

"Oh yeah? How's that?

"Because you have—How should I say it?—a healthy ego, and you like the power of office, the prestige. You're not about to give that up if you can help it. And with me and our little plan, you *can* help it."

"So now what?"

"There's really nothing much for you to do. After we hang up, I'll go next door and talk to Mrs. Lawrence—her name is Jillian—and sell her on your firm. She trusts me, and I'm sure will take my advice. I'll tell her to call Brad tomorrow morning and set up a meeting to sign the fee agreement and get the ball rolling. I suggest you call your son tomorrow afternoon to see how things are going. That way you can make sure he received her call and is going to take the case with the usual fee agreement. There shouldn't be any reason for us to talk until after the case is settled. I'll handle it at this end and make sure Brad receives the settlement draft at least eight weeks before the general election. That should give you and your reelection team plenty of time to convince the voters that you're the right man for the job."

"And how do I know I can trust you with this, Fitch?"

"Because when you're reelected, you'll be very valuable to me, Senator. That's how. Here's to our success."

"Yeah."

"Bye for now," said Fitch, and hung up.

Max held the receiver to his ear as he stared at his reflection in the mirror. It was a new low. *God, help me.* Max hung up and reached for the vodka tonic. He would need several more before the day ended.

16

Fitch looked out his kitchen window and saw the big black Mercedes pull up his neighbor's driveway and stop outside the front door. Mrs. Lawrence and her two kids got out looking very somber and entered the house without talking. Two months had passed since Dr. Lawrence's death, and they still looked like zombies. He waited a couple of minutes before heading out the door to talk with Mrs. Lawrence.

Fitch walked under the grape arbor that ran along the side of his house—mansion was more like it. An expansive garden filled with flowers, fountains, statues, topiary, and other ornamental trees took up the entire yard on both sides of the arbor from his home to the stone wall separating his property from the Lawrences'. The crunch of pea gravel under his feet was the only sound he heard other than the tinkling of a fountain and the twitter of a pair of wrens darting from tree to tree. Fitch surveyed his estate as he walked. A satisfied smile curled his mouth as he thought how he had it all and was about to get even more once the Senator was doing his bidding in Sacramento. Midway down the arbor, a gravel walkway turned to the left and led to a massive wooden door in the stone wall. The door served as a shortcut to the Lawrence property.

Before opening the gate, Fitch took out his pocket knife and cut a vibrant bouquet from the flowers near the path. He figured flowers would endear him to Jillian and help convince her to entrust her case to the law firm he was about to recommend. After closing the gate, he headed through the Lawrences' side yard, around the corner of the house, and up to the front door. He paused for a moment before ringing the bell, listening to the faint sound of a string quartet playing "Spring" from Vivaldi's *The Four Seasons*. He considered himself well-versed in classical composers and their music, and particularly enjoyed works from the baroque era. He and Jillian had similar tastes in music.

Fitch pressed the button and heard the rich tone of high-priced chimes echo throughout the house. He inspected the bouquet, pulled off a couple of yellowing leaves, and deposited them in a planter as the staccato clicking of heels approached the door and stopped.

Jillian opened the door and smiled. "Adrian, good of you to stop by. Please, come in." She was beautiful in spite of the fact the past two months had dimmed the usual sparkle in her eyes and created dark circles in otherwise flawless skin. Her black hair was pulled back in a ponytail, and a large diamond dangled from each ear.

"Good to see you, Jillian." Fitch gave her a neighborly hug and handed her the fresh-picked bouquet.

"Thank you so much. They're beautiful, and I'll bet from your garden."

"They are. Only the best for my favorite neighbor."

As Jillian led the way into the living room, Fitch asked, "How are you and the kids holding up?"

"Oh … we're getting by. Still going through most days in a fog. I'm constantly forgetting things. Just the other day I was supposed to meet a girlfriend for coffee and remembered it when she called from the cafe to make sure I was OK. The kids spend more time in their rooms than before, and not a day goes by that we don't have a good cry. But I sense we're making progress."

"It takes time. You're having to deal with a significant loss."

"I'll say."

"Listen, Jillian, I don't want to keep you, but I promised to check around for a good lawyer and get back to you."

"Yes, thank you. I've been seeing television ads for the Gomez firm in Pasadena and thought I might check them out. The ads make it sound like they can't lose."

Fitch hoped Jillian didn't notice the sudden shift in his expression as the thought of losing Max Johnson's Sacramento power flashed through his mind. Without missing a beat, he said, "I know the ones you're talking about, but I wouldn't use that firm if I were you." Lying through his teeth, Fitch continued, "I have a colleague whose friend hired them for an accident he was involved in a few years ago. He was captured by the flashy advertising too. Unfortunately, a young lawyer right out of law school handled the case and lost. The guy wound up getting nothing and still had to pay litigation costs. You're better off with a less flashy firm where your case will be managed by an experienced trial lawyer."

"Wow. I had no idea that sort of thing happened. Thanks for the tip."

"No problem. I did some checking and found a great firm in San Diego. Johnson and Associates. Ever heard of them?"

"No, not that I recall."

"You've heard of Senator Max Johnson?"

"Yes, of course. He's a well-known name in California politics. Although, I hear he's not doing very well in the polls this year."

"I've heard that too. He's a good man as far as I know, so he'll probably be able to turn things around. Anyway, Senator Johnson founded Johnson and Associates, and his son still runs the firm." Again lying, "Word on the street is he's a good lawyer. It's a two-lawyer firm with a good support staff, and the son personally manages each case. He's got a great track record and has won some big ones."

"Isn't San Diego a bit far?"

"Not really. The case would be filed in Los Angeles, and the attorneys will come up here to meet with you, take depositions, and attend court appearances and trial, if a trial becomes necessary. It's not uncommon for attorneys to travel to other areas if it means getting a good case."

"Well, I suppose, if you think that's the way to go."

Continuing to deceive, Fitch said, "I talked with several attorneys I know who don't handle PI cases.

They had all heard of the Johnson firm and believed it would be a good choice. I called the firm the other day to get some basic information. I feel comfortable recommending them to you."

"Thanks, Adrian. I appreciate your advice. How do I get in touch with them?"

"Brad Johnson is the son's name." Fitch handed Jillian a note and said, "Here's the attorney's name and contact information. I'd give him a call in the morning so he can get started before memories fade and evidence is lost."

"Thanks again, Adrian. I really appreciate all you've done. I'll call him tomorrow."

With that, Fitch turned and walked to the door. Jillian followed.

"Give us a call if there's anything you need. Theresa and I will do whatever we can to help."

At the door, Jillian hugged Fitch and said, "Say hi to Theresa for me. You're a lucky man to have such a terrific wife."

"Don't I know it? Let me know how it goes on Monday."

"I will. Bye, Adrian."

"See you soon."

Fitch walked out the door and headed home. A slight smile crossed his thin lips as he contemplated beating the system and greatly increasing his clout in Sacramento.

17

Jan spent a kick-back Saturday sunning around the pool, grocery shopping, and reading the latest Alex Delaware novel. On Sunday, she and a neighbor ate an early breakfast at Major's Diner about forty-five minutes east of San Diego. Major's was popular for its hearty meals served in a throwback-to-the-50s atmosphere: including walls adorned with photos of Elvis, 45 records, and COCA-COLA signs. After breakfast, they took a four-and-a-half-hour hike on Secret Canyon Trail. The trail meanders beside Pine Valley Creek through a beautiful, oak-filled valley. In the 1990s, the valley was trafficked by illegal immigrants from Mexico walking their way to what promised to be a better life. But Operation Gatekeeper pushed most of that traffic farther east to the desert.

After her relaxing weekend, Jan was back at her desk by 8:00 a.m. Monday. She liked getting to the office before the others arrived. It gave her time to organize her day, take care of personal matters, and enjoy a cup of coffee before the buzz of official business kicked into gear.

By 8:30 a.m., Jan was on the phone checking with one of her clients who was visiting his parents on the East Coast while rehabbing from an attack by his neighbor's pit bull. The dog had escaped through a hole in the neighbor's fence and attacked the man as he sat on his porch reading the paper.

Her client's right arm was broken when he tried to fend off the attack, and his other arm was bitten in several places. The wounds required forty-seven stitches, and a nerve was damaged resulting in numbness to his left thumb and forefinger. Jan filed a complaint alleging negligence and requesting compensatory and punitive damages. Punitive damages were more difficult to prove because the plaintiff had to establish the defendant's wrongdoing by clear and convincing evidence rather than the preponderance of evidence standard required for compensatory damages.

Jan felt confident the court would award punitive damages in this case because the dog had a propensity to be very aggressive, and the owner knew it. Within the past year, the dog had killed a neighbor's cat and bit a small boy who was visiting his grandmother. The dog also escaped several times from the owner's back yard through a gap in the fence, and Jan's client had a copy of the letter he wrote to the owner requesting the fence be repaired. Another piece of damning evidence was the fact the dog's owner previously bragged to another neighbor that his pit bull belonged to the most dangerous dog breed in the world. What an idiot. All of this would help prove the dog was dangerous and the owner knew it yet did nothing to make the dog less aggressive or ensure it could not escape the back yard. Given the fact Jan's client lived next door to the dog, it was reasonably foreseeable he could be attacked if the dog was not properly restrained. Although there were no guarantees in litigation, Jan believed the case would most probably settle before trial in the hundred to hundred-fifty thousand range.

Jan was finalizing a settlement demand letter to one of the insurance carriers when she heard Brad in the hall. She stopped him as he passed by on his way to the kitchen for his caffeine jump start.

"Morning, Brad. Got a minute?"

"Hey, Jan. What's up?"

"Have you found anyone to replace me yet?"

"Are you kidding? You're irreplaceable. I'll be lucky to find someone who can do half of what you do around here."

"Thanks, but I'm sure you'll find someone who can handle it just fine. Speaking of which, I have a friend from law school who passed the bar and is looking for work. He's a great guy and would be a real asset to the firm."

"Awesome. That's fantastic. If he's a friend of yours, I'm sure he'll fit in. Have him give me a call ASAP."

"Will do."

"What's his name?"

"Tom. Tom Davidson."

"I'll be waiting for his call. Thanks, Jan." Brad tapped his knuckles against the door frame and headed for the coffee.

18

Tom woke up and rubbed the sleep from his eyes at 8:03 a.m. Monday morning. He didn't often get a chance to sleep in on weekdays, but he did this morning. The last project his supervising attorney had given him was finished and turned in on Friday. The report requested by the managing partner wasn't due until 9:00 a.m., and his supervisor would be out of the office until early afternoon. He sat up and leaned against the headboard trying to remember the dream he had. Something about a beautiful girl with long golden hair riding through the forest on a white unicorn. *Was she naked?* He couldn't recall, but really wished he could. She held a sword above her head and cradled a small furry kitten. He wondered who she was and what it meant. Maybe it had to do with seeing Jan again.

Forty sit-ups, twenty push-ups, and a few curls with dumbbells followed by a hot shower got Tom's blood flowing and ready for the day. Breakfast consisted of orange juice and half a California Burrito left over from the day before graduation. Awake, showered, and nourished, Tom picked up Jan's card and reached for his phone to give her a call about the job prospect she'd mentioned.

One ring. Two rings. "Johnson and Associates. This is Barb. How may I direct your call?"

"Hi, Barb, it's Tom Davidson calling for Jan Bennett."

"Good morning, Mr. Davidson. May I tell her what this is regarding?"

"I'm a friend from law school. She asked me to give her a call."

"Please hold and I'll see if she's available."

"Sure. Thank you." After a brief pause, Led Zeppelin came on the other end of the line singing "Stairway to Heaven." It was a welcome change from the typical elevator music Tom usually heard while on hold: and an interesting choice for a law firm.

Tom was getting into the song when Robert Plant's vocal was cut off. "Good morning, Tom. I'm glad you called."

"Hi, Jan, good morning. How was your weekend?"

Sensing a smile spread across her face at the sound of his voice, Jan said, "Great. Went for a hike near Pine Valley with one of my neighbors on Saturday. It was nice to get out of town for a few hours."

"Sounds fun. Do you hike often?"

"Every chance I get. I did it a lot with my dad when I was a kid. It's good for the soul."

"I agree. I love to hike. We should plan one sometime."

"I'd love it. You're on."

"Jan, I'm calling about the possible job with your firm."

"You're timing's perfect. I mentioned you to Brad about ten minutes ago, and he said to have you call him ASAP. I'm pretty sure you've got the job if you want it."

"That's awesome. Thanks, Jan."

"My pleasure. He's here, so I can transfer you if you want to talk with him now."

"That'd be great. Hey, Jan, let's do go for a hike sometime."

"You got it. Hold on and I'll put you through. Talk soon."

Zeppelin was back. "There's a sign on the wall … But she wants to be sure … 'Cause you know sometimes words—"

"Tom. Brad Johnson. Jan said you might call."

"Yes, sir. Good morning. Jan told me you may be looking for an attorney."

"Please, drop the sir, it's Brad, and yes, we are looking for an attorney. Are you available today to come in for an interview?"

"Yes, sir, er, Brad. I have to drop a report off at Benson and Reilly at nine, and then I'm free until one if that works for you."

"Perfect. How about eleven?"

"I'll be there at eleven."

"Great. Bring your resume. I'll see you then. Do you know how to get here?"

"Yes. I drive by your office on my way to work."

"Super. See you at eleven."

The line went dead as Tom pumped his fist and let out a whispered, "Yes." The prospect of his first job as an attorney was exciting and made even more so by the possibility of seeing Jan again. It was turning out to be an awesome day.

19

It was 9:37 a.m. Monday morning, and Brad had just finished reading an article in *Cigar Aficionado* magazine about the art of hand rolling cigars. He read the magazine and smoked an occasional cigar over drinks with a friend, not because he particularly liked the taste of cigars, but because he thought it gave him a certain air of sophistication—an attitude not shared by his wife. Brad typically showered, brushed his teeth, gargled, and doused himself with cologne at the club before going home. In spite of his efforts, his wife could detect cigar odor as soon as he got near her, and it would lead to a ten-minute tirade on the harm smoking caused to him, the kids, her, and the environment.

Brad put down the magazine, turned on his computer, and was about to start a game of Solitaire when Barb buzzed him. "Brad, I have a Mrs. Lawrence on the line from L.A. Says she wants to talk with you about a PI matter."

Disappointed at having his leisure time interrupted, Brad responded, "OK, Barb, thanks. Put her through."

"Here you go."

After a brief pause, he said, "Hello, this is Brad Johnson."

"Oh, good morning Mr. Johnson. My name is Jillian Lawrence. My neighbor Adrian Fitch suggested I call you to discuss a possible case involving my husband's death."

"Thank you for calling, Mrs. Lawrence. I'm so sorry to hear of your loss."

"Thank you. It's been a difficult couple of months. Is this a good time to talk?"

"Absolutely. I don't believe I know Mr. Fitch. How is it he recommended us?"

"His wife, Theresa, and I have been good friends for several years. When he heard of Peter's death—that's my husband—he graciously offered to help me find a lawyer. He contacted several of his lawyer friends and your firm came highly recommended."

"Well, thank you. That's nice to hear. I know this will be hard for you, Mrs. Lawrence, but I need to ask you some questions about your husband and the circumstances surrounding his death to properly evaluate your case."

"I understand."

"I assume from what you said a moment ago your husband died approximately two months ago?"

"Yes, that's right."

"How did he die, Mrs. Lawrence?"

"He was driving home from work"—Jillian sucked in a short breath and fought back tears—"on the 405 freeway when he was hit head-on by a semi-truck. The driver was intoxicated."

"Oh, my goodness," said Brad, as he felt a surge of excitement at hearing semi-truck and intoxicated used to describe the defendant. He hoped the truck was part of a large company and well insured. An intoxicated driver would make a strong case. So far, Brad was hearing all the right things. "How do you know the driver was intoxicated?"

"That's what the police officer who investigated the accident told me."

Brad couldn't wait to see the police report. "What did your husband do for work?"

"He was a neurosurgeon. You may have heard about it on the news. He was well-regarded in his field. Peter ... Peter Lawrence is his name."

"Yes, ma'am. I did read about it." Brad had to contain his enthusiasm. He'd read about Dr. Lawrence and the accident on an Internet news site and knew the man was tops in his field. That meant he made a lot of money which Mrs. Lawrence would no longer benefit from. The damages could be big, and big damages were what made PI lawyers rich. "Do you have children, Mrs. Lawrence?"

"Yes, our daughter, Meredith, is eight. Our son, Greg, is six. This is a very difficult time for them as you might imagine."

Cha-ching. Kids losing their father made it an even better case—for the lawyer, not the kids. Brad wished he could get Mrs. Lawrence to sign a fee agreement on the spot. Unfortunately, she was in L.A., and propriety dictated he should offer to meet her in person before suggesting a contract. Keeping his voice concerned and professional, Brad said, "I'm sure it is for all of you."

"Mr. Johnson, would it be possible to meet, discuss the case further, and see if it's a matter you'd be interested in handling?"

See if I'm interested? Is she kidding? I'm definitely inter-ested. I've never had a case this big. Maintaining his com-posure, Brad said, "Of course. We should meet. I want you to feel comfortable with me and my firm since we'll be working together for some time." To get the deal signed, Brad lied and said he was plan-ning to be in L.A. the next day on business and would be happy to meet at her home if that was convenient for her.

"Tomorrow would be great. The kids will be in school from eight thirty to two thirty. Any chance we can get together around ten?"

Since he had no plans for the entire next day, Brad said, "Ten is perfect." He spent a couple more minutes getting the address, telephone number, and some basic information for the fee agreement be-fore ending the call. After hanging up, a smile crossed Brad's face as he leaned back in his chair, clasped his fingers together behind his head, and placed his feet on the desk. *Dad will be proud.*

20

Adrian Fitch arrived at his office at 8:30 a.m. Monday morning to meet with Todd Burns: the claims adjuster assigned to the W. T. Trucking Company's fatal accident case involving Dr. Lawrence. He pulled his black Bentley into a parking lot filled with the cars of adjusters, appraisers, and clerical staff: most hoping to get through their assigned mountain of paperwork in time to be home for dinner and pour a stiff one to numb the effects of monotonous work. The morning was dark from the thick marine layer trapped along the coast. The air hung heavy with the pungent, bleach-like smell of smog so familiar to Angelenos.

Fitch pulled into his spot by the entrance and turned off the engine. He continued to listen to Bach's "Toccata and Fugue in F Major"—his favorite organ piece—while breathing in the rich scent of leather upholstery. He was excited to be at work knowing this was the day Mrs. Lawrence would be contacting the Johnson firm: a major step toward increasing his influence in Sacramento. As Bach concluded, Fitch grabbed his briefcase and got out.

Although Fitch's private life was lavish, with no expense spared, the face of his business was austere. The home office was one story and occupied twelve thousand square feet of a corner shopping center in a residential neighborhood. The exterior was boring, adobe-colored stucco in need of a face lift. A plain glass door with a narrow glass panel on each side served as the entrance. The company name was printed in black and gold letters on the left panel. Fitch thought it a waste to spend money beautifying the company headquarters. He was probably right since customers never came to the office to buy insurance. All applications were received by email, fax, or regular mail. All policies were delivered via email or USPS. Customer inquiries were handled by calling the customer service department or through live chat online. Fitch didn't want customers to know how rich he was getting off their premiums.

After dropping his briefcase in his office and glancing at his calendar, Fitch headed to Todd Burns' office for a briefing. Todd had been promoted to head adjuster two years earlier and was one of the few employees not stuck in a sea of six-by-six cubicles. Fitch entered the office without knocking and found Todd bent over his cheap oak veneer desk reviewing documents. Todd was fifty-six and had worked various jobs in the insurance industry since completing his AA degree at the age of twenty. A diminutive man with a natural tonsure encircled by short gray hair, he possessed too-large lips that never seemed to completely close. An ever-present spot of white spittle dotted each corner of his mouth and stretched between the upper and lower lip when he spoke. Very distracting. He was round-shouldered with age spots and wrinkles that made him look much older than fifty-six. Despite his appearance, Todd Burns was a very capable adjuster.

Looking up from his work, he said, "Good morning, sir."

"Morning, Burns. How was your weekend?"

"Fine, sir. Thank you."

"What have you got for me on the Turner truck accident?"

"Well, sir, as you know, the truck was a total loss due to the fire. The contents were insured by another carrier, but the replacement cost of the cab and trailer was a hundred-eighty thousand dollars. A check was sent to Turner Trucking three weeks ago."

Shaking his head and frowning, Fitch responded, "God, I hate it when we lose one like that. What's happening with the liability end of it?"

"Well, we've not received a claim yet, but I imagine we'll be getting one soon. I've tried to contact the doctor's widow, but my calls haven't been returned." Shuffling through the stack of papers on his desk, Todd continued, "I have a copy of the police report here somewhere, and it doesn't look good. The officers found three empty beer cans in the cab, and the blood sample obtained at the scene indicated a .18 blood alcohol concentration. That's four and a half times the legal limit for commercial drivers."

Fitch interjected, "Any witness statements."

"Yeah, several, and it doesn't look good for the driver. A woman who was behind the truck when it lost control said she was on her way home from dinner and had been following the truck for several miles. She said the truck kept weaving back and forth between the lines and crossed part way into another lane two or three times. Some drivers had to switch lanes or slam on their brakes to avoid being sideswiped. She didn't see any turn signal on the truck when it swerved into the other lanes. She indicated traffic flow was normal, and there didn't seem to be any reason for the truck to suddenly brake and veer into the center divider. Two other witnesses said they had to brake hard to avoid being hit as the truck shot across the fast lane. The man who pulled the driver out of the truck said he could smell alcohol on his breath. All in all, I expect we'll be paying some money on this one."

"I'm afraid you're right," said Fitch, as he repressed a smile at the thought of what that pay out was going to buy him. "Listen, Burns, I want you to keep me updated on this one, and I don't want anyone else working the file. I'll have my assistant help with data entry. Let me know right away if anything significant occurs and give me an update first thing every Monday morning."

"Yes, sir, I'll do that," said Todd, as Fitch turned and walked out of his office.

21

Tom pulled his beat-up VW Bug into the Johnson firm parking lot at 10:56 a.m.: four minutes before his scheduled meeting with Brad. He headed for the far end of the lot and an empty space between a large SUV and a big sedan, hoping the larger vehicles would screen any view of his rust bucket from the office. He grimaced as he cut the ignition, but relaxed when the usual loud backfire didn't erupt to draw unwanted attention as he stepped out of his poor excuse for a car.

The car may not have looked good, but Tom sure did. His recently barbered dark-brown hair looked very lawyer-like, and the sunburn he'd received from his beach snooze on Saturday was now a deep, golden tan. His medium-gray herringbone suit was set off with a light-gray pinstriped shirt and Jerry Garcia tie: all gifts from his mother the last time he saw her before she died. He was wearing that outfit and standing next to his mother's bed in the last photo taken with her.

Tom entered the office and walked to the reception desk. Barb was talking on the phone as she looked up at Tom, flashed a big smile, and held up her index finger while mouthing the words "one minute." Tom glanced around the reception area and noticed how low-key it was compared to his current employer, Benson and Reilly. He liked that. Not as stuffy. It exuded homeyness. There were six simple wooden chairs with dark-brown leather seats and backs positioned against two walls. They faced a wooden coffee table bearing a vase of fresh-cut flowers, several magazines, and a bowl of various hard candies. The walls were painted light-green and decorated with five framed photographs depicting scenes from around San Diego.

Barb finished jotting down a name and phone number, hung up, and still smiling, said, "You must be Tom. Brad told me to expect you."

"Yes. I believe we spoke on the phone earlier this morning."

"We did. Please have a seat, and I'll let Brad know you're here."

"Thank you."

Tom took a seat close to the table and picked up the latest copy of *San Diego Magazine*. He wondered if Jan was in and if he'd get to see her. He hoped so.

Barb called Brad and let him know Tom was waiting. She was thinking what a hunk Tom was, and how nice it would be to have him around the office. In the hope of making that happen, Barb looked over at Tom and said, "So, you're here about the attorney job?"

"Yes, that's right."

"It's a pretty good place to work. The people are laid back, friendly, and everyone gets along. There's plenty to do, but it isn't as hustle-bustle as some of the big firms. I like that."

"Yeah, me too," said Tom, as an interior office door opened, and Brad stepped into the reception area.

"Tom, good of you to come on such short notice. I'm Brad."

"Hi, Brad. Nice to meet you."

"I see you met Barb. She's the one that keeps this place running," said Brad, as he gave a wink in her direction.

"Yes, I did."

"Barb, hold my calls while I'm with Tom." Brad opened the door to the hallway leading to his office and motioned for Tom to follow. "Come on in Tom. Let's talk."

Tom looked around as he walked down the hall, hoping to catch a glimpse of Jan. It didn't happen. But he heard her voice because she was talking on the phone. *Great. She's here.* He'd try to see her before he left.

As he took a seat behind his desk, Brad offered Tom coffee and water: both of which he declined. "Jan tells me good things about you," said Brad.

"*That's* good to hear." Tom took his resume out of his briefcase and handed it to Brad.

Brad took it, settled back in his chair, and spent the next thirty seconds reading. "Wow. That's pretty impressive. Your GPA is up there, and it looks like you've gotten some significant clerking experience along the way. How do you like Benson and Reilly?"

"They're a good firm, and they've given me a lot of practical experience."

"My dad was in the law school class a year ahead of Bill Benson. Bill's a first-class lawyer."

"I agree."

Brad drummed his pen on the desk, glanced down at the resume, and back up at Tom. "Listen, Tom, I don't want to beat around the bush. I spoke with Bill this morning after you and I talked, and he has nothing but good things to say about you. With that, plus your resume, and the fact Jan highly recommends you, I'm prepared to make you an offer and see if we can make some money together."

Tom felt a surge of excitement at the thought of having a real job as a lawyer. It was the goal he'd spent so many hours staring into books to achieve. He hadn't expected things to move so fast, and it took him a couple of seconds to respond. "Well, I'm interested."

"Good. We start new lawyers at sixty-two-fifty a month, and if after six months things are going well, that will be increased a thousand a month. We also provide medical coverage and pay your state and local bar dues."

Tom knew that wasn't the highest starting salary in town, but it was in the ball park, especially after the six-month raise kicked in. The fact he wanted to work in a smaller firm, plus the fact he didn't have any other offers pending, made his decision easy. "At the expense of sounding overeager, I'll take it. When are you thinking of having me start?"

"I asked Bill when he could let you go if things worked out between us. He said all your current assignments have been completed, and they hired a recent grad last week who should be able to take over any new projects. So if you want to, you can start right away. It would be good for you to work with Jan as much as possible before she leaves so you can get up to speed on her files."

Thinking he couldn't agree more, Tom said, "That's great. Yeah, I'd like time to get to know the office and familiarize myself with the files." *And spend time with Jan. Perfect.*

"I'd like you to hit the ground running. Can you start at seven tomorrow morning?"

"You bet."

"Super. I got a call from a potential new client this morning about a case that could be huge. I'm meeting her in L.A. tomorrow morning at ten, and I want you and Jan to come with me. I'd like her meet the team that will be working with her."

Tom thought about spending the next day with Jan and said, "I'll be here at seven. What should I bring?"

"Just yourself, and dress like you are today. We want to look sharp for this lady. I'll have Barb prepare our contract, and you can review it tomorrow."

Brad stood and extended his hand. "Tom, nice to meet you. I look forward to us working together."

Taking Brad's hand, Tom said, "Thanks. Me too."

As Tom left Brad's office, he hoped to drop by and say hi to Jan. But she wasn't at her desk, so he turned and walked to the reception area. *Oh well. I'll be with her all day tomorrow, and with luck, for many days after.*

22

Max awoke with a start at 5:00 a.m. Monday morning after a restless night's sleep. He felt his body tense as he remembered this was the day Mrs. Lawrence was to call Brad. He lay in bed trying to relax and assure himself everything would work out fine. Unable to calm down, he got up and headed for the shower.

The hot water both calmed and energized him. By the time he was toweling off, Max had pretty much convinced himself the plan could work. But misgivings continued to plague his mind as his thoughts bounced from current bills he'd sponsored, to the upcoming election, to potential scenarios concerning how the Fitch scheme would play out.

After breakfast, Max headed to his study to try to get some work done before the rest of the house was up and distractions set in. Although his ability to concentrate was off, he managed to review a bill he'd been asked to co-sponsor before Sanford knocked on the door. Knowing Claire wouldn't be up that early, Max said, "Come on in, Sandy."

The door opened, revealing a wide-awake Sanford Toddman dressed in his usual crisp, white uniform. He was carrying a silver tray with a matching coffee pot and creamer next to a bone china cup and saucer. "Good morning, sir. I noticed you were up early and thought you might like some coffee."

Continuing to look at the bill before him, Max said, "Thanks, Sandy. That sounds great."

Sandy entered the room, placed the coffee service on the corner of Max's desk, poured the right amount of half-and-half, and filled the cup with steaming hot coffee. Setting the cup and saucer near Max, Sandy asked, "Would you care for breakfast? I picked up some beautiful, fresh blueberries yesterday that are begging to become one with a pancake."

The corners of Max's mouth turned up in response to Sandy's mild attempt at humor. Looking at Sandy over the top of his readers, he said, "Sandy, you're too good to me, but no thanks. I had a bite when I first got up. I'll hold off until lunch."

Turning to go, Sandy said, "You got it, sir." He crossed the room, and as he reached the door, turned and asked, "Is there anything else I can do for you?"

Sitting back and thinking for a moment, Max said, "Yes, there is. I have to catch a two thirty-five flight to Sacramento this afternoon. Would you pack a suitcase of my usual things? I should only be gone for two or three days."

"I'll get right on it, sir." Sandy left the room and closed the door behind him without making a sound.

Alone again, Max felt the distraction regain control of his mind. He sat staring out the study window as a light breeze brought life to the leaves. His jaws were clenched, and his stomach felt empty even though he'd eaten a short time before. Drumming his fingers on the desk, Max looked at the steam rising from the coffee and realized he didn't need anything to amp him up. He needed the opposite. Something to calm him down and take away the uncertainty creeping back into his thoughts. He knew the perfect thing for the job. Although it was early morning, Max got up and went to the liquor cabinet in his study. Johnnie Walker, his good friend for many years, was the ideal antidote for jangled nerves. He removed his friend's cap, poured amber liquid in a tumbler, and topped it off with ice cubes. Raising his glass in a toast to the bottle, Max said, "Johnnie, my good friend, you're always there when I need you."

Realizing productive work was not an option, Max took a sip, settled into his chair, and switched on Fox News. At least he could catch up on national and world events.

After his third encounter with Mr. Walker, the droning talking heads and lack of REM time sent Max into a deep sleep. Around 11:00 a.m., the cacophony of an unhappy raven jolted him back to the present and the uneasy feeling in his gut. A Fox reporter was breaking the news North Korea had launched another missile that landed near its eastern sea border with the South. He'd heard the same report before falling asleep. News channels were notorious for repeating stories over and over again, ad nauseam. Although tempted to summon his liquid friend for assistance, Max decided against it, remembering he had to call Brad and head to the airport in a couple of hours.

Back at his desk, Max paid a few bills, checked his email, and responded to those needing an immediate reply. He sent emails to a couple of friends, put the paperwork he needed in his briefcase, and went to find his wife. Claire was gone, having left for the club while Max grabbed much-needed shut-eye. Just as well. Dealing with her wasn't high on his list of priorities. He wondered how much her bar tab would be and what embarrassment she might bring to the family.

Max went back to his room, checked the suitcase to see what Sandy had packed, added a few things, and moved to the bathroom to splash cold water on his face. He stood staring in the mirror as water dripped from his chin. He had to pull it together if Fitch's plan was going to work.

As he changed into travel clothes, a grumbling in his stomach reminded Max it had been several hours since his modest breakfast. He grabbed his suitcase and walked down stairs to the kitchen as Sandy put the finishing touches on his blue-ribbon Cobb salad.

Idle conversation with Sandy took Max's mind off his present concerns as he devoured the salad. Sated, he walked to the study to collect his briefcase and call Brad.

Seated at his desk, Max stared at the phone but couldn't lift his arm to make the call. After a moment, and a couple of deep breaths, he got the phone to his ear and dialed the office.

"Good morning, er, good afternoon, Johnson and Associates, this is Barb, how may I direct your call?"

"Barb, it's Max. How was your weekend?"

"Great, sir. Thanks for asking."

"Barb, is Brad in?"

"He is." As soon as Barb said, "I'll put you through," Simon and Garfunkel came on the line singing, "Hello darkness my old friend. I've come to talk with you again." Max hoped that wasn't an omen. Before he could give it more thought, Brad answered.

"Hey, Dad. What's up?"

"Well, I'm heading to Sacramento for a couple of days and wanted to check in before I go."

"I'm glad you did. I have some news I think you're going to like."

Max felt his stomach tighten as he said, "Oh, what's that?"

"I got a call from a lady in L.A. this morning whose husband was killed a couple of months ago by a drunk driver. You may have heard about it. He was a world-renowned neurosurgeon. Doctor Peter Lawrence."

"No, I don't believe I have," said Max, realizing he was lying to his son.

"Yeah, and it gets even better. He made huge money and has a wife and two young kids. This could be a big one. I'm going to L.A. in the morning to meet with her and sign her up."

Already knowing the answer, Max asked, "How is it she contacted our firm?"

"That guy who called last week, Adrian Fitch, referred her. Did you ever talk with him?"

"No," said Max, lying to his son for the second time in thirty seconds. "I tried to return his call but didn't get through. It does sound like this could be big. Listen, Brad, I'd appreciate it if you'd keep me in the loop on this one."

"Definitely. Will do."

"Thanks. Congratulations, and good luck tomorrow. I'll see you in two or three days."

"OK. Have a good trip."

The line went dead, and Max sat holding the phone to his ear. *God. What am I doing lying to my own son?* A shudder coursed through his body as he hung up. With almost an hour to kill before heading to the airport, and against his better judgment, Max got up and walked to the liquor cabinet. He would kill the time with his good buddy Johnnie.

23

Wearing the same suit from the day before but with a different shirt and tie, Tom turned his light-blue and rust Bug into the Johnson parking lot at 6:50 a.m. Tuesday morning. He stopped in one of the few shady spots and killed the engine. A loud backfire erupted—sounding more like a shotgun blast—as Jan pulled into the spot next to him. Embarrassed, he looked at Jan who was laughing, gave her a sheepish grin, gestured by raising both hands, palms up, and mouthed, "What can I say?"

Tom got out of the car as Jan walked toward him, still smiling. "Tom, I'm sorry. I didn't mean to laugh, but that backfire brought back such memories. I've been there. Oh, my God. Did you ever see what I was driving when I graduated?" Tom nodded he had. Jan continued, "It was a death trap on wheels. Didn't start half the time and died at least once every time I drove it."

"Yeah, I'm looking forward to having a real car," said Tom.

They went into the office so Jan could grab her briefcase, and to wait for Brad. Pushing the start button on the coffee maker, Jan asked, "Did Brad tell you much about why we're going to L.A. this morning?"

"No, not really, other than we're meeting some lady about a case that could be big."

"I don't know much about it either except that it involves a doctor killed by a drunk truck driver about two months ago. I know Brad wants you to come along because he's planning to have you do most of the work on it. That's typical though. You'll be doing most of the work on all the cases here."

The sound of the front door opening was followed by Brad entering the kitchen. "Good morning, guys. Thanks for coming in so early."

Jan and Tom both responded with, "Good morning."

"Make sure you each have a legal pad and pen. I'd like you to take notes while I interview Mrs. Lawrence. OK, let's get going. I'll bring you up to speed on what I know while we drive."

They each filled a paper to-go cup with coffee and headed to Brad's car. Tom opened the front passenger door for Jan and took the back seat behind Brad, so he'd have a better view of her on the drive up. The trip to L.A. was uneventful. Brad filled them in on what he knew about the case, and except for a pit stop in Costa Mesa necessitated by their morning coffee, they spent the rest of the ride alternating between silence and idle conversation: covering topics from growing up, to favorite restaurants, to the practice of law. Tom spent his quiet moments staring at the side of Jan's face and wondering what she thought of him. Jan spent *her* quiet moments staring out the front windshield and wondering what Tom thought of *her*.

Brad took the Mulholland Drive exit off the 405 freeway and turned east. The road meandered along the top of the eastern Santa Monica Mountains with spectacular views to downtown Los Angeles: punctuated by an occasional glimpse of gorgeous homes set back from the road and secluded by trees, shrubbery, and cleverly constructed walls.

"Wow. This is beautiful," said Jan.

Brad said, "Yeah, it is pretty awesome. Mulholland Drive was named after William Mulholland. He was the civil engineer who supervised the building of the Los Angeles Aqueduct that brings water out of the Owens Valley and into the San Fernando Valley. That water supply allowed L.A. to grow into the megalopolis it is today."

"How do you know so much about L.A.," said Jan.

"I don't. I had to write a paper on a famous Californian when I was in high school, and I chose William Mulholland. At the time, I thought I wanted to be an engineer."

A lady's voice came on the GPS and announced, "Arriving at destination on your left." Brad saw the large brass address numbers attached to a massive stone column to the right of the entrance. A gravel driveway, bordered by a low curb, disappeared as it curved to the left amid thick foliage, flowers, and trees. The house itself was not visible from the road. There was a matching stone column to the left of the entrance. An ornate wrought-iron gate spanned the drive with a corresponding arch over the top. Each column supported an elegant light fixture resembling a flame. Brad pulled up to the intercom and pressed the button. A woman's voice came on and said, "Mr. Johnson, is that you?"

"Yes, good morning."

"Good morning. Here you go. I'm opening the gate. Pull up to the front door and I'll meet you there."

"OK. See you in a bit."

There was a metallic click as the gate began to open.

"Man, this is impressive. What kind of doctor was this guy?" asked Tom.

"He was a neurosurgeon, and a pretty darn good one," said Brad.

Brad headed down the drive and followed the curve to the left. The property opened up, revealing a large two-story Spanish-style home and a spacious, well-manicured lawn. The driveway continued along the side of the property, passed in front of the house, and ended in a large circle that surrounded a fountain and low shrubs. Mrs. Lawrence was standing in the entry and waved as Brad brought the car to a stop. Brad, Jan, and Tom got out.

Walking toward the driver, Jillian said, "You must be Brad. I'm Jillian Lawrence."

"Yes, Mrs. Lawrence. Nice to meet you."

Jillian stopped in front of Brad and took his outstretched hand in both of hers. Looking up into his eyes, she said, "Please, it's Jillian." With tears forming in the corners of her eyes, she put her arms around his neck, hugged him, and said, "Thank you so much for coming."

"I'm happy to be of service." He turned and introduced Jillian to Jan and Tom, and said, "Jan and

Tom will be working with me on your case. I wanted you to meet them so you know the people who'll be representing you."

"I appreciate you all for coming. I've never had to deal with anything like this, or any litigation for that matter," said Jillian, as she led them into her home.

A woman entered the living room as they each took a seat on the leather couches separated by a rough-hewn coffee table that matched the Spanish decor. Jillian introduced her and said, "Brad, Jan, Tom this is Lupe: the woman who has kept us all going around here for the past sixteen years. I don't know what I'd do without her."

Lupe smiled, gave a slight nod, and asked if she could get them anything. They all agreed on coffee, and Lupe disappeared in the direction of the kitchen. The meeting lasted a little more than an hour. Jillian provided information about her husband, his practice, the family, and the grief. Brad explained the litigation process and his hope the matter could be resolved short of trial. Jillian signed the fee agreement.

When Brad asked if she had any questions, Jillian said, "I received a couple of voicemail messages from a gentleman claiming to be with the insurance company that insures the trucking company. I haven't called him back because I wanted to speak with you first. Would you like his information?"

Brad said he would, and Jillian reached for her notebook on the coffee table. Finding the page with her notes, Jillian said, "His name is Todd Burns, and he's with California Affiliated Insurance Network." Turning the notebook to Jan who was seated next to her, she pointed to the bottom of the page, and continued, "That's the number he left."

The meeting concluded, and on the way back to the car, Jillian said, "Brad, you're Senator Johnson's son, right?"

"Yes, ma'am."

"Well, I hear very good things about him. He seems like a good man. You're lucky to have him for a father."

"I agree," said Brad, as he shook Jillian's hand goodbye. "Very nice to meet you. We'll be in touch soon, and please, give any of us a call if you ever have a question."

"I'll do that. Thanks again for coming up."

Jan and Tom said goodbye to Jillian and took the same seats they had on the trip up from San Diego. Before driving off, Brad lowered his window and said, "I know your neighbor Adrian Fitch referred you to us. Please tell him thank you for me."

Pointing to her left, Jillian said, "He and his wife live right there on the other side of the wall. I'll be sure to tell him."

With that, the trio headed back to San Diego.

24

Brad called Jan and Tom to his office first thing Wednesday morning to outline a plan for handling the Lawrence matter. He wiped donut glaze from the corners of his mouth and said, "Guys, this looks like a real good case." Directing his attention to Tom, he asked, "Have you ever worked on a PI case before?"

"No. This is my first. My work at Benson and Reilly involved real estate transaction matters and construction defect litigation."

Shifting his focus to Jan, Brad said, "I'd like you to help Tom get started while you're still here. Show him how to prepare the Complaint and take him through the initial PI discovery steps. Be sure to get the CHP accident investigation report and medical records. Contact the CHP in L.A. and find out where the accident report is located: send the request to that office. Jillian gave us a copy of the Certificate of Title to the Porsche indicating she's listed as an owner with her husband. Attach that to her authorization for release of information to us. Los Angeles Fire Department paramedics were the first medical personnel on the scene, so get their records. Life Flight transported Dr. Lawrence to the UCLA Medical Center where he later died: be sure to get the records from both of those entities and the doctors who treated him. We have a copy of Dr. Lawrence's HIPAA form authorizing Jillian to obtain any of his medical records. Attach a copy of that form to her authorization for release of medical information to us. Once we have the accident report, we can try to get a written declaration from any favorable witnesses listed."

Tom followed Jan to her office to start work on the case. Barb had already set up the Lawrence file and scanned the fee agreement, HIPAA authorization, and authorizations for release of information into the computer documents folder entitled LAWRENCE, JILLIAN. Jan showed Tom how to access and use the firm's case management and billing program, how to record time and expenses, request a check, and locate the firm's forms folder. Because his only litigation experience concerned defects in large residential construction projects, the forms folder would be a great benefit for Tom when preparing the pleadings, motions, discovery requests, and other documents that were the tools of a personal injury practice. They split up the work. Jan prepared the Complaint and drafted the requests for records from the UCLA Medical Center and Dr. Lawrence's treating physicians. Tom prepared requests for records from the CHP, Los Angeles FD paramedics, and Life Flight. Jan made all correspondence for Tom's signature since she would be gone in a couple of weeks and he would be responsible for handling the case.

By the end of the day, the Complaint had been filed, the initial round of discovery requests was ready to go, and Tom had a better understanding of how the office operated. He was happy when Jan asked if he'd like to go to happy hour for a drink and some spicy wings to celebrate his first full day in the office.

Jax Bar and Bistro was two blocks from the office, so Jan and Tom left their cars in the office lot and walked. Jax was a favorite after work hangout for lawyers and other business types in the area. It was small, intimate, and decorated with large plants, original art, and high-back chairs. Happy hour prices were reasonable, and the food and drinks were excellent. Jazz aficionados flocked to Jax on Friday and Saturday nights when some of the best jazz musicians in Southern California jammed there until well past midnight.

Seated in a corner away from the boisterous crowd at the bar, Jan and Tom ordered Cadillac Margaritas and a plate of Jax signature Hot 'n' Spicy Wings. As the waitress headed toward the bar with their drink ticket, Jan said, "What fun. I haven't gone to happy hour in forever."

"Yeah, me neither. I haven't been able to afford it until now. Another perk of having a real job."

Jan agreed. "It's great, isn't it … having enough money to do some of the fun things life has to offer?"

Tom looked at Jan, smiled, and nodded.

When the drinks arrived, Jan and Tom clinked their glasses together, and Jan said, "Here's to success handling your first big PI case."

Tom was about to respond when Eric Collins, a classmate of Jan's, walked up to the table, and said, "First big PI case, huh? Do tell." Eric gave Jan a quick kiss on the cheek and extended his hand to Tom. "Hi, I'm Eric Collins. Jan and I were in the same section together in law school."

Feeling a tinge of jealousy about the kiss, Tom said, "I'm Tom. Nice to meet you."

"So tell me what's up with the PI case."

"A semi-truck hit a car head-on, killing the driver," said Tom.

"Sweet. I know that sounds sick, but semi-truck smells of deep pockets. I trust liability is in your favor?"

"I think so."

"Awesome. Who's the carrier?"

"California Affiliated Insurance Network."

"Oh boy, good luck with that. C.A.I.N. is notorious for being tight-fisted and slow to pay claims. I hear the owner, Adrian Fitch, is a real bear to work with."

Tom and Jan exchanged quizzical looks at the mention of Adrian Fitch's name as Eric waved to a woman entering the bar. "Well guys, gotta run. My date's here. Good to see you again, Jan. Nice to meet you, Tom, and good luck with your case."

Looking puzzled, Jan said, "Adrian Fitch. Isn't that the guy Ms. Lawrence said referred her to our firm?"

"Yeah, it is. That's strange. I wonder why he referred her to a lawyer when his company insures the trucking company at fault. You'd think he'd want to try to make it go away without involving lawyers.

"Too weird. Maybe he didn't realize his company insured the trucker. Or maybe he was being a good friend and neighbor."

"I don't know. But that adds an interesting twist to the matter," said Tom.

"It sure does. Oh well, it's great our firm got the case. Maybe you'll get a nice bonus if you get a big settlement or verdict."

"That'd be great. God knows I could use it."

Jan and Tom spent the next hour sipping their margaritas, savoring the wings, and getting to know one another. They walked back to the firm parking lot, exchanged a quick hug, and went home.

25

Trudy Greene set up the Lawrence file when California Affiliated Insurance Network received the claim two months ago. She'd worked for C.A.I.N. since moving to Los Angeles after graduating from Southside High School in Greenville, South Carolina. She was plain looking except for her thick red hair and freckled face. She married her high school sweetheart, who she thought was the love of her life, and moved to the West Coast. Her small-town hubby found the bevy of ready and willing L.A. females irresistible and moved out five weeks after arriving. Trudy was devastated. She had been hired by C.A.I.N. on her second day in town, and the work kept her mind occupied and off the pain of lost love.

Trudy started out in the mail room and rapidly advanced to assistant for one of the junior claims adjusters. Her intelligence, upbeat personality, and hard work did not go unnoticed, and she became Adrian Fitch's assistant six months after hire. Her position gave her access to all of C.A.I.N., including Fitch's office.

It was Saturday, and Trudy's roommate dropped her off at the office to catch up on the work that piled up while she was out with the flu. She would have driven herself, but her car battery was dead.

Trudy set her purse and keys on her desk and went to the ladies' room. Her stomach was a bit queasy, and the breakfast she'd eaten an hour ago wasn't settling well.

With her stomach calmed, Trudy was on her way to the lounge to grab a 7-Up when she heard Fitch's voice coming from his office. She changed course and walked toward his office to say hi and see if there was anything he needed. Trudy stopped short as she was about to enter his office. Fitch was talking on the phone, and she didn't want to interrupt. Standing outside the door, she heard Fitch say, "Senator Johnson. Fitch here. I wanted to let you know our little plan with the Lawrence matter seems to be working, and no one knows about it but you and me. Sweet, huh? Make sure Davidson gets a policy limits demand letter to us ASAP."

Trudy's stomach let out a loud gurgle and she froze; afraid Fitch might have heard it. He didn't, and continued, "It looks like the case isn't worth more than ten million, but as agreed, we'll pay the twenty-two million policy limits. It's perfect. You'll have the funds needed to win the election, we get around the campaign contribution laws, and I'll have more political influence in Sacramento. A win-win for everyone." Then after a brief pause, Fitch said, "Calm down, Senator. You remember our deal." With that, Fitch hung up.

Trudy was panicked. She didn't know what was going on but sensed something was not right. She glanced at her desk. Her purse and keys were sitting in plain sight where she'd left them. There was no way she could get them without Fitch seeing her, and she didn't want that to happen. She turned and slipped back into the ladies' room, hoping Fitch would leave soon and not see the things she'd left on her desk.

She held the door open a crack and peeked out of the restroom. Her fingers grew tired after a few minutes and slipped off the edge of the door, causing it to close with a loud click she'd never noticed before when the office was abuzz with activity. Afraid Fitch heard the click, she held her breath and listened before opening the door again. Although it seemed like hours, she saw Fitch leave his office about fifteen minutes later without looking in the direction of her desk. A whispered "Thank God" escaped her lips when she heard him leave the building and lock the door.

Trudy's heart was pounding, and her palms were damp. She opened the door wider and peeked out. She had a clear view of the front door and saw Fitch's Bentley pull out of the parking lot. She sucked in a deep breath and noticed her hands were shaking from the weight of the door, and fear. Fear predominated. She left the restroom and tiptoed to the front door to make sure there were no cars in the lot. Satisfied it was empty and the front door locked, Trudy went to her desk and plopped down on her chair, feeling drained.

After taking a moment to process what she'd heard, and with her breathing returning to normal, Trudy realized Adrian Fitch and Senator Johnson were up to no good, something illegal. *What should I do? Should I tell someone? Maybe I should forget what I heard and let it go.* She leaned forward with her elbows on her desk, hands pressed together as if praying, and pushed her index fingers hard against her lips. Her eyes darted around the office as she contemplated her next move.

Trudy thought about contacting Todd Burns since he was the adjuster assigned to the Lawrence claim. But she didn't know him well, and he seemed so cold and aloof. She didn't feel comfortable confiding in him and wasn't the only one who felt that way. Burns's own assistant told her she didn't know how to approach the guy. And for all Trudy knew, Burns could be involved in whatever was going on. After all, Fitch had put Burns in charge of the Lawrence claim.

Trudy was responsible for most of the data entry on the claim. She found that unusual because it was customary for data to be entered by the adjuster managing the claim, or by his or her assistant. She didn't question why she was doing work on the claim and was thrilled to see Tom Davidson's name as the attorney representing the plaintiff, Jillian Lawrence. The best part was that Tom was in San Diego a few miles south of L.A.

Trudy and Tom had been in the same class at Southside High. She'd had a silent crush on him ever since freshman year. After graduation, Tom went off to college, and Trudy got married and moved to L.A.

Trudy wondered if Tom was involved with whatever was going on between Fitch and the Senator. The thought was dismissed as soon as it entered her mind. Tom was an honest, upstanding person and wouldn't be tangled up in anything illegal. Besides, she heard Fitch say no one knew about the plan except for himself and the Senator.

Trudy had to do something. She wasn't the kind of person to ignore what she'd heard and pretend all was well. Morality—standing up for what was right—had been instilled in Trudy by her parents from an early age. She decided to contact Tom. He was someone she knew and trusted, a good person, and a lawyer. He'd know what to do.

Trudy turned on her computer and opened the Lawrence file. The Johnson firm telephone number was on the front page of the case data sheet. She wrote the number on a yellow sticky and turned off the computer. Staring at the number, Trudy contemplated her various options, trying to convince herself calling Tom was the best thing to do. She felt nervous and realized it was caused by both the conversation she'd overheard and the thought of talking with her secret flame again after all these years. Would Tom remember her? She guessed there was one way to find out. She picked up the phone and dialed the number, hoping Tom would be in his office on a Saturday.

The phone rang once, twice, three times. An answering machine picked up after the fourth ring. "You've reached Johnson and Associates. The office is currently closed, but your call is very important to us. To leave a message for Brad Johnson, press one. For Tom Davidson, press two—"

Trudy pressed two, and after a brief pause, the phone began to ring again. On the second ring, she heard, "This is Tom."

Trudy froze for a moment, not sure what to say, then said, "Uh, Tom … I don't know if you remember me or not. It's Trudy Greene from Southside High."

"Trudy Greene. Oh wow, hi. Of course I remember you. We played together in the band freshman year. How are you?"

"Fine, I guess. I can't believe you remember me. It's been a long time."

"As I recall, you played a pretty mean clarinet. Do you still play?"

"Not really. I still have it but don't play much."

"Trudy, it's great to hear from you. What's up?"

"I'm not sure where to begin. You're handling the Lawrence case for the Johnson firm, right?"

"Yeah, but how do you know that?"

"Well, I work for C.A.I.N. I've been with them since high school and have done most of the data entry on the Lawrence matter. I'm Adrian Fitch's assistant. I saw your name on the file and wanted to talk with you. Do you know Mr. Fitch?"

"I know he owns C.A.I.N. and referred Mrs. Lawrence to the firm, but I've never met him."

"How about Senator Johnson, do you know him?"

"I've met him a couple of times, but I don't really know him. I know he started this firm. His son runs it now. Why?"

Her voice shaking, Trudy said, "Tom, something's come up with the Lawrence case, and I'm not sure what to do about it. I'm scared and don't know who else to talk to but you."

"What is it, Trudy?"

"I'm alone in the office right now, but if some-one comes in, I'll have to hang up and call you back later. I came into the office about twenty minutes ago to catch up on some work, and I heard Mr. Fitch talking with Senator Johnson about the Law-rence matter. Oh God, Tom, I'm so scared. Mr. Fitch told the Senator their plan with the Lawrence case was working. He said to make sure to have you send a policy limits demand letter soon, and C.A.I.N. would pay the twenty-two million policy limits even though the case wasn't worth that much. He said that way the Senator could keep his seat, they'd get around the campaign contribution laws, and the Senator could do things for Mr. Fitch in Sacramento. Something's not right, Tom. I'm sure whatever they're planning is illegal."

"Whoa, are you serious? Are you sure Fitch was talking to Senator Johnson?"

"Positive. He mentioned the Senator's name."

"Does Fitch know you heard him?"

"No, I don't think so. He walked out of his of-fice without looking toward my desk and drove away. He's a scary guy. I don't know what he might do if he found out."

"Wow. I need to think about what to do, Trudy. For now, continue doing your work like normal and don't talk to anyone about this. Do you have a cell phone?"

"Yes."

"Great. Let's exchange numbers so we can stay in touch outside work."

After entering the number in her phone, Trudy said, "Tom."

"Yeah."

"Thanks. I feel better knowing you're there to help."

"I'm glad you called me. Nice to hear from you, Trudy, even if it is under less than desirable circumstances. Take care of yourself. Let's talk soon."

With that, they hung up.

26

Tom sat at his desk and thought about the conversation with Trudy. He felt a knot growing in his stomach and a distinct sense of unease. What to do with the information he received? *Should I tell Brad? Maybe he's involved. What then? Even if he's not involved, I'm not sure I want to be the one to break the news to him.* Tom contemplated calling the police but felt he needed more concrete proof of wrongdoing before taking that step. He decided to call Jan because she'd been involved with the case, knew Brad better than he did, and might have a suggestion about how to proceed. Besides, they'd both been so busy with work that he'd only seen her a few times since she left the firm six weeks ago. It would be good to hear her voice.

Tom opened the contacts list on his cell phone and pushed the number for Jan. She picked up after three rings and said, "Tom. I'm glad you called. It's been awhile. How are you?"

"Hi, Jan. Fine, I guess. Jan, something weird just happened, and I need to run it by you."

"Of course. What's up?"

Tom told her about his conversation with Trudy and his uncertainty as to how to handle the situation. When he finished, Jan said, "Oh my God, Tom. That's intense."

"I know. I thought about calling the police, but I need to be more certain it's all true before doing that. If it's not true, and the rumor gets out, Fitch's and Senator Johnson's reputations could be ruined, not to mention the fact I'd lose my job."

"Yeah, that's a good call."

"Do you think Brad may be involved?" said Tom.

"I suppose it's possible, but I doubt it. I don't think his dad would trust him with that kind of information, and he wouldn't want to put that burden on Brad. The little I've been around the Senator, I sense he loves his son. Brad may be lazy, but I think he's a pretty honest person, aside from the affair he's having with a lady from the tennis club."

"An affair? Really?"

"Oh, yeah. I think most everybody knows about it except his wife. Maybe she figured it out too but just wants to keep the family together. Who knows?"

"That's sad. Jan, I think I'm going to call Mrs. Lawrence and fill her in on what I know. Maybe she'll have some insight. It's her case, and she has a right to know what's going on."

"I agree. Let me know what she has to say, and call me if there's anything I can do to help."

"Thanks, Jan. I appreciate your support."

"Good luck. Talk soon."

"Bye." Tom hung up and stared into the blur of empty space. Alone, without Jan on the other end of the line, the tenseness in his stomach returned. He sat in his office tapping his pen on the desk while looking out the window and wondering how this could be happening. Law school hadn't taught him how to deal with this situation. A sparrow landed in the ficus tree on the patio outside his window, chirped, and cleaned its beak on a branch. Tom watched it for a moment and thought how wonderful it would be if he could be as free as that bird—simply fly away and never have to deal with the Lawrence matter again. But the moment passed, the sparrow flew away, and Tom realized he did have to deal with the situation at hand. He opened the Lawrence file, found Mrs. Lawrence's number, and dialed.

Tom listened to the phone ring at the other end of the line while thinking about what to say. He was ready to hang up after the seventh ring when Mrs. Lawrence answered. "Hello."

"Mrs. Lawrence, this is Tom Davidson. How are you?"

"Fine, Tom. Good to hear from you, but it's Saturday. Shouldn't you be at the beach or out with some lucky lady?"

"Yeah, I suppose so. That would be nice, but there's always something to do here. Catching up a little on the weekend takes some pressure off when Monday rolls around."

"I know what you mean."

"Mrs. Lawrence, something's come up, and I need to talk with you about it."

"Sure. What is it?"

"How well do you know your neighbor, Adrian Fitch?"

"Well, he and his wife, Theresa, have been friends of ours for several years. I've been at parties with both Adrian and Theresa, but I'm closer to Theresa. She and I used to play tennis together once a week, and we volunteered at a local nursing home for three or four years. Why?"

"Just curious. Do you know what Mr. Fitch does for a living?"

"I know he's involved in the insurance business, but I don't know what he does. I assumed he was in sales. I'm not sure why I thought that. He must be good at it given their gorgeous home and all the traveling they do."

"He owns C.A.I.N., Mrs. Lawrence. They insure the trucking company responsible for your husband's death?"

"Oh?"

"How did it happen that he referred you to our firm?"

"Gee, I was talking with him at some point after my husband's accident and asked if he knew of a lawyer who might help me. I was thinking about contacting the Gomez firm in Pasadena after seeing their television ads, but Adrian told me not to go with them. He said Johnson and Associates was great at handling personal injury cases and told me to contact you."

"You know Senator Max Johnson is Brad's father, right?"

"Yes. Why?"

"Mrs. Lawrence, I received a disturbing phone call today from someone close to Mr. Fitch. This person claims to have overheard a telephone conversation between Mr. Fitch and Senator Johnson concerning an agreement to pay the trucking company's policy limits in order to get around the State campaign contribution laws, provide the Senator with the funds needed to win the election, and increase Fitch's political clout in Sacramento. The Senator is chair of the Senate Standing Committee on Insurance and could be valuable to Mr. Fitch and his company."

"Oh my goodness. Tom, that's terrible."

"I know, but I don't have enough information to go to the police. I'd hate to accuse them of anything that wasn't true. For now, I wanted to let you know what may be going on and see if you have any information that might be helpful."

"Thanks for letting me know. I'm sorry I can't be more help. I'm going to talk with Adrian to see if I can find out more about this."

"I don't think that's a good idea, Mrs. Lawrence. My source said he's a scary guy. I don't know what he's capable of, especially when it involves something as serious as this."

"I suppose you're right, Tom, but I can't imagine Adrian being involved in something sinister. He's been a real gentleman to me."

"I'm going to look into this further to see if I can confirm what I heard. I'll keep you posted, but in the meantime, don't confront Mr. Fitch."

"OK, Tom. Thanks for telling me. This is so unsettling."

"I know. I'll call you when I have more information."

"OK. Bye."

"Talk soon." Tom hung up and felt the stomach knot return. He hoped he'd made the right decision confiding in Mrs. Lawrence. He reached across his desk for another file to review and write a status report to the client. After reading the same paragraph several times and not retaining what he'd read, Tom realized his concentration was shot. He closed the file, turned off his computer, and drove home.

27

Trudy felt a little better after talking with Tom, but her hands continued to shake, and she felt a shudder course through her body. She needed to get out of the office and go home but didn't have her car and was dependent upon her roommate, Carla, to rescue her. She grabbed her cell phone, pressed Carla's number, and prayed she'd answer. On the fourth ring, Carla's voicemail picked up, "Hey, Carla here. You know what to do. Ciao."

In a fear-tinged whisper, Trudy said, "Carla, I need you to pick me up right away. Please call me as soon as you get this message. I'm scared. Hurry."

An eerie quiet permeated the office, broken by the intermittent buzz of a dying fluorescent light. Trudy decided to go outside, walk the few blocks to a little coffee shop she knew, and wait for Carla's call. At least she'd escape the tomb-like ambiance. Fresh air, sunshine, and the presence of other people might help take her mind off the conversation she'd heard.

Trudy picked up her purse and keys and started toward the front door. As she passed Fitch's office, the thought dawned on her that she might find a memo or some other document to confirm the conversation. She made a visual sweep around the rest of the office to make sure she was alone and walked to Fitch's desk. She set her purse and keys on the credenza and started going through the calendar he used to keep track of important events. She searched the entries for January, February, March, April, and May but found nothing. As she turned the page to June, a deep voice behind her said, "May I help you?" It was Fitch.

Trudy's body bolted upright, knocking the calendar to the floor as she turned to face him. He was not smiling, and his steely eyes seemed to bore right through her. The shock evident in her voice, Trudy said, "Mr. Fitch, I didn't know you were here. I just came in to catch up on some work."

"Really, Trudy. When did you get here?"

"Just a couple minutes ago. I was looking for a file I thought you might have taken for review."

"Oh, what file is that?"

Her mind racing, Trudy replied, "Uh… the Petit file. You know, the one where the little girl was shot in the eye with a BB gun."

"Interesting. You know that file was closed two months ago."

Fumbling for words, Trudy said, "Oh, you're right. I forgot."

Fitch's gravel voice was mordant, when he said, "Trudy, when did you get here?"

Panic swept her body. "Like I said, a couple of minutes ago."

The sarcasm turned menacing and cold. "Trudy don't lie to me. I got here thirty minutes ago, and I didn't see you. I was here for twenty minutes, then left. I pulled out of the lot and realized I'd forgotten something, so I made a U-turn and came back. I've been in my car talking on the phone. I didn't see you come in. Now, Trudy, tell me when you really got here."

Trudy's lower lip quivered, and fear choked back her words as she stared into her boss's sinister eyes. After a moment the timid words formed. "A few minutes ago, Mr. Fitch. I swear."

In a flash, Fitch was standing nose to nose with Trudy. His black eyes bored into her. One strong, thick hand squeezed her throat and cut off her air while the other hand pinched her face so hard it felt like her cheeks would tear. Trudy thought she was going to pass out. "Now. One last time. When did you get here?"

Tears oozed from her eyes as she tried to speak through Fitch's vice-like grip. With a choked whisper, she said, "Thirty-five minutes ago."

Fitch loosened his grip but kept his hand around her throat. "I didn't see your car, and I didn't see you when I came in. Where were you?"

"My roommate dropped me off. I was in the bathroom because my stomach was still upset from being sick." Without thinking, and before she could stop herself, she blurted out, "I didn't hear anything, honest." Trudy realized what she'd said. Terror flashed in her eyes, and the blood drained from her face as she sucked in a short, quick breath.

Fitch's face twisted into a maniacal grimace as his hand compressed her trachea. With a slow, deliberate growl, he said, "You … damn … liar." His right hand struck her face with such force it knocked her to the floor. Dazed, Trudy lay on the floor with blood trickling from her nose and the corner of her mouth.

Fitch moved to the front of his desk, opened a drawer, and removed a roll of packing tape. Stepping back to Trudy, he knelt, jerked her into a sitting position by her hair, and pressed tape over her mouth. He yanked her arms around to her back, bound her hands together with tape, and shoved her back down on the floor. The tape on Trudy's mouth pressed her lips into her teeth, cutting her lower lip, while the tape on her hands cut off circulation, numbing her fingers.

Fitch stood and paced back and forth behind his desk, planning his next move. He had to get her out of the office and to some place secure. But where? It dawned on him that his wife was out of town visiting relatives and wouldn't be home for at least another week. That should give him time to deal with this dilemma.

Fitch walked back to Trudy and yanked her to her feet by her arm, causing a searing pain to shoot through her shoulder. He squeezed her face until it felt like her jaw would break. With a look of hate on his face, he said, "You're gonna walk with me to my car. You make one sound or any sudden move and I'll kill you. Do you understand?"

Feeling faint, Trudy nodded. Blood continued to drip from her nose and mouth.

Fitch grabbed her purse and keys from his credenza, pushed her out of his office, and guided her toward the front door. At the door, he shoved Trudy face first into the wall as he scanned the parking lot to make sure it was clear. Satisfied they were alone, he unlocked the door and pulled her into the sunlight. He grabbed Trudy's elbow and walked her to his car, surveying the area for anyone who might see them. The office was elevated from the street, and the parking lot was secluded—surrounded by brush and trees with no buildings in sight—making the exit easy.

Fitch opened the door to his Bentley, had Trudy get in the back seat, then pushed her to the floor. He stuck his head into the car and said, "You don't move or make a sound, understand?" Trudy nodded. He slammed the door, striking the bottom of her foot, and jamming her knee into the metal driver's seat support. A sharp pain shot through her knee, causing her to cry out. She was lucky the door was shut: Fitch didn't hear her. He got behind the wheel, started the car, and drove out of the lot.

A few blocks from the office, a police cruiser emerged from an alley and pulled in behind the Bentley. Fitch saw it in his rearview mirror, and whispered, "Shit," as he checked the speedometer to make sure he wasn't speeding. At the next light, he turned right to get the cop off his tail, but the black and white followed him. His hands clenched the wheel while his eyes darted back and forth between the road ahead and the rearview mirror. He drove for several blocks before turning left in another attempt to ditch the cop. The policeman stayed right with him. Fitch pounded his hand on the steering wheel and continued down the street, certain the cruiser's lights would start flashing at any moment. The cop made a right at the next corner and disappeared. Fortunate for Fitch, not so for Trudy.

Fitch made a U-turn and headed back to the 405 freeway—and home.

28

Back at the C.A.I.N. parking lot, Billy "Big Bill" Turley sat on his crusty sleeping bag in the bushes at the far end, drinking his half pint of cheap gin straight from the bottle and thinking about what he'd seen. The years of alcohol abuse played havoc with his memory, and the fact he was three-quarters through a half pint of gin didn't help. He was sure the girl he saw worked in the building. It looked like her hands were tied behind her back and tape covered her mouth. Billy recognized the big man with her as the guy who drove that Bentley. He knew it was a Bentley because he'd walked by the front of the office and seen the hood ornament with outstretched wings and a white "B" in the middle of a black circle. Billy knew that symbol because he used to see them in the exclusive Manhattan neighborhood where he grew up. That was years ago—before the war and booze got the best of him.

Billy wondered if he should tell the cops but decided against it since he was sure they'd never believe him. And he didn't want to get busted again for public intoxication and spend another night in jail. It was summertime and too nice to be locked up with a bunch of smelly, pee-stained derelicts. Nope. He'd mind his own business.

Billy took his last swig of gin and tossed the bottle into the bushes. He relieved himself against a tree, picked up his sleeping bag with his left hand, grabbed the black plastic garbage bag containing all his worldly possessions with his right, and started on his daily rounds of looking in trash bins for cans, plastic bottles—and with luck—a half-eaten burger and fries.

29

Fitch breathed a sigh of relief as he turned off Mulholland and into his driveway—home at last. He pressed the garage door opener as he rolled down the drive so he wouldn't have to stop before entering. No need to chance having a nosy neighbor see him. Halfway into the garage, he pushed the remote to close the door. The car came to a stop as the garage door made contact with the concrete floor.

Fitch sat in the quiet of the garage and stared straight ahead. He clenched his jaws and ground his teeth while formulating a plan to deal with his captive.

Trudy looked out of the corner of her eye and could see the side of Fitch's face in the space between the front seats. She was in pain from the slap to her face and the tape pushing her lip into her teeth. The fingers on both hands were numb, and although her lip and nose had stopped bleeding, dried blood covered her chin and right cheek. She wondered what this maniac planned to do with her. For the first time in her life she was beyond scared—petrified.

Fitch got out and stood staring at a bone-handled hunting knife lying on the workbench next to the car. He wondered if he should get rid of her now. She knew too much and could ruin him. His better judgment told him to take his time and not do anything foolish. After all, he had plenty of time to take care of this problem: his wife was out of town, and no one knew he'd taken Trudy hostage.

Fitch found a five-foot chain bicycle lock in the workbench that his wife used to secure her bike. He opened the car door and pulled Trudy up to a sitting position by her arm like he'd done back at the office. Trudy heard a popping sound in her shoulder that was accompanied by agonizing pain—worse than the one before. Her face scrapped the back of the driver's seat, tearing the tape off of her mouth so that it hung from her cheek. She managed to get her feet out the door and scooted forward until they touched the garage floor. Fitch jerked her the rest of the way out and to a standing position. She didn't hear another pop, and there was no pain except that caused by the tight grip of Fitch's beefy hand. Standing was difficult due to the pain in her left knee from having it jammed into the metal support of the driver's seat.

As Trudy limped to the door leading into the house, she saw Fitch pick up the hunting knife from the workbench. A shiver ran through her body, and with terror in her voice, she said, "What are you going to do with that?"

"Nothing, at the moment. I like having it with me. It could come in handy."

"Please don't hurt me. I promise I won't say a word. Please."

Fitch didn't respond. He fastened the tape back over her mouth, opened the door, and shoved

Trudy into the kitchen, making her trip and almost fall.

The kitchen was huge: bigger than any Trudy had seen. A vast array of stainless-steel cookware hung from a large metal oval attached to the ceiling above the central island. An expensive range was surrounded by a sea of gorgeous marble and other top-of-the-line appliances. It was either a gourmet chef's kitchen or that of someone who wanted to impress.

Fitch pushed Trudy to a door next to the double-wide refrigerator. He opened the door and ordered her down the dark stairway. A cool breeze brushed her face. After she'd taken a few tentative steps, Fitch switched on the light, revealing an expansive wine cellar with bottles racked along the walls as far as she could see. The cellar was complete with a heavy, wooden table surrounded by eight overstuffed chairs. It included an ornate chandelier centered over the table, shelves of wine glasses against the far wall, and a glass top humidor filled with Cohiba cigars. A door to the right of the table led to a half bath. The cellar was secluded, soundproof, and the perfect location to hold a captive.

A large support beam extended from floor to ceiling in the center of the cellar. Fitch stopped Trudy short and shoved her down to a sitting position in front of the beam. He wrapped the bike chain around her waist, pushed her shoulders against the support, and brought the ends of the chain around the post, securing them with the lock. She winced as the chain dug into her waist.

Fitch stood and looked down at Trudy, penetrating her terrified eyes with a cold, sadistic stare. He turned without saying a word, walked up the stairs, and shut off the light. Trudy heard the heavy wooden door close and the deadbolt engage. She was alone in the cold and total darkness.

30

Carla Bodean and Trudy had been roommates since Carla moved to L.A. from Fresno over three years ago. Trudy was the first person Carla contacted after searching Craigslist for roommate wanted ads. Carla appeared at Trudy's door with her straight brown hair pulled back in a ponytail, lips colored bright red, and wearing a gray T-shirt emblazoned with the words GIRLS ROCK. Her cheery personality, quick wit, and love of chocolate, red wine, and romantic movies convinced Trudy she'd found her roommate. The girls hit it off, and over time, became best friends. Last year, Trudy spent Christmas with Carla and her family in Fresno, and the year before, Carla flew to South Carolina to spend Christmas with Trudy's family.

Back home after running Saturday morning errands, Carla walked into the apartment and saw her cell phone lying on the coffee table. She never went out without her phone but had forgotten it in the rush to get to her hair appointment. The icon on her phone indicated one voicemail was waiting, so she entered the code to retrieve the message. Carla heard Trudy's voice and knew something was wrong. She was whispering like she didn't want anyone to hear her, and there was fear in her voice.

Carla flipped to her contacts list and pushed the CALL button next to Trudy's name. The phone rang once, twice, three times: on the fourth ring it went to voicemail. "Trude, it's me. Are you OK? Your message sounds weird. Call me as soon as you get this." Carla closed her phone, and a worry crease formed between her eyebrows. Trudy took her phone with her that morning and had called Carla less than an hour ago. It was not like her to not answer even if to say she was busy and would call back.

Carla went to the kitchen, poured a glass of orange juice, and sat on the couch sipping her juice while leafing through a copy of *Elle* magazine. A shiver ran up her spine when she read her horoscope for the day. *Expect the unexpected with friends today.* She looked at the time on her cell phone and realized it had been twenty minutes since she'd tried Trudy. Thinking Trudy may have found another ride, Carla called their mutual friend Tammy. No luck. Tammy hadn't seen Trudy since they walked out of work together Tuesday afternoon: the day before Trudy called in sick. Calls to several other friends brought the same response. No one had talked to Trudy or seen her today.

Ten more minutes passed while Carla flipped through *Elle* and contemplated what to do next. She couldn't just sit there. It was clear her friend needed her.

Carla tossed the magazine on the coffee table, grabbed her purse and cell phone, and headed to her car. Not certain how to proceed, she decided to drive to Trudy's office: the last place she'd seen her.

Why was everyone driving so slow, and why did she hit every stop light?—lights that seemed to be stuck on red forever. It was twenty minutes before Carla pulled into the empty parking lot at C.A.I.N. She came to a stop near the entrance. The place looked dead.

Carla got out, walked to the door, and pulled the handle like she'd done a hundred times before. It was locked. Cupping her hands around her eyes and pressing her pinkie fingers to the glass, Carla searched the office for any sign of Trudy. No one was there. It was dark. She banged on the door but got no response.

Frustrated, she got back in her car, grabbed the steering wheel, and rested her head in the space between her hands. What to do now? She thought about calling the police, but there was no way they would do anything given the current information and the fact Trudy had only been missing—if indeed she *was* missing—for a couple of hours. She remembered the coffee shop down the street from the office. Trudy often went there on breaks, after work, and to wait for Carla on the days she needed a ride home.

Certain that must be where Trudy had gone, Carla drove to the coffee shop. She pulled into the fifteen-minute parking spot in front of the shop, hoping to see Trudy waiting for her at one of the sidewalk tables. They were all empty except for one where a young girl was sipping coffee and surfing the net on her laptop. Carla panned the front windows of the shop to see if she could spot Trudy. The glare from the sun made it difficult to see into the shop, but her friend was not one of the visible faces sitting near the windows.

Carla got out of the car and approached the girl at the outside table. She described Trudy to her, but the girl said she'd only been there about fifteen minutes and hadn't seen anyone matching Trudy's description. Carla entered the shop and scanned the interior from left to right and back again, but no Trudy. Madge, the proprietor of the shop, was manning the cash register near the entrance. She knew Trudy and Carla from the many times they'd been in the shop drinking coffee and splitting a pastry. Madge told Carla she'd been at the register all morning and hadn't seen Trudy. She promised to have Trudy call Carla if she showed up.

Carla left the shop and looked up and down the street hoping to see her friend. No pedestrians in either direction. Distressed and at a loss for what to do, she got in her car and drove home.

31

Trudy's rear end was cold and sore from sitting in one position on the hard, wooden floor of the wine cellar. Her entire body was chilled, and her teeth were chattering as a result of the perfect fifty-five-degree temperature. Perfect, that is, for the wine, but not so perfect for a slender young woman wearing a sleeveless tank top. She'd worn jeans, socks, and tennis shoes that helped her retain some body heat: although at this point, the cold was winning.

The last of her morning coffee had worked its way through her system, and Trudy's bladder felt like it was going to burst. She tried to think of things to keep her mind off the discomfort of having to go. She thought about files at work, friends from high school, her crush on Tom, and the last time she hiked in the desert: but it wasn't working, and the pain was becoming unbearable. She didn't want to wet herself. Although the initial warmth would feel great, she knew it would soon make her feel colder and more uncomfortable than she already was. She tried to call out, but the tape sealed her mouth, and all she could do was make a moaning sound, not loud enough to be heard outside the soundproof cellar.

Trudy closed her eyes and was about to give in to Mother Nature when the lock clicked in the cellar door. The light flicked on, splitting the blackness, causing Trudy to squint. Fitch slowly descended the stairs, stopped in front of Trudy, and stabbed her with the same cold stare she remembered from earlier.

The bladder pain reminded her she needed to go—now. Unable to talk, Trudy made a pained face, crossed her legs, and leaned forward, moaning. She looked up at Fitch as a slight smile played the corners of his mouth.

"So, you have to pee, do you?"

Trudy nodded and mumbled "mm-hmm" through the tape.

Fitch said, "Wait," and went back up the stairs.

Trudy didn't think she could wait, but after what seemed like an eternity, Fitch came back down the stairs carrying a short piece of rope. He knelt in front of her and tied her ankles together, leaving just enough slack in the rope so she could shuffle along taking baby steps. The smell of alcohol was heavy on his breath.

Fitch unlocked the padlock securing her waist chain and pulled Trudy to a standing position by grabbing both of her shoulders. He pointed to the half bath and followed Trudy as she shuffled toward the toilet. Inside the small bathroom, Trudy turned and faced Fitch. Her hands were taped behind her back, making it impossible for her to undo her pants and finish her business. Fitch stood directly in front of her, his face inches from hers, and expelled air through his nose in a silent laugh as he reached for the button on her jeans. A shiver ran through Trudy as Fitch's fingers found the zipper and slowly began to pull it down. He hooked his thumbs in the top of her pants and dropped to a kneeling position, pulling her jeans and panties to the floor with one steady, unhurried motion. His eyes moved gradually from the panties on the floor, up the inside of her legs, and stopped, staring straight ahead at her femininity. The neatly trimmed, curly red triangle brought a sensation to Fitch's groin he hadn't felt in a long time. His mind flashed on his first sexual experience: the thirteen-year-old neighbor girl he'd forced into his parents' garage when he was eighteen. He was lucky he'd scared her enough, so she didn't tell. No one ever found out.

Fitch wondered what it would be like to force himself on Trudy like he did to his neighbor. His eyes wandered up her stomach, over her navel, across her tank top, and came to rest looking directly into her terrified eyes. A knowing smile formed on his lips as he decided this was not the time. He'd keep the thought alive in his head and revisit it later. As he stood, Fitch couldn't resist lightly brushing his fingers across the triangle, making Trudy flinch, and causing a few drops of urine to escape. He liked that, and his smile broadened.

Fitch backed up a step but didn't turn around. He stood there waiting for Trudy to pee. Something about watching a woman pee excited him. It had for as long as he could remember. An erotic indulgence his wife had agreed to one time when they first began dating, but never allowed again. This was his chance to relive the fantasy, and with a captive. The element of complete control, total domination over a helpless woman, enhanced the experience. He knew many people would consider it sick, but what the heck, no one would ever find out, and he really needed it.

Trudy stood there for a moment, barely able to contain the flow. Realizing Fitch was not going to turn around, she sat and experienced the orgasm-like release of a bladder on the verge of bursting.

When the tinkling sound ended, Fitch—eyes still glued to Trudy's face—reached for the toilet paper, tore off a few sheets, wadded them into a ball, and put his hand between her legs. She turned her head in disgust and tried to press her legs together, but his strength forced them apart. Remembering what he'd heard or read years ago, Fitch wiped from front to back. Something he never had to think about as a man. And he was definitely a man. Just look at him now. He brought the paper to his nose and inhaled deeply before dropping it into the toilet. The smile on his face made Trudy feel sick.

Fitch grabbed Trudy by the shoulders and pulled her off the toilet. He bent down, and taking another glance at the crimson curls, pulled up her panties and jeans. He zipped and buttoned the jeans and led her back to her support-post cell. He tightened the chain around her waist and clasped the lock. Before standing, he leaned over and kissed Trudy's cheek. She snapped her face to the side to avoid his repulsive gesture.

Undaunted, Fitch gave her neck a quick kiss and stood to go. He walked up the stairs and flicked off the light, encasing Trudy in total darkness—cold and alone.

As the cellar door closed and the deadbolt snapped into place, Fitch heard the faint sound of a cell phone ringing in Trudy's purse on the kitchen counter. He opened the purse and snatched the still-ringing phone. The name on the screen indicated the call was from Carla, Trudy's roommate. He'd met Carla several times when she came to see Trudy at the office. The ringing stopped. Fitch waited for the sound indicating a voicemail had been received. He was lucky Trudy hadn't created a password to retrieve calls. He pushed the VOICEMAIL button and waited to hear Carla's message. After the recorded voice, he heard, "Trude, it's me again. Where are you? I've called everyone, and I've been looking all over for you. No one knows where you are. I'm worried. Call me."

Fitch was relieved. Carla had no idea where Trudy was or that he'd taken her. And it appeared she didn't know of his deal with Senator Johnson. That was a good thing. He scrolled through Trudy's list of recent calls and discovered one that was particularly disturbing. A call she made to Tom Davidson, the lawyer at the Johnson law firm handling the Lawrence matter. It was made about the time he caught her in his office. That was not a good thing.

32

Jillian Lawrence sat in her living room staring out the window, drinking a glass of Riesling, and thinking about her conversation with Tom. It just didn't make sense. Theresa was such a wonderful person, and Adrian always seemed such a gentleman: although he could be a bit gruff at times. She'd assumed it was just his way of dealing with the pressures of work and life in general.

Although she almost never drank wine or any other alcoholic beverage during the day, Jillian was enjoying her second glass after finishing the first as a complement to a shrimp salad she'd prepared for lunch. The kids were in Olympia, Washington, for their annual two-week summer visit with her parents, and she was on her own: not responsible for anyone but herself. The warming effect of the wine helped take her mind off the sadness of losing Peter, and the shocking news she'd received about her neighbor Adrian. Although the first was real, the latter couldn't be. Adrian Fitch seemed like way too nice a guy to be involved with anything illegal, let alone scheming to violate the campaign contribution laws to buy political influence in Sacramento. The more she thought about it—and with the wine taking the edge off her usual good judgment—

Jillian felt she had to talk with Adrian and get to the bottom of this silliness.

Although Tom had advised her not to discuss it with Adrian, Jillian had always been someone to confront situations head on. She'd learned early on that being open and honest and talking things out usually proved most fears to be unfounded, and most misunderstandings to be just that, misunderstandings. She took the last sip of her wine, set the glass on the coffee table, and decided to pay a visit to her neighbor to clear up the unsettling rumor she'd heard.

Jillian grabbed her keys from the side table next to the front door and stepped outside, locking the door behind her. It was a perfect Southern California day, sunny and seventy-two degrees. A raven perched high atop the magnolia tree at the far end of the lawn was calling to a mate that could be heard replying way off in the distance. A Black-chinned Hummingbird was busy flitting from flower to flower drinking the life-sustaining nectar that kept its wings moving at seventy to eighty beats per second. Amazing. Jillian took a moment to soak in the beauty and peacefulness of nature before walking down her side yard to the wooden gate that separated her property from the Fitches' estate.

As she walked down the path through the Fitches' garden, Jillian found the sound of pea gravel crunching under her feet relaxing. It brought back a childhood memory of walking down the driveway leading to her grandparent's farm house. Those were wonderful times: but little did she know that as she reminisced, she was being watched by a sinister, semi-inebriated, and nervous Adrian Fitch.

Fitch set down the half-empty glass of scotch and backed away from the kitchen window. He wondered what the hell Jillian was doing? Why was she coming over when she knows Theresa's gone? Did she know about the deal with Johnson? This was not good. He had to stay calm.

Although he knew the wine cellar was sound-proof, Fitch ran to the cellar door, opened it, and took several steps down. He jabbed an index finger at his startled and terrified captive, and with a hate-ful look, whisper-yelled, "You make one sound and I'll kill you. Got it?" Trudy, cold and shivering, just looked at him. Fitch went back up the stairs and locked the door as the front entry chime sounded. On his way to confront Jillian, he stopped at the kitchen window, took another swig of whiskey and a deep breath, then calmly walked to greet his neighbor. He hoped it was a neighborly visit.

Fitch took another deep breath as his hand grasped the door handle, exhaled, put on the best smile he could muster, and opened the door. "Jil-lian, what a surprise. Good to see you. I saw you walking up the path. Come in."

With an uncertain, forced smile, Jillian said, "Hello, Adrian," and stood there looking into his eyes. Looking for some sign of innocence or guilt or whatever: something to give her a clue as to wheth-er what Tom had told her was true.

Her questioning look told Fitch all he needed to know. She had been told something: just what he wasn't sure, but something. He had to stay calm. He could handle this. Continuing to meet her gaze, Fitch's smile noticeably dimmed. He hoped she didn't catch it, and again said, "Come in, please." Lying, he continued, "It's nice of you to drop by."

Jillian did notice the change in his smile and wondered what it meant. She looked past him into the house and stepped through the doorway, silently praying she was doing the right thing. She considered what Fitch might do if Tom was right. It wasn't pretty. Maybe she shouldn't confront him.

Fitch showed her to a chair in the living room and offered to get her a drink, "Wine? Water? Juice?" Jillian declined, sat in the chair, and licked her lips. They were bone dry.

Fitch took a seat opposite her, crossed his legs, attempted a superficial smile, and stared at her. "How are you doing, Jillian? I know this is a very difficult time for you. I imagine with the kids being gone it may be even more difficult. Kids do provide a certain distraction."

Jillian looked at him and said, "No ... uh, no, I'm fine. Although I do miss the kids." Her gaze shifted to a white rose wilting in a vase on the coffee table. It was evident Theresa was gone.

Wanting to get to the point and find out what she knew, if anything, Fitch said, "Did you ever contact the lawyer I suggested? The Johnson firm."

Jillian blinked as her eyes shifted from the rose, to Adrian, back to the rose, and to the trembling hands on her lap. She looked back up at Fitch, this time without a smile, her expression strained. Her effort to appear normal by pasting on a smile caused her lower lip to tremble. She noticed an imperceptible twitch dance at the corner of Fitch's eye as he glanced to his left before locking her in his gaze. Knowing conversation was inevitable, she replied, "Yes, yes I did."

"And what do you think? Are you happy with them?"

"I am. Yes. Adrian, that's why I'm here. I heard something that greatly disturbs me, and I want to talk with you to clear it up." She looked deep into Fitch's eyes. Having broken the ice about her reason for the visit, Jillian felt a surge of confidence.

Fitch felt his jaws tighten. A knot formed in his gut. His shoulder raised up as his head tilted down to meet it: an involuntary reaction to relieve the tension in his neck. Knowing full well she was on to him, Fitch said, "Sure, Jillian, what is it?"

Her voice subdued, but continuing to look Fitch in the eyes, Jillian said, "Well, you mentioned Senator Max Johnson's name when you recommended the Johnson law firm to me, and I was wondering what you know about him?"

Fitch knew from the reference to Johnson she was on to the deal. The lump in his stomach tightened. The remnant of his wary smile faded. His jaw muscles popped with each clench of his teeth. Despite his obvious tension, Fitch gave a slight nod and responded with, "I remember, yes. I really don't know much about him. The lawyers I contacted told me he's a State Senator from San Diego and founder of the Johnson firm."

"Yes, I recall you telling me that when you suggested I contact them."

"Why do you ask?"

Jillian noticed the shift in Fitch's demeanor in response to her question and again wondered if she was doing the right thing by confronting him. She'd come this far and there was no turning back now. "This sounds so crazy I hate to bring it up. But I was told that you and the Senator may be exploiting my case to get money to him so he can win the election and use his influence to your benefit." In an attempt to mitigate her accusation, Jillian continued, "I don't believe that, Adrian. But since that's what I was told, I thought the best thing to do was face it head on, talk with you about it, and clear up the nasty rumor. It's really been bothering me."

Regaining composure, Fitch said, "My God, Jillian. That's terrible. I'm so glad you came to me with it." Certain it was Tom Davidson who told her about the plan, he feigned ignorance, again lied, and continued, "I don't know anything about the Senator other than what the other lawyers told me. Where did you hear this terrible accusation?"

"I'd rather not say just now. I don't want to get anyone in trouble for repeating something they heard."

Sensing he was defusing the situation, but not wanting to take any chance she was not completely convinced, Fitch said, "No. I understand. I can't believe anyone would spread such an awful rumor." With a forced laugh, he continued, "Perhaps I have an unknown enemy. I would never do such a thing, and I assume the Senator wouldn't either. This is extremely upsetting. It could ruin my business if such a fabrication became public."

Not certain Fitch was telling the truth, but wanting to get out of there and back home, and believing she was not going to get any more information out of him, Jillian said, "I didn't think it was true. Thank you for being so understanding, Adrian, and clearing that up for me."

Feeling a bit relieved, a tentative smile reappeared on Fitch's face, and he said, "Absolutely. Thank you for coming to me to talk about it. I can't believe anyone would try to sabotage me like that. Please tell whoever told you that fantastic story, it's not true."

As Jillian assured Fitch she would not repeat a lie, he heard the muffled ring of Trudy's cell phone coming from her purse on the kitchen counter. His eyes shifted toward the sound for a moment. The ring and eye movement did not go unnoticed by Jillian. Fitch thought he'd turned the sound off. *Shit.* He hoped Jillian didn't hear it and wondered if the damn thing would ever stop ringing?

Coercing a smile and hoping to get Jillian out of the house without her hearing the phone, Fitch stood, extended his hand, and said, "Jillian, I'm so glad you came to me, and we had this talk. Please, call me or come over again if you have any other concerns."

Jillian stood, took his hand, and hoping to get a glimpse of his soul, looked into his eyes one last time. They were empty.

When she was gone, Fitch returned to the kitchen window, killed the last of his glass of whiskey, and watched Jillian walk home. She seemed deep in thought. He poured another glass of whiskey, neat.

Raising the glass to the window and Jillian, he said to himself in a menacing voice, "You will not harm me.

33

The phone kept ringing, and like the other calls, went to Trudy's voicemail after the fourth ring. It was the fifth time Carla had called her since receiving the earlier message. Something was not right. It was unlike Trudy not to return her calls. Carla disconnected the call and leaned back into the overstuffed sofa. She felt sick. She'd called everyone she could think of and checked all the places where Trudy might have gone. No Trudy. She had to do something. Her friend needed her. She couldn't just sit there and do nothing. Although it had been less than six hours since Trudy left the voice message, Carla decided to call the police. Maybe she could convince someone to bend the twenty-four-hour missing person rule and start to search for her friend. She entered the San Diego PD number into her phone and pressed CALL.

A pleasant, official-sounding voice said, "San Diego Police Department. This is Sergeant Wilkins."

Relieved to be talking with the police, Carla said, "Sergeant Wilkins, thank you for taking my call."

"Yes, ma'am. How may I help you?"

Desperation colored Carla's voice. "Sergeant, I dropped my roommate off at her office this morning, and she left a voicemail for me shortly afterward asking me to pick her up right away. She said she was scared. I keep calling her, but I get no answer or returned call. It isn't like her to not call back. She's not at her office. I've checked with her friends and all the places I know where she might have gone. No one has seen or heard from her. Sergeant, something's wrong. I need your help."

Sounding a bit like he was reading from a script, Sergeant Wilkins asked, "How long ago was it she called you?"

"About six hours." And before Wilkins could respond, Carla continued, "Sir, I know about your twenty-four-hour rule. Please don't tell me to wait. My friend is in trouble. I know she is. Please, try to find her now. Please."

"Ma'am, we don't have a twenty-four-hour rule to report a missing person. If you believe she's missing, I'll take your report and forward it to the Missing Persons Unit where it will be entered in the national data base of missing persons. But most likely your friend is fine and will contact you. That's how these things usually work out. I know it's difficult but try to be patient."

"Oh, thank you, Sergeant. Can I make the report now over the phone?"

"Yes, ma'am."

Carla gave him the requested information, and asked, "Sergeant, can you start to search for her now? She said she was scared, and I know she's in trouble. Trudy wouldn't say that unless she needed help."

"I'll have a unit swing by her office to see if she's returned and to look for anything that would warrant a further search at this time. But unless the person is a minor, suffers from a physical or mental impairment, or foul play is suspected, there isn't much more we can do. Every competent adult has a right to not be found if that's what they choose to do."

"I understand. Thank you."

"In the meantime, we'll contact you if we locate her, and please, let us know if she returns."

"OK. Thanks again."

Carla hung up and fell back onto the sofa as a tear rolled down her cheek.

34

Back in San Diego, Tom finished the last of a tuna salad sandwich as he contemplated what he should do about the disturbing information he'd received from Trudy. He had to do something but didn't feel he had enough solid facts to go to the police. He didn't know if Brad was involved and certainly didn't want to confront him if he was. After weighing various options, Tom decided to go back to the office, and if no one was there, see what he could find.

He guided his rusty Bug onto the I-5 freeway southbound and was immediately stuck in stop-and-go traffic. All he could see was a never-ending line of trucks and cars, four lanes wide, with no apparent cause in sight. An ambulance approached from behind in the emergency lane with its lights flashing, indicating a distant accident was the culprit: an occurrence becoming more and more frequent as San Diego continued to attract snowbirds and people hoping to find work in the city. Tom was able to get off at the next exit and navigate the rest of the way to the office on surface streets. He'd only been delayed about five minutes by the time he pulled into the firm parking lot. It was empty. That was good.

Tom parked in a space that couldn't be seen from the street. He killed the engine and wondered why he'd chosen a secluded spot since no one in town—other than Jan—knew what he'd been told. And he had every right to be at the office on a Saturday catching up on work. But for some strange reason it made him feel safer.

Tom entered the building and found the reception area empty. He checked the offices, conference room, kitchen, and restroom to make sure he was alone. He walked into Brad's office and opened the blinds a bit so he could see anyone approaching the front from the parking lot. It was a sunny day, and he was able to see around the office without having to turn on the lights.

Brad's top desk drawer was open a crack, so Tom started there. He found pens, pencils, yellow legal pads, Post-it Notes, a half-eaten bag of M&Ms, rubber bands, and paper clips: but nothing relating to the Senator and Mr. Fitch. Two other drawers contained more of the same, plus phone books and a few closed files. The bottom-drawer was locked, and Tom couldn't find the key. Brad must have taken it with him. He would have to try to get into it another time: assuming he could get his hands on the key or be lucky enough to have Brad forget to lock it. Brad's computer would also have to be checked another time since Tom didn't have the passcode to access it.

There was nothing on top of the desk except the computer monitor, a wireless mouse, a plastic bin for outgoing and incoming mail, and Brad's calendar. Tom flipped the calendar open to the first page and methodically worked his way through each page. It was filled with reminders for court hearings, meetings, lunch dates, tennis dates, and a few encrypted notes he couldn't decipher. There were two entries that caught Tom's attention. One on May 9th read: **Adrian Fitch (213) 888-8666 dad call**. The other on May 13th read: **Fitch = Lawrence's neighbor**. The entries made a connection between Fitch and the Senator, but standing alone, didn't prove any wrongdoing. They also established Brad was aware of a connection between his dad and Fitch. But they didn't prove he was in any way involved in illegal activity. They also didn't prove he wasn't involved.

Tom closed the calendar and returned it to the spot on Brad's desk where he'd found it. He leafed through a few papers scattered on top of Brad's credenza but didn't find any useful information. As he turned to leave, there was a loud bang on Brad's window. Tom involuntarily shouted, "Hey," and whirled around to face the window. He dropped to the floor—his heart racing. After staring at the window for a full minute, he regained his composure and got to his feet. He walked to the window and looked out but saw nothing unusual except a single gray feather stuck to the glass, confirming his suspicion it was a bird strike.

Other than Brad's note linking Fitch to the Senator, Tom didn't have anything more to establish criminal activity than what he had when he arrived at the office: and he didn't have enough to know if Brad was involved. He'd play it safe for now and not say anything to him. He believed Trudy, but at this point no crime had been committed—other than perhaps conspiracy to commit a crime. And that would be very difficult to prove since there was no settlement in the case and no money had changed hands. It would be hard to prove wrongdoing even if there was a large settlement because cases settled every day for huge sums of money. Without more, it was just Trudy's word against Fitch and Senator Johnson. Not likely enough to sway a jury.

Tom left the office and headed back home. Perhaps Trudy had discovered something since he talked with her that would substantiate the conversation she'd overheard. He'd give her a call again later.

35

Fitch sat at the desk in his study swirling the last of his fifth whiskey in a crystal tumbler Theresa had given him fifteen years ago. A few drops of amber liquid spotted the desk, the result of vigorous swirling. He was calmer now and more certain of himself than he was when Jillian left. The study's hunter green walls produced a relaxing effect and created a sense of security. He gazed out the window to the back yard with its manicured hedges. Granite stairs led to a crystal-clear pool, Jacuzzi, and a pool house with bar and sauna. Ahh, the sauna. A place he'd enjoyed on many intimate occasions eight or nine years ago with the maid when Theresa was shopping, playing tennis, or out with her girlfriends. Maybe he'd try to look her up again one of these days.

What was he going to do about Jillian? She obviously knew way too much and possessed the power to ruin him. He could not allow that to happen.

Fitch retrieved his keys from his pants pocket and unlocked the desk drawer. He slowly opened the top drawer and sat staring at the revolver he'd kept concealed in his desk for years. It was a Smith & Wesson .38 Special his father had given him when he turned eighteen. It was originally his grandfather's gun and had been given to his father back in the 1920s. The gun had never been registered, and its existence was not known to any living person, except Fitch. Perhaps it could solve his Jillian problem.

After downing the rest of his whiskey, Fitch reached into the drawer and gripped the revolver. It felt sure, solid, and cool against his skin. He paused for a second before withdrawing his hand from the drawer. The weapon was loaded with six deadly rounds: it had been since he moved into the house.

Fitch stood and felt a slight dizziness with the sudden movement. He let his head clear, locked the desk, and with the revolver firmly grasped in his hand, walked out of his office. He didn't have a plan but knew he had to get to Jillian before she had a chance to talk to anyone else.

With his liquid courage at its peak, Fitch slipped the gun into his pants pocket and walked through the kitchen. He paused at the window and looked at Jillian's house to see if she had any visitors. Her car was parked near the front door, but there were no other vehicles in sight. The gardeners did her yard on Saturday, but the truck that had been parked in the driveway earlier in the morning was gone. They'd moved on to the next client.

Fitch went out the front door, stopped, and did a visual sweep of his property to make sure he was not being watched. Seeing no one, he quickly walked down his side yard toward the gate leading to Jillian's.

Jillian was changing the sheets on her bed when she saw Fitch round the corner of his house and start down the path toward the gate connecting their lots. She felt a momentary panic when she realized she was alone. Since the kids were at their grandparents for two weeks, Jillian had let Lupe off for a much-needed vacation to visit her family in Mexico. Lupe hadn't been home in three years and missed her close-knit family. Reassuring herself she'd convinced Fitch she didn't believe the rumor about him and Senator Johnson, Jillian dropped the pillow case she was holding and headed downstairs to meet him.

The door chime sounded as she reached the bottom of the stairs. It sounded again before she could get to the door: Fitch seemed impatient. That was unusual since he'd always come across to her as a very calm person.

Jillian opened the door and saw Fitch leaning against the entry wall. He immediately straightened up when she said, "Adrian."

He forced a weak smile and said, "Hi, Jillian."

His eyes looked glazed, and she caught a faint whiff of alcohol on his breath. She also detected a slight slur when he said her name. Feeling uneasy, she was about to shut the door when Fitch started through it, causing Jillian to move aside to avoid being bumped. The aggressive behavior was uncharacteristic of the Adrian she knew, and her sense of unease heightened.

Continuing to hold the door open, Jillian said, "What can I do for you, Adrian?"

He turned, took two steps toward her, and shut the door. "You can talk to me, Jillian. That's what you can do for me. You can talk to me." Standing in front of her, his face inches from hers, the scent of alcohol was unmistakable. He turned toward the living room, and reaching for her elbow but missing, walked to the nearest sofa and sat down. Jillian contemplated running out the door. But never knowing Adrian to be violent, she followed and stood behind the sofa across from him.

"Adrian, why are you acting this way? Are you drunk?"

Fitch responded with a more pronounced slur, "Perhaps jus' a bit. But that's beside the point. Righ' now, you need to tell me all you know 'bout the rumor you heard. Tell me who told you."

Contemplating her response, Jillian's arm pits dampened as her fingers worked the pleat on the back cushion of the sofa. With Fitch staring straight into her eyes, she did her best to keep the fear out of her voice when she answered. "Adrian, I've already told you all I know. And I told you I believe it's only a sick rumor. I don't know who started it or why. I certainly would never pass such a thing on to anyone. I assure you."

Without shifting his gaze, and with an ice-edged tone in his voice, Fitch said, "Let's jus' assume I believe you, which I don't. But, let's jus' say I do." Continuing, Fitch shouted, "I still wanna know who told you such garbage."

Sensing she was in danger, Jillian looked around the room as her mind raced through different scenarios as to what she should do next. How could she get away from him? Where could she hide? She remembered the .22 revolver Peter had always kept in the night stand next to the bed but wasn't sure it was still there. She'd only fired it once and that was years ago. Anyway, such drastic action wasn't going to be necessary. Adrian will calm down, and this will be resolved without resorting to violence.

Fitch yelled, "Jillian, tell me who told you."

Startled, Jillian looked back at Fitch and said, "Adrian, I told you I don't want to involve anyone else in this, especially since it's just rumor."

Fitch jumped to his feet, causing Jillian to fall back a step. With an evil look in his eyes, and his voice deliberate and menacing, he said, "It was that damn lawyer of yours, wasn't it? What's his name? Tom something.

"No, Adrian—"

Pulling the revolver from his pocket, Fitch screamed, "Don't you lie to me. I know it was him."

As he raised the gun and pointed it toward Jillian, she bolted to her right and headed up the stairs. Her foot hit the first step as a shot rang out. The decorative sconce at the bottom of the stairs exploded, sending shards of glass flying everywhere, and striking the side of her face. The alcohol, combined with the fact Fitch was not a trained marksman, worked in Jillian's favor as she took the stairs three at a time. Half way to the second floor, another round hit the hand rail to her right, causing splinters of wood to dust the stairs in front of her. She topped the stairs and sprinted toward the master bedroom as a third shot blew a hole in the ceiling plaster directly in line with where her head had been a split second before.

The sound of Fitch's feet hitting the stairs echoed in Jillian's ears as she raced into the bedroom, closed and locked the door, and dashed to the night stand on—what used to be—Peter's side of the bed. She jerked the drawer open with such force it pulled completely out of the cabinet and crashed to the floor, spilling the contents around her feet and under the bed. She looked down but didn't see the revolver: three shells lay at her feet she assumed were for the gun. Dropping to her knees, Jillian frantically swept her hands across the carpet beneath the bed. Nothing. She flattened on her stomach to look under the bed as she heard Fitch's body slam into the door. Thankfully, it was a solid door, and it held. Jillian made a visual sweep and saw the weapon on the floor beneath the center of the bed. She stretched her arm out as far as she could but was still a couple of inches shy. Fitch crashed into the door again, and this time she heard a cracking sound. As solid as it was, the door couldn't withstand much more. She pushed with all her might and forced her shoulder a bit farther under the bed, just enough so her fingertips touched the handle of the gun. Scraping with her fingers, she managed to move it closer and was able to grab the handle and pull it out from under the bed. She rose to her knees and picked up one of the shells as Fitch hit the door: this time she heard a loud snap. He'd be in the room on his next try. Jillian checked the cylinder. It was empty. She attempted to insert a round but was shaking so badly she dropped it.

Fitch, exhausted from the stair sprint and body slams to the door, paused, and yelled, "You're not going to get away, Jillian. So jus' open the door and make it easy on yourself. We can talk 'bout this."

Jillian retrieved the bullet she'd dropped, and with convulsing hands, managed to insert it into the chamber. She remembered Peter telling her it was a single-action revolver, and she'd have to cock the hammer before it would fire. She pulled the hammer back as Fitch struck the door for a fourth time, splintering the frame and breaking through the door, revealing his demonic presence. The sudden burst of the door caused Jillian to wheel around with the gun raised and pointed in Fitch's direction. Without thinking, she pulled the trigger, and a loud bang erupted from the weapon. The shot was wide and struck the door frame to Fitch's left.

Fitch ducked and moved to the right while firing off two shots in rapid succession. One hit Jillian in the left shoulder, and the other produced a liquid-red spot in the middle of her chest. The force knocked her into a sitting position against the night stand as her finger involuntarily pulled the trigger of the uncocked gun. Her eyes stared blankly at Fitch as she attempted to raise her arm in defense. Her lips moved as though she was trying to speak, but there was no sound, just a gurgling noise from deep in her throat, as a trickle of blood began to flow from her mouth. Her arm dropped to the floor, and her head fell forward onto her chest. Jillian Lawrence was dead.

Fitch dropped to his knees with his eyes locked on Jillian. He felt a sense of panic course through his body. He'd never killed anyone before and felt like he was going to vomit. *No, don't puke. Don't leave anything behind. Think. Think. What should I do?*

The initial panic passed after a couple of minutes, and Fitch stood. He retrieved the two spent shell casings, and after turning to confirm Jillian was not breathing, walked out of the bedroom and into the upstairs hall. As he was about to go down the stairs, he paused. *Did I touch anything? Yes, the bedroom door handle.* He walked back to the door, and using the end of the tennis shirt he was wearing, wiped the handle to eliminate any finger prints he may have left. Although he didn't remember grabbing the stair railing as he ran up, he used his shirt to wipe it from the top of the stairs to the bottom. You can't be too careful in a situation like that. He picked up the two shell casings at the bottom of the stairs and the one next to the sofa, stuffing them in his pants pocket along with his revolver.

Although he knew both kids and the housekeeper would be gone for at least another week, he looked around to be sure no one was there. That should give him enough time to get this unfortunate matter resolved before anyone discovered the corpse.

Adrenaline was racing through Fitch's body, and his breathing was labored. He was out of shape and not used to the intense activity he'd just experienced. Previously unnoticed, a sharp pain was running up and down his right thigh. He must have pulled something racing up the stairs. Fitch made his way to the front door, and using his shirt to turn the handle, opened it a crack. He peered out the door and surveyed as much as was visible through the small opening. Satisfied the immediate vicinity was clear, he opened the door wider and scanned the entire front area of Jillian's property. There was no one in sight. Fitch cautiously stepped through the open door and onto the portico. Without turning around, he pulled the door closed behind him with his foot. He limped back down the side yard: his eyes continually searching for any sign someone might be watching him.

When Fitch reached his side entrance, he opened it, walked in, closed the door behind him, and leaned back against the door frame. He was exhausted, and thankful for the privacy provided by large estates endowed with lots of trees, shrubbery, and walls. He'd made it back undetected.

36

It was a beautiful San Diego Saturday afternoon, and Tom had just finished his regular five mile run on Mission Bay, trying to make sense of what Trudy had told him, and mulling over what he should do next. A mild breeze blew the scent of the sea from the west, filling Tom's lungs with the redolence of seaweed, salt, and fish, and bringing a sense of peace to an otherwise disturbing day.

Tom opened the door to his Bug and grabbed the towel from the front seat. He stood next to his old clunker and dried off before getting in. A family of four was having a picnic on the grass near the water. A half-dozen twenty-something guys were engaged in an intense game of basketball, while a dad pushed his young son on the swing set next to the basketball court. It all seemed so peaceful. How could the gross lack of conscience and moral perversion that Trudy had conveyed to him coexist on the same planet with all this apparent normalcy?

As a bead of sweat ran down the middle of his back, Tom tossed the towel on the front passenger seat, got in, and drove home. It was a short drive back to his apartment, and the whole way he kept replaying the conversation he'd had with Trudy over and over again in his mind. It didn't make sense that a successful State Senator and the owner of a major insurance company would risk it all to retain a State Senate seat on the one hand, and perhaps gain some political influence on the other. It didn't jibe with the image of the Senator he'd met at graduation. Or maybe it did. The Senator did seem intent on talking with and touching everyone at the graduation. But then again, that's what politicians do: they try to make contact with as many people as possible to create a sense of connection and garner votes.

Dot Harmon wasn't out and about performing her normal managerial duties when Tom pulled into his parking space at the apartment. Although he usually enjoyed chatting with Dot, it was a good thing she wasn't around. He wasn't in the mood for small talk: too many confusing issues clouding his mind. Tom gathered his things from the car and headed to his unit. He wiped the remaining sand from his legs and feet before he went in. Once inside, he checked his cell to see if there were any new messages from Trudy. Nothing. He decided to clean up before trying to contact her. He dropped his T-shirt, shorts, and socks into the hamper and adjusted the shower temperature to tolerably hot. The running water helped take his mind off the craziness of the world.

Shower finished, Tom grabbed a Gatorade from the refrigerator and sat at the kitchen table to give Trudy a call. Her voicemail picked up after the fourth ring. Tom almost hung up to give it a try later. Instead, he said, "Hey, Trudy, it's Tom. Just checking to see if you found out anything more about the conversation you heard. I called Mrs. Lawrence to give her a heads up and told her not to confront Fitch. Anyway, give me a call when you can."

Tom hung up and sat sipping his drink. He assumed Trudy was either on another call or not near her phone. He had no idea that the phone with the message he'd just left was sitting on Fitch's kitchen counter. He decided to call Jan to give her an update and see if she had any more ideas about how to handle the situation. Although he hoped she might have some sagely advice, he mainly wanted to make plans to get together with her. He dialed, and she picked up on the second ring.

"Hi, Tom. I've been thinking about you. I can't get the thing with Fitch and the Senator out of my mind. Anything new?"

"Well, I called Mrs. Lawrence and filled her in on what I heard. She seemed surprised: always thought Fitch was a really nice guy. I advised her not to contact him about it because who knows how he might react? Oh, I drove to the office and went through Brad's desk and calendar but didn't find much. Just a couple of calendar entries that show he knows about Fitch, but nothing indicating he's involved. One of his desk drawers was locked, so I'll have to try it another time if I can get the key. And his computer was password protected, so I couldn't check it either."

"I know his password, unless he changed it in the last four months. He called me one day needing some information from his contact list and gave me the password so I could check. It's *tennisman*. All lower case. Brad thinks he's such a great tennis player, so it was easy to remember."

"Thanks, Jan, that's great. I'll try to get down there tomorrow and check it out. I really appreciate your help. Hey, if you're up for it, let's do lunch, drinks, or something one of these days."

Hoping for a chance to see Tom again, Jan said, "I'd love it. Let's talk on Monday and pick a time that's good for both of us."

Tom's cheeks flushed. "Great. I'll call you Monday. Thanks again. Have a good rest of your weekend."

"You too."

With that, they hung up. Unbeknown to one another, each sat smiling while thoughts about the coming week occupied the moment.

37

Fitch awoke with a start at the sound of a loud bang against his door. He sat there, confused, still deep in the stupor of alcohol and sleep. He looked around the room. For a moment he couldn't remember where he was. Then the disorientation caused by his profound REM state wore off, and he realized he was in his study. There had been no bang against the door. It was simply a dream, or perhaps a nightmare. Anyway, he was back in the real world and safe in his recliner. He picked up the whiskey bottle from his desk and poured a full glass. No need for ice. That would require him to get up and walk to the minibar: too much effort required for so little gain. He turned on his computer and found his favorite Pandora station: classical solo piano. Soothing music played as he ran his finger around the rim of the Waterford tumbler. Leaning back in his chair and sipping the amber elixir always seemed to alleviate stress. The seriousness of his situation faded further and further into the ether with each drop from his glass.

Fitch pushed himself up from his chair after consuming two glasses of alcohol and almost fell over his desk in the process. He managed to make it to the study door, open it, and bounce off the door frame as he proceeded through to the kitchen. The walls, floor, and appliances all seemed to be moving in different directions as he worked his way to the sink—where he threw up.

With his stomach emptied, and after splashing cold water on his face, Fitch felt a little better: more stable on his feet. He looked outside and noticed it was getting dark. There was the slightest hint of pink in the western sky. *God, how long have I been asleep?* A glance at the clock on the microwave told him it was almost 8:30 p.m. When he turned to lean against the sink, he saw Trudy's cell phone lying on the counter. Curious as to who may have tried to call her, he made it to the phone and noticed the VOICEMAIL icon indicated three new calls. He pushed the button to retrieve the messages and was relieved to hear the first two were from her roommate, Carla: still trying to contact her, and still having no idea where she was. The third message was a different story—very disturbing. It was that lawyer, Tom somebody, trying to find out if she had any new information about the conversation she'd heard. *Damn.* Now he knew for sure the lawyer was involved. That would not do. He had to put a stop to that kid before knowledge of his plan spread any further. Fitch disconnected the voice message and slammed the phone on the counter with such force it cracked the glass front. He grabbed his head with both hands, entwined his fingers in his hair, and pulled so hard he jerked out a few strands. The pain helped him to briefly sober up a bit.

Realizing he hadn't checked on Trudy for several hours, Fitch stagger-walked to the cellar door. He unlocked it, flicked on the light, and stumbled down the stairs: relying on the handrail to keep from falling. He balanced himself against the wall at the bottom of the stairs and looked at Trudy with unsteady eyes.

Trudy had fallen asleep as a result of terror-induced exhaustion and the total darkness of the cellar. Her chin jerked up from her chest when her coma-like sleep was shattered by the light, causing her head to strike the support post. She was immediately aware that Fitch was standing a few feet away, staring at her. Sleep had caused her entire body to relax, including her bladder. Her jeans were wet, and a puddle of liquid surrounded her thighs and buttocks.

Awake now, Trudy's entire body began to shake from the fifty-five-degree temperature of the cellar. The initial warmth provided by the release of urine had long since dissipated. The now cold liquid only added to her discomfort. The skin on her face had taken on the look of alabaster with a slight bluish tint to her lips. She tried to say she was cold, but the tape was so tight on her mouth the sound that emanated from her throat was an unintelligible moan.

Despite his drunkenness, Fitch could tell by looking at Trudy she was cold. Whether a remnant of kindness emerged from the deep recesses of his dark soul, or because he didn't want her to die just yet, Fitch turned, and using the handrail for balance, ascended the stairs.

Walking the straightest line he could manage, but occasionally using the kitchen counter top and appliances to keep him on course, Fitch made it to the garage where he found an old, dusty moving blanket left behind by the crew who delivered the Steinway grand piano he'd surprised Theresa with on her fiftieth birthday. Generally considered the first choice in pianos for serious concert pianists, its craftsmanship far surpassed Theresa's skill at the keys. But, when you're filthy rich, what the heck.

Fitch grabbed the blanket, gave it a drunken shake, and headed back into the kitchen. As he passed the refrigerator, he realized he never gave Trudy anything to eat, and she probably hadn't eaten since breakfast, or perhaps the night before. Not so much out of a concern for her, but more out of his desire to keep her alive and functioning in case he wanted to partake of her feminine pleasures later, Fitch opened the fridge and grabbed a bottle of Tasmanian Rain water and the leftovers of his deli-dinner from two nights ago: a broiled chicken leg and a half pint of coleslaw. He picked up a dirty fork from the sink and made his way back down the stairs to Trudy.

She winced as Fitch dropped the blanket and plopped down cross-legged next to her, causing the dirty fork to bounce off the floor and into the urine puddle next to her thigh. Fitch draped the blanket over Trudy's shoulders, letting the bottom end soak up the liquid from the floor. He ripped the tape from her mouth with such force that it tore her skin in a couple of places. The pain brought tears to Trudy's eyes even as the warmth from the blanket calmed her shaking.

Fitch picked up the fork from the remains of the urine and wiped it dry on Trudy's jeans. He scooped up some coleslaw and held the fork to her mouth.

From the looks of the dirty fork, and knowing where it had just been, Trudy contemplated whether she should accept his offering. But the hunger pangs won, and she opened her mouth.

Chained to the support beam with her hands tied behind her back, Trudy accepted the slaw and chicken Fitch shoveled into her mouth, interspersed with sips of water. She took each bite and chewed slowly, keeping her eyes averted so as not to have to look at the devil feeding her. She knew she had to eat to keep up her strength if she was ever going to survive this ordeal.

Fitch grimaced as he lifted the bottle of water to Trudy's lips. He thought Tasmanian Rain water was a real joke. At five dollars for a 750ml bottle, what a waste. He remembered Theresa discovering it on a visit to Tasmania several years ago. She was so impressed with the fact it was collected straight to the bottle from the sky without touching the ground that it instantly became her favorite water: and the only water she drank at home. She found an independent distributor in LA and had it delivered to the house once a month ever since. Why not just collect rain in a bucket in the back yard and save the expense? But then again, as the song says, it hardly ever rains in Southern California. And the rain that does fall undoubtedly contains more solid garbage than the rain that falls in remote Tasmania. Who knows? Anyway, just another way to squander money when you're wealthy.

The feeding finished, Fitch got to his knees, collected the fork, bottle, and plastic container and leaned over to give Trudy a kiss. She jerked her head to the side, causing him to lose his balance and smack his forehead on the beam. In spite of her fear, a slight smile tickled the corners of her mouth as Fitch dropped the items he was holding, raised a hand to his forehead, and yelled, "Shit!"

Fitch grabbed Trudy's face, pulled it to within an inch of his, and growled, "You bitch. You will pay for that. You and your lawyer friend." Panic returned to Trudy's eyes as he continued, "That's right. I know about your little conversation with Tom. The message he left on your phone confirms it. He will pay too. Neither of you will get away with trying to mess with me. I'm much bigger than the two of you put together."

After a long, silent stare into Trudy's eyes, Fitch pushed her head back into the beam, retaped her mouth, picked up the things he'd dropped, and went back upstairs.

38

Carla leaned against the arm of her sofa and stared out the window while the dark eastern sky softened, progressing from lighter and lighter shades of gray to deeper and deeper blue tones. The dawn was highlighted by a few wispy, pink clouds. It was becoming another beautiful Southern California day, but Carla's mind was fixed on her friend Trudy, and the fact she hadn't heard from her in almost twenty-four hours. The afghan she'd used to repel the night chill still covered her legs, but it had done nothing to eliminate the inner chill she felt when thinking about Trudy.

Carla hadn't eaten since breakfast the day before, but she didn't feel hungry. The Ibuprofen she'd taken at 5:00 a.m. failed to allay her unease. At 8:46 a.m., she dialed Trudy's cell one more time in hopes that by some miracle she'd answer, be unharmed, and on her way home from spending the night with some wonderful, romantic new lover. Carla knew it was wishful thinking. That wasn't Trudy's style. The call went straight to voicemail, and Carla hung up without leaving a message. She brushed the afghan off her legs and went to the kitchen to make coffee. With only two hours of restless sleep, she'd need the kick of caffeine if she was going to get through the day and make the inevitable call to Trudy's parents.

The light on the coffee maker switched to green, indicating the caffeine buzz was ready and waiting. Carla poured a large mug of the brew and headed back to the sofa as the clock slipped slowly on toward 9:00 a.m., making it a whole day since she'd last seen Trudy.

After a few sips of coffee, and needing to know what the police were doing, Carla navigated to the recent calls menu where she'd stored the main number for the Los Angeles Police Department. She pressed the CALL button.

The phone had rung for what seemed like an interminably long time for a call to the police department, when a familiar voice finally answered with, "Los Angeles Police Department. This is Sergeant Wilkins. How may I help you?"

"Sergeant Wilkins. Oh good. I'm glad it's you. This is Carla Bodean. I called you yesterday about my missing friend Trudy Greene."

"Yes, Ms. Bodean, I remember. Have you heard from Trudy?"

"No, sir. That's why I'm calling. I was wondering if you'd found her and what's being done to search for her. There's no way she wouldn't have contacted me by now if she was all right."

"I understand. We haven't located her, but a unit was sent to her office after we spoke. They didn't find any evidence of foul play so there's nothing more we can do at this time. We'll let you know if we find her."

"Thank you, Sergeant. I just know she needs help. You asked if I have a photo of Trudy, and I remembered one I took a few months ago. Do you want me to bring it to you?"

"Yes. A picture can be very helpful."

"I'll be there in twenty minutes. Should I ask for you?"

"Yes, ma'am. I'll send the photo to the officer assigned to Trudy's case."

"Oh, thank you so much, Sergeant. I'll get there as fast as I can. Thank you."

"My pleasure, Ms. Bodean. See you when you get here."

With that, Carla hung up, jumped off the sofa, and headed to the shower to wash off the sweat and stress-induced odor brought on by the anxiety of the past twenty-four hours. The hot water helped relax the tension in her muscles as she leaned against the shower wall with eyes closed and said a silent prayer for her friend.

Feeling rejuvenated, Carla toweled off, brushed her teeth, and applied deodorant. She combed her hair back to dry before picking up her phone to call Trudy's parents. She'd avoided making the call until now because she didn't want to needlessly worry the Greene family. Trudy was very close to her mom, dad, and other relatives back in South Carolina, and Carla knew the news of her disappearance would devastate them.

Dolores Greene, Trudy's mom, picked up on the third ring with, "Hello."

"Dolores, this is Carla Bodean."

With a smile in her voice, Dolores said, "Carla. How nice to hear from you. It's been too long."

Carla's mind flashed on the name Dolores, and the one Latin class she'd taken in high school. Although she'd forgotten almost everything she'd learned in the class, hearing the name reminded her that Dolores was derived from a Latin word meaning sorrows. How sadly appropriate given the news she was about to deliver.

"Yes, it has been a while. Dolores, I'm calling because I took Trudy to work yesterday morning and haven't heard from her since, except for a voice message she left not long after I dropped her off. I thought maybe she'd been in contact with you."

Fear pervaded Dolores's response. "Oh no. Oh God, no. No, I haven't heard from her. Have you called her friends?"

"I've called everyone I can think of since she left the message yesterday. I've driven to all the places where I thought she might go, but no one has seen her. I filed a missing person report and am on my way to the police station now with Carla's picture. The police put her information in a national data base and went to her office, but they won't do much more at this time because she's a healthy adult and there's no evidence of foul play."

Fighting through sobs, Dolores managed to say, "Oh ... I think ... I'm going to be sick. Carla, please let me know if you hear anything. Oh dear ... I don't know if Ted can take this. He's been having some heart issues. Oh God, keep her safe. Carla, we'll be on the first plane we can get out of here."

"I'll call you as soon as I know more. She's going to be alright, Dolores. They'll find her." Carla heard a loud cry on the other end of the line as Dolores hung up.

Carla pulled on a pair of faded jeans, a wrinkled T-shirt, and sandals: then grabbed a photograph of Trudy she'd taken three months earlier on a hike in the San Bernardino Mountains. Trudy hated the picture because she thought it made her face look fat. Fat or not, it just might save her life. Carla picked up her purse, ran out the door, and was at the station eight minutes later.

39

At 8:43 a.m. Sunday morning, Carrie Sullivan dialed Jillian's cell phone for the third time in ten minutes to let her know she'd be a few minutes late picking her up for their weekly tennis game. Each time her call had gone to voicemail. Something wasn't right. Jillian never forgot their tennis date and always answered her cell when Carrie called to say she was on her way. They'd played tennis together every Sunday at 9:00 a.m. for the past eight years unless one of them was sick or on vacation.

Carrie considered Jillian to be her best friend, and the two of them spent a great deal of time together having lunch, wine tasting in Santa Barbara, shopping, and just hanging out talking about kids, school, and life in general. They often kidded one another that if they were lesbian they'd wind up together. On one occasion several years ago, they did kiss. It started out innocently enough and startled both of them. They were on one of their trips in the mountains above Santa Barbara. They decided to spend the night and hit a few more wineries the next day. A bottle of Cabernet Sauvignon was shared during dinner, and they were back in their room getting ready for bed. The lights were low, and soft jazz drifted up from the patio below. Carrie was standing naked at the bathroom vanity wiping mascara from her eyes when Jillian stepped out of the shower. Jillian's body was tanned and nicely toned: water dripped from her jet-black hair. Their eyes locked in the mirror above the vanity, and after an erotic moment, Carrie turned and walked over to Jillian. Their lips touched and tongues met, but at the same instant both pulled back and silently whispered, "No." Not wanting to do anything to hurt their families, they stopped right there and never discussed the incident again. Although the wonder of "what if" remained ever present in their minds.

Concerned that Jillian was either having a problem with her cell phone or needed help, Carrie grabbed her car keys and tennis bag and headed to her car. It was a short drive down Mulholland to Jillian's house. They only lived three-quarters of a mile apart. Concern for her friend helped Carrie make the trip in less than half her normal time. She turned into Jillian's driveway, punched in the gate code, and as the house came into view, she saw Jillian's car parked near the front door where she usually left it. At least it looked like she was home. That was a good sign. Maybe it was just a cell phone issue.

Carrie stopped behind Jillian's Mercedes and shut off the engine. She glanced through the living room window but didn't see any lights on or any sign of activity. She got out, walked to the front door, and rang the bell. She could hear the chimes reverberate throughout the house but heard neither footsteps nor Jillian's cheery voice saying she'd be right there. Carrie pushed the doorbell again with the same result. Becoming increasingly worried, she pounded on the door but was again greeted with an eerie silence from the other side. She walk-ran to the front window, and leaning as far as she could over the bushes in front of the window, cupped her hands to the glass and peered in. From her limited vantage point she didn't see anything unusual. She walked back to the front entry and dialed Jillian's cell. No answer.

Her worry turning to fear, Carrie tried the door handle, and much to her surprise, the door opened a crack. Something was wrong. Jillian never left the front door unlocked. In fact, she was very anal about it being locked: a trait instilled by her parents when she was a child.

Afraid to open the door any wider for fear of what she might find, Carrie called out through the opening, "Jillian?" Then louder, "Jillian. It's me, Carrie." No response. A chill ran up her spine as she instinctively looked behind her to make sure no one was there. Taking a deep breath, and mustering all the courage she had, Carrie gave the door a push, opening it fully. Her eyes fell first on the shattered glass sconce at the bottom of the stairs. There clearly was a problem.

Still standing at the open door and afraid to enter, she called out again, "Jillian? Jillian, answer me. Are you OK?" No answer. Just a deadly stillness that sent a shiver through Carrie and caused the hair on her arms to bristle. Her heart was pounding in her chest, and her knees felt like rubber. Terrified an intruder might still be in the house, and not thinking to call the police, she slowly stepped through the open door, her eyes frantically scanning every direction at once, her body poised to flee at the first sight of someone who didn't belong there.

Carrie made her way through the living room and didn't see anything unusual other than the broken glass at the bottom of the stairs. "Jillian? Jillian, please answer me if you're here." She looked in the kitchen, dining room, and laundry room but didn't see a thing out of place. While in the kitchen, she grabbed a large knife from the cutlery block on the center island and checked the back door. It was locked, and everything she could see of the back patio, pool, and cabana looked normal.

Not finding any sign of Jillian on the first floor, Carrie worked her way back through the living room to the stairs. Her hands were shaking, and her breathing was erratic, coming in short gasps, almost like sobbing. She tightened her grip on the knife as she turned to head up the stairs.

She slowly worked her way up one step at a time, her eyes glued to the landing above for any sign of movement. About six steps up, she saw it. Wood fragments on the stairs and what appeared to be a bullet hole in the banister. Her pulse quickened and the palms of her hands were damp. It became more difficult to grasp the knife. "Jillian? Talk to me, please." Before taking the next step, she looked up and saw the chipped ceiling plaster above the second-floor landing. There was a perfectly round, bullet-sized hole in the center. Carrie felt like she was going to throw up and pass out—all at the same time. After a moment's pause, she continued to vigilantly work her way to the top of the stairs. She stopped on the landing and looked down the hall toward the bedrooms and bath: her hearing acutely tuned to the slightest sound. Jillian's bedroom door was ajar, and a thin strip of wood the color of the door was lying on the floor just outside the room. Although she couldn't see the inner edge of the door frame, Carrie was sure the strip of wood resulted from someone breaking in the door. She wondered if they were still in the bedroom waiting for her and prayed to God they weren't. She put her back against the hall railing and inched her way toward the bedroom with the knife clutched tightly in both hands and the blade pointing straight in front of her.

When she was opposite the bedroom door, Carrie looked to her left and right to make sure she was alone. She strained to look through the small crack in the door but didn't see anything out of place. She leaned to her right for a better view inside the bedroom but still didn't see anything abnormal. Hoping for the best, Carrie crept across the hall to the door with her knife at the ready. She paused at the door and listened for any sound coming from the bedroom. Nothing. Just deadly quiet. She whispered a silent prayer, waited a moment, and pushed the door open with her foot. Nothing could have prepared her for the horrific scene that slammed into her senses like a speeding car into a wall.

The visual image of her lifeless friend, slumped against the night stand with a bullet hole in her chest and her blouse soaked with blood, burned an indelible image into her brain. The smell of death permeated her nostrils as a scream caught in her throat and she collapsed against the door frame.

Tears streamed down her face. Little sobs grew into uncontrollable wailing, culminating in the loss of her breakfast on the bedroom floor. The knife dropped from her hands as strength drained from her body. She looked at her friend one last time as she slowly got to her feet and backed out of the door, silently mouthing, "Oh no. Jillian. No."

A moment later, Carrie found herself at the bottom of the stairs with no recollection as to how she got there. With trembling hands, she pulled her cell phone from the pocket of her tennis skirt, dialed 911, and collapsed back on the stairs to wait for the police.

40

Fitch heard a woman scream, muted at first, but then the sound became more intense until he thought his ear drums would burst. He covered his ears with his hands to block out the noise. But then another woman began to scream, then another, and another. *How many are there? Why are they screaming?* Their screams were faint at first but got louder and louder. Just when he thought he could take no more, they stopped, and silence returned. *Are those voices I'm hearing?*

Fitch awoke with a jolt as the last woman's scream was silenced, and he fell off the sofa onto the floor. Those weren't women screaming at all. They were emergency sirens, and they were very close. And yes, he was hearing people talking. *Where are they? Who are they?* With his sleep-heavy eyes adjusting to the light pouring into his living room, Fitch could see what appeared to be a dim red light pulsing on his ceiling. He'd never seen that before. *What the hell?*

He got to his knees, and using the coffee table for support, pushed himself to a standing position. A headache banged away at the back of Fitch's head: the result of way too much booze the day before and sleeping with his neck bent against the arm of the sofa. The voices were faint, and he couldn't make out what was being said, but they seemed to be coming from the direction of Jillian's house. *Shit.* He took two quick steps toward the sounds and fell to the floor when his feet became entangled in the throw Theresa always kept on the arm of the couch. *Dammit.* He hated that thing. Always had. Thought it made the place look too girlie. He freed his feet, got back up, and made his way to the window. The source of the commotion was immediately apparent when he saw cops everywhere around the Lawrence house.

Fitch jumped to his left and away from the window, standing with his back pressed against the living room wall. His vision blurred, and beads of sweat formed on his forehead as his mind raced with thoughts of what to do. The pulsing red lights from the many police vehicles permeated his living room and seemed to beat in time with his racing heart. A staccato hiss burst from Fitch's mouth. "Shut. Those. Damn. Lights. Off."

Fitch wondered why the cops were there already. No one should have found out about Jillian for at least a few days. She was alone for God's sake. He wiped the sweat from his forehead with the sleeve of his shirt and tried to slow his breathing. No need to panic. After all, no one saw him with Jillian, and he was very careful not to leave any fingerprints or other evidence in the house. And what if they did find his DNA? He was a neighbor and had been in the house many times over the years. He'd have to get rid of the revolver and the box of .38 shells as soon as possible. Although his gun wasn't registered, the police could still do ballistics tests on it and match the slugs to those found in Jillian's body. If the striations on the bullets test-fired from the weapon matched those found on the slugs removed from Jillian, it would be the end of him. The gun had to go. He'd either throw it into the ocean along with the shells or bury them both in some remote place where they'd never be found.

Fitch figured there was no way the police could connect him to Jillian if he just kept his cool: except for the one person who could get the police looking in his direction—that damn lawyer in San Diego. He was a very dangerous loose end. So far it appeared he was still trying to contact Trudy to get more information before going to the police with what she told him. Fitch knew he'd have to act fast to put a stop to this Tom character before things really got out of hand.

He peeked out the window keeping his body hidden, except for just enough of his face so he could watch the scene unfolding next door. There were cops everywhere, and two more cruisers and the coroner's van had parked in the drive since he last looked out. He didn't see anyone looking in his direction, so he figured he wasn't going to be questioned anytime real soon. But it wouldn't be too long until the cops were at his door to ask if he saw or heard anything unusual at his neighbor's place.

The gun. Where's the gun? The last thing Fitch remembered was sticking the gun in his pants pocket as he was leaving Jillian's. He felt in his pocket, but it wasn't there now. He sidled back to the sofa making sure he stayed clear of the window. The gun wasn't in sight. He lifted each cushion, but the .38

was nowhere to be seen. He dropped to his knees and looked under the sofa and at the area around the sofa. Not there.

Fitch recalled falling asleep on the chair in his study after returning from his business with Jillian. Maybe it was locked in his desk. He got back up, and walking on the side of the room away from the windows that looked out on Jillian's, he started for the study. Passing through the kitchen, he noticed the weapon lying on the counter next to the sink, directly in front of the window, in plain view of anyone who happened to look in. *Damn. How careless can you be? You idiot.*

Fitch grabbed the gun and shoved it in his pants pocket. Without passing in front of the window, he leaned over the counter and looked down the side yard to see if anyone was snooping around. No one was there. That was a good thing. He bent down so his body was below the bottom edge of the window and duck-walked to the other side of the sink. Again staying away from in front of the window, he peered over the counter to check for any unwanted visitors in the yard to his left. Thank God the coast was clear in that direction too. Two cops were walking down Jillian's side yard checking the windows, lawn, and bushes for any evidence that might lead to her killer. It wouldn't be much longer before they were at his door. He had to hide the gun, now. He began to feel a heightened sense of panic as he thought of where to stash it. Then his more rational side kicked in. *Wait. Wait. Slow down. There's no need to panic. I'm not a suspect. The worst that can happen is the cops come to the door to ask if I saw or heard anything. They're not going to search the house.*

Regaining a modicum of calm, Fitch walked into his study and locked the gun back in his desk drawer with the box of bullets. Feeling a need for even greater tranquility, he went to the liquor cabinet and opened another bottle of his favorite sipping whiskey. *Oh, thank you booze.* He put two ice cubes in a tumbler, filled it to within a quarter inch of the top with the sweet-smelling liquid, and slumped down in his recliner to wait for the inevitable visit from the cops—and to consider his strategy.

41

Jillian's house was now crawling with several police officers, the deputy coroner and his assistant, and the district attorney assigned to the case. All worked quickly and efficiently as a team, trying to determine the sequence of events that led to the death of the attractive woman in the upstairs bedroom. A television news truck and two reporters, one from a local newspaper and the other from an area radio station, were already parked on Mulholland in front of the house. A rookie cop was assigned the duty of making sure they stayed on the street and off the property.

Carrie was in the living room being questioned by Robert "Bobby" Daniels, one of the homicide detectives, while his partner, and lead detective, Chase Banning, was inspecting the body and talking with the coroner about time of death. The coroner had been working at his job for fifteen years and was one of the best in the business. Although he could only give an estimated time of death at the crime scene, he told Detective Banning, based on body temperature and the state of rigor, she most probably died mid-to-late afternoon on Saturday.

The coroner photographed the body while a ballistics expert dug slugs out of the wall at the bottom of the stairs, the stair railing, the ceiling above the second-floor landing, and the bedroom door frame. A crime scene investigator was dusting for prints on and around the bedroom door, while the police videographer was capturing the entire scene from the front door to the body.

On his way out of the bedroom, Banning asked the officer handling finger prints if she'd found anything. She told him it appeared the killer was either wearing gloves, didn't touch anything, or had wiped things down pretty well before leaving. But she did find a complete right hand print on the hallway side, upper-right panel of the bedroom door that could lead to something. It was a rather unusual place to find a print, but who knows, perhaps the killer placed a hand on the door while trying to break it down. She said the print was large, so it probably belonged to a man. Banning complemented the technician on her work and made his way down the stairs and out the front door.

Although he'd cut way back on his habit, Banning knew he really should quit completely. He found the craving too irresistible, however, and usually grabbed a smoke at some point during every one of his crime scene investigations. Today was no different. He stood in the driveway leaning against the hood of his car and enjoyed his only vice while reflecting on the things he'd just seen and heard. It always seemed to help him solve a case by taking time to pull back and think about what he'd learned so far.

While he was taking a final drag on the first, and hopefully last, cigarette of the day, Banning noticed the large house—estate, really—directly in front of him on the other side of the wall from the Lawrence property. He looked around and realized it was the only home with a fairly good view of the crime scene surroundings. Maybe whoever lives there saw or heard something that could help the investigation. There was no time like the present to get a jump on neighbor interviews—the sooner, the better. Banning usually left witness statements to a subordinate, unless the prospect of gaining valuable information from the person seemed particularly promising. Given its proximity and partly unobstructed view of the Lawrence house, he decided to take this one himself. He put out his smoke with the bottom of his shoe, picked up the butt, and put it in his pocket. He gathered his notebook from the hood of the car and headed down the side yard to the gate he'd observed earlier that connected the two properties.

Fitch was still sitting in his recliner, about midway through his second tumbler full of whiskey and ice, when the door chime sounded. He knew immediately who it was and froze for a moment with the glass almost touching his lips: his pulse quickening. He contemplated not answering but realized they'd only be back later, and this was probably as good a time as any to get it over with. And if it goes well, he may not have to deal with them again. When the chime sounded a second time, he downed the rest of the whiskey, set the empty glass on the desk, and went to answer the door.

Detective Banning looked just like Fitch imagined a detective should look: mid-fifties, thinning hair, graying on the sides, about six foot one or two, in decent shape, with the beginnings of a slight paunch. He couldn't remember when or why that image of a detective formed in his brain. Maybe from movies or TV.

Banning matter-of-factly introduced himself, showed Fitch his badge, and asked him if he'd noticed anything unusual at the house next door. Fitch said, "No. Nothing out of the ordinary, Detective. Why?"

Getting a whiff of booze on Fitch's breath, Banning replied, "Well, a body was found in the house, and I thought you might have some information that could help us find out what happened."

Sounding as shocked as he could, Fitch said, "Oh no! Poor Jillian. Why would anyone kill her? She was such a lovely lady."

Staring directly into Fitch's eyes, with a frown contracting his brow, Banning asked, "How do you know the deceased is Jillian, and that she was killed?"

Realizing he'd said way too much, Fitch's left eye twitched as he back peddled and said, "I, uh, I just assumed it was Jillian since she lives there, and I-I-I believe her kids are away visiting their grandparents. With you here asking questions, I figured foul play was involved. How did she die?"

Without answering Fitch's question, Banning made a mental note of the eye twitch, the comment about Jillian being killed, and the beads of sweat forming on Fitch's forehead and upper lip. He handed Fitch his card and told him to call if anything came to mind that might help. Fitch promised he would.

Banning started to leave, but before Fitch could close the door, the detective turned around, and putting on his best casually inquisitive demeanor, said, "Mr. Fitch. One more thing, if I may. Where were you yesterday afternoon and evening?"

Feeling the muscles in his jaws tighten, Fitch struggled with his response, but finally managed to say, "I … let me see. Yesterday. I ate lunch at home, worked in my office until five or six, read awhile, watched a movie, and went to bed around nine or nine thirty."

Banning followed up with, "Really. Seems we have some things in common. I like to read sometimes and watch movies too. What movie did you see?"

Thrown by the question, and unsuccessfully scrambling to remember a recent movie he'd seen, Fitch gave a little laugh, and replied, "Gee, I'm so bad at remembering movies. I can see a great film and not remember the name, who was in it, or much about it the next day. My wife kids me about it all the time. I usually sleep through half of 'em."

Pressing a little, the detective asked, "So, do you remember anything about it, like who was in it, generally what it was about, or who directed it? You know, anything like that?"

Fitch felt his stomach turn and thought he was going to vomit. With a forced smile and equally insincere laugh, he said, "I feel like an idiot. I'm drawing a total blank right now. I hope this isn't a sign of early dementia." His phony smile faded as he figured he'd just screwed himself.

Banning quieted Fitch's fear somewhat when he responded with, "Don't worry about it, Mr. Fitch. I do the same thing." Then he continued, "Oh, by the way, did you see it in the theater, rent it, watch it on TV, stream it on Netflix, Hulu—"

Without thinking, Fitch said, "Netflix."

Banning knew he'd be able to check Fitch's viewing history to see what he watched, or if he watched anything at all. He thanked him for his time, turned, and walked away: certain he'd be talking with Mr. Fitch again soon.

42

Patrol Officer Shawna Wilson and her partner, Darryl Harms, were assigned the area that included C.A.I.N. and Trudy Greene's apartment. Officer Wilson had been on the force eight years and had been partnered with Officer Harms for the past six months. Wilson was a dedicated cop and had graduated number two in her class from the academy. Harms, also very committed, graduated six years after Wilson and was ranked number three in his class. Although graduation requirements had become much more difficult to achieve in the six years since Officer Wilson graduated, she never let a day go by without mentioning his lower class standing—all done with good humor and much respect for her partner. Harms always feigned disgust but was well aware his partner thought very highly of him and was glad to have him riding shotgun with her.

Wilson and Harms had been patrolling their beat since 6:00 a.m. that morning without much activity. That was typical for a Sunday morning because most Saturday night partiers had long since gone home—or passed out naked in the arms of a one-night-stand lover who'd provided animalistic release after a night of bacchanalian indulgence.

As they were passing by C.A.I.N., Wilson slowed and pulled into the parking lot. They'd already cruised the lot earlier in the shift, driven past Trudy's apartment, and patrolled her neighborhood three times. Although they hadn't observed anything unusual so far, their training and experience told them to keep vigilant, keep searching. You never could tell what might turn up around the next corner: perhaps a clue that would help solve the mystery of Trudy's disappearance, or possibly Trudy herself. Who knows? Just stay alert.

Wilson stopped the car in front of the building, and Harms got out. He tried the door for the second time that morning, and again finding it locked, peeked through the glass to see if anyone was in the office. Nothing had changed. The place was dark. He knocked on the door just to be sure no one was there, and when he got no response, headed back to the patrol car.

Wilson turned the car around and drove slowly back toward the exit while both officers scanned the surrounding area for anything that might lead to finding Trudy. Wilson was preparing to turn out onto the street when she stopped the car and said to her partner, "You remember Big Bill don't you?" Seeing a frown produce wrinkles between Harms's eyebrows, she continued, "You know. The big homeless guy that hangs out in this neighborhood."

Recognition caused the creases to disappear. "Oh, Billy Turley. Sure. I know him. Why?"

"Well, one of his favorite places to camp is up in the bushes at the far end of this lot. Did you see anything over there?"

Harms thought for a moment and said, "No, but I didn't look very close. And it is kind of hard to see him when he's sleeping: especially when he's covered up with that old blanket he carries around. He blends right into the dirt."

Wilson made a sharp turn back into the parking lot and said, "Let's check him out. Who knows what he might have seen or heard?"

The patrol car moved at a snail's pace around the far edge of the lot as both officers scanned the bushes for any sign of Big Bill. Wilson brought the car to a stop when she reached the end of the lot, and asked, "Did you see him?"

"No. Nothing. Maybe he's at the park by … wait. I see a spot of red near that tree where he usually sleeps. Could be the red baseball cap I've seen him wearing lately. Let's have a look."

Wilson radioed in their location, shut off the engine, and got out to join Harms. They walked along the edge of the lot until they found what looked like a trail that Billy probably used to enter his sometimes open-air home. Beer cans, liquor bottles, and other assorted trash became more prevalent the farther up the hill they walked. The stench of urine, and God knows what else, became more pungent with each step—and they were outdoors. Harms tried to imagine what it would be like in an enclosed environment.

The officers found Big Bill about thirty feet up the trail from the parking lot: sound asleep with a half empty gin bottle still clutched in his hand. His crotch was wet from a recent bladder evacuation.

He probably didn't even feel the urge to go, or maybe was too drunk to care. What a life.

Wilson and Harms both genuinely empathized with Billy. They'd each been in the military and served a tour of duty in Iraq. What a hell that was. No human being should be exposed to the horrors of war. It destroyed good minds, and for what? Because a bunch of egomaniacal politicians around the globe put greed, their aggressive natures, and the fear of appearing weak before a sense of compassion for their fellow human beings. What crap.

Wilson took her baton out of its holster and gave Billy a light tap on the sole of his shoe while calling his name. No response. She tried again, this time with a little harder tap of the baton. Still nothing. Harms knelt down next to Billy, gave his shoulder a strong shake, and called, "Billy. Billy. Wake up. We need to talk to you. Hey, Billy."

Finally, with a loud grunt, Billy jerked upright with his right fist cocked and ready to strike, spilling the remainder of his precious gin on his sleeping bag. "What? Stay away. Leave me alone or I'll beat you." Then, the sleep and booze fog lifted, and his bleary eyes brought the officers into focus. He relaxed his fist, fell back onto his elbows, and with intoxicated-sounding speech said, "Oh, Officers. I do 'pologize. I'm sorry. I didn't know it was you. Can't be too careful. I been robbed twice this week already. Sorry."

Wondering how she managed to come back in one piece and not wind up like Billy, Wilson responded, "Not a problem, Billy. I understand. We just want to ask you some questions."

"I ain't done nothing wrong. I swear."

Wilson responded, "No, Billy. We don't think you've done anything wrong. We just want to ask you some questions about what you may have seen or heard around here lately. That's all."

Tipping his wobbly head back so he could look at Officer Wilson's face, Billy said, "I betcha this is about that girl I seen."

Surprised by Billy's comment, Wilson and Harms simultaneously said, "What girl?"

"I seen this girl here yesterday. I think it was yesterday. What day is it? Oh yeah, I remember. It *was* yesterday. Just before I pulled outta here, I seen this girl get in the car with that man. I can't swear to it 'cause I was a little tipsy, but it looked like her hands was tied behind her back, and he was treatin' her kinda rough. Maybe there was tape or something on her mouth."

Pulling his notebook and pen out of his shirt pocket, Harms asked, "What time did you see that?"

Struggling with his memory, Billy looked out over the brush and off into the distance. The synapses finally fired, and returning his gaze to Harms, Billy said, "Well, let's see. I was getting ready to break camp, so it musta been nine or ten. Somewheres in there."

Harms wrote in his book, while Wilson continued with, "Can you describe the girl?"

"Well, I didn't get a very good look at her. It happened pretty quick." Then, pointing toward the C.A.I.N. offices, Billy continued, "But I know she works in that building over there because I seen her come and go a lot. And ya can't miss all that red hair."

The red hair comment cinched it for the officers. Billy had to be talking about Trudy Greene. Her profile describes her as having a lot of red hair, an employee of C.A.I.N., and last seen in this very parking lot when she was dropped off at the office yesterday morning.

As Harms continued to take notes, Wilson asked, "What about the man she was with? What can you tell us about him?"

Billy was becoming more alert, and although his response came faster, it still reflected the intonation of inebriation. "Ya know, I don't know who the guy is. But I'm pretty sure he's some bigwig over there. I seen him here a lot. Always dressed in some fancy suit or other. And he always drives that big old Bentley. He gotta be a big shot to drive that thing. Ya know?"

Wilson and Harms immediately knew who Billy was talking about. It had to be that guy, Fitch. They'd responded to a civil disturbance call at C.A.I.N. about five months ago. Some dissatisfied customer decided to take it upon herself to show how displeased she was with something the company had done, or not done. She'd pushed over a file cabinet and knocked over a computer monitor on one of the agent's desks, while screaming obscenities at the top of her lungs. They'd gotten a statement from Fitch after cuffing the woman and securing her in the back seat of the patrol car. They'd commented to him about his nice ride before driving off and taking the woman to the central jail.

Hoping to get more out of Billy, Wilson asked, "Is there anything else you can remember about the man and woman you saw here yesterday?"

Billy rubbed his unshaven chin between his thumb and index finger as if deep in thought, then responded with, "Nah. Nothin' I can think of now." Then Billy's eyes brightened as if a light bulb had gone off inside his head, and he snapped his fingers. He focused his eyes on Wilson's face as a smile parted his lips, exposing what was left of his gray-black, scum encrusted teeth, and he said with a laugh, "Yes, Ma'am. There is something more I do remember. One day I was setting up here just watching the comings and goings when that man walked out and started to get into his car ... boat's more like it. When all of a sudden, some lady come out waving her arms all frantic like and yelled at him. 'Adrian. Hey, Adrian.' Well I just about blew a nut. Pardon, ma'am. But alls I could think of was when Rocky Balboa says to his girl, 'Adrian. Hey, Adrian.' " With that, he bent over laughing hysterically until it generated a violent coughing spree, and he threw up what remained of the gin. Embarrassed, and no longer laughing, Billy wiped his mouth on the sleeve of his shirt and propped himself back up on his elbows.

Harms finished taking notes. He slipped his notebook and pen back into his shirt pocket as Wilson thanked Billy for his cooperation. She told him he'd been most helpful. As they started back down the hill to the parking lot, Wilson turned back to Billy and said, "Sorry about the gin, Billy."

Billy looked down at his gin-soaked sleeping bag, then back up at Officer Wilson, and said, "No problem. Probably better it dumped anyways."

The officers got back in their car and immediately radioed dispatch with the new details they'd collected from Billy. Within five minutes, dispatch had issued an APB for all officers in L.A. County to be on the lookout for Adrian Fitch as a person of interest in the disappearance of Trudy Greene. Now every on-duty officer in the County had a description of Fitch and his car, including the personalized license plate, 1LUCKY1.

43

At 10:49 a.m. Sunday morning, Max was walking off the court with Claire at the San Diego Tennis and Racquet Club. They had just won the doubles match they'd played against another couple who were considered two of the best doubles players at the club. The win felt good, but it was made extra special by the fact Claire was sober, and it was the first time in over two years she and Max had been on the court together. Claire could be really fun when she wasn't drinking. Max too for that matter.

They toweled off and walked to the clubhouse bar together for a mimosa to celebrate their victory. They had an hour or so before Claire's next match with a girlfriend, and Max would head home to prepare for a Monday morning meeting with a bunch of San Diego business leaders. They shared a cordial conversation while enjoying the sun and celebratory libation as they watched the activity in the pool from the patio deck chairs. It was the first time in over three months they'd had a conversation that at some point didn't include snide remarks and foul language. It was a nice change. As Max got up to leave, they exchanged a kiss that was, although not passionate, somewhat longer than usual, and tinged with an emotion Max had not experienced with Claire in quite some time. Perhaps things were going to change. Perhaps they could recapture a loving relationship.

At 11:52 a.m., Max got in his car and drove out of the club parking lot. He was driving down Sea World Drive, heading home to Point Loma, when his phone rang. He pushed the CALL button on the steering wheel and said, "Hello, this is Max."

In a voice edged with agitation and evoking the tonality of too much alcohol consumption, Fitch said, "Max, it's me. Things have turned to shit. You gotta help me."

"Whoa. Whoa. Whoa. Slow down. What do you mean things have turned to shit? I thought you said everything was going according to plan."

"It was, 'til that meddling secretary of mine overheard me talkin' with you yesterday and stuck her nose into it. Now things have changed. But don't worry about the girl. I got her tied up in my wine cellar. She's not gonna say anything to anyone. Neither is your firm's client, Jillian Lawrence. Unfortunately, she met with misfortune and is no longer with us. Poor thing."

Anger, fear and confusion mixed together to color his words, as Max said, with the pitch of his voice rising, "Fitch. What the hell have you done? What do you mean she's no longer with us?"

Doing his best to keep his cool, Fitch lowered his voice and clenched his jaw. "Just how it sounds, Max. She's gone … dead."

Max squeezed the steering wheel, and his vision started to tunnel as he almost drove off the road. He caught himself just in time and jerked the wheel back to the left, bringing the car into the center of the lane and avoiding what would surely have been a multiple fatality accident: two bicyclists had been riding on the shoulder of the road just ahead of him. They were very lucky.

Max's face turned crimson and his heart began racing as he tried to stay focused on his driving. Any remaining calm he possessed dissolved, as he yelled, "Fitch, you dirty bastard. Murder was not part of the plan. You've gone way too far. You're sick. I won't have anything more to do with it. You're on your own."

Struggling from the effects of an elevated blood alcohol level, Fitch did his best to regain the cold, calculating demeanor and voice for which he was so well known in the business world and said, "Oh, Senator, you *will* have more to do with it. Unless, of course, you want me to destroy you."

"Go to hell, Fitch. I'll tell the police you tried to bribe me, and I'll deny any involvement with your scheme. I'll leave you holding the bag. You'll fry for what you've done."

With a voice sounding even more menacing, Fitch responded, "You'll do no such thing, Senator. The suspicion of you being even remotely involved in our plan will destroy any chance you have of winning re-election now or any time in the future. So listen to me, and listen carefully. My girl contacted your lawyer Tom Davidson and told him about the conversation she overheard concerning our arrangement. He's the last loose end that could destroy both of us. Neither one of us wants that to happen. So, Senator. Your job is to stop him. Get rid of him. Immediately."

Max sounded very rattled, almost like he was sobbing, as he said, "You monster. I'll do no such thing. My political career be damned. I'll go to the police if you ever contact me again." With that, Max ended the call and continued on his way home, very shaken, but determined to distance himself from Fitch and the scheme he should never have considered in the first place. What was he thinking?

44

Fitch convulsed with rage as the cell phone connection went dead and ended his conversation with Max. His hands were trembling, and veins bulged from his neck as he held the phone to within an inch of his mouth and screamed at the top of his lungs. "You son of a bitch. Don't you ever hang up on me. You're a dead man. Do you hear me? A dead man." He threw the phone down on the nearest chair with such force it would have shattered had it struck the floor. He then stormed off to his study.

Fitch went straight for the minibar and filled a tumbler with ice and whiskey. It was becoming his routine whenever he felt the onset of stress. He sat in the chair at his desk, took a swig, sat back, and contemplated what to do next.

Now he had two loose ends that had to be tied up—Davidson *and* the Senator. Based on the voice messages to Trudy, it appeared Davidson was still trying to figure out what was going on. Being a lawyer, he'd probably not go to the cops until he had more information. Max on the other hand, knew what was going on and was already threatening to go to the police. That was not going to happen. Fitch realized both of them had to be stopped as soon as possible, and there was no one else to handle it but himself. He knew both men were in San Diego, so a trip down south seemed like his next logical move.

A cop had already been at his door asking questions, and Fitch knew it wouldn't be long before he returned. He needed to get out of there before that happened. He also needed to stop Davidson and the Senator before they did anything that could compromise him. He downed the last of the whiskey in his glass as his resolve solidified. He would go to San Diego and stop those who could do him harm.

Fitch set the empty tumbler on his desk, got up, and headed to the gun cabinet he had specially built into the wall of his study. He retrieved a key from under his favorite sculpture of all time—Charles M. Russell's solid bronze *Bronco Twister*—inserted the key into the cabinet lock and opened the door.

Fitch had never been an avid hunter and didn't consider himself a gun enthusiast. The weapons he owned were given to him by his dad when he was in junior high and high school. His dad loved to hunt and took Fitch with him every year in search of pheasant, duck, squirrel, rabbit, deer, elk, or whatever was in season at the time. He hadn't fired a gun in years until yesterday when he used the .38 revolver to take care of one of his problems. His array of firearms was just as he'd left it several years ago after showing a friend his collection. There was a Marlin semi-automatic .22 caliber rifle, a Mossberg 500 pump-action 12-gauge shotgun, and a Remington Model 700 bolt-action 30-06 rifle.

Fitch considered his options and thought about what he might need to get things done in San Diego. He decided to take the 30-06, so he could take care of business from a distance and lessen the chance of being seen. The rifle had a great Nikon scope mounted on it that allowed him to clearly see his target at one hundred, two hundred, three hundred yards, or more if necessary. He'd just have to remember to allow for windage and elevation if he was to hit his mark. He'd also take the .38 revolver, just in case things became more up close and personal. He was sure taking both guns would cover all the bases. There'd be plenty of time to dispose of the .38 after business was taken care of in San Diego. Who knows, he might have to dispose of the 30-06 too.

Fitch grabbed the 30.06 and a box of Springfield cartridges with soft tips, then headed to his desk to retrieve the .38. The soft tips on the cartridges would ensure greater penetration of the target, while still allowing for expansion of the bullet to cause greater internal damage. He unlocked his desk and removed the .38 along with a box of cartridges. There was one cartridge still in the cylinder after his meeting with Jillian, so he loaded five more rounds, snapped the cylinder closed, and stuck the gun in his front pants pocket. He considered what else might come in handy on his little journey down south and headed to the minibar. Alcohol just might be the companion he'd need to complete his San Diego operation and return home safely to celebrate *mission accomplie*. Perhaps then he could enjoy the fruits of his captive before he decided what to do with her. No need for a glass, ice, or other accoutrements of the minibar for this trip. A chug straight from the bottle now and then would do just fine.

Fitch got his backpack down from the top shelf of the closet, stuffed the revolver and both boxes of cartridges in the center compartment, and went to the kitchen for supplies to get him to San Diego and back. He didn't want to have to stop and eat if the trip took longer than anticipated. He found a bag of dry-roasted almonds, some dried apricots, an apple, and a box of chocolate chip cookies and put them in the pack. He grabbed two bottles of Tasmanian Rain water and dropped them in with the other items.

Fitch had Max's home address written in the calendar he kept in his desk drawer. He'd done some research and found it when he first considered using Doctor Lawrence's accident as a way to get Max reelected as his Sacramento puppet. He went back into the study, got the calendar out of his desk, and entered the address into his phone.

On the way to the garage, Fitch opened the wine cellar door to check on Trudy. The odor that hit him as soon as the door was open told him Trudy could have used his assistance earlier. He thought about helping her get cleaned up but decided it would take too long. He needed to get to San Diego. He shut and locked the door without turning on the light or seeing how Trudy was doing.

Fitch slung the backpack over his shoulder, grabbed the rifle, and went out into the garage. He started to open the trunk of the Bentley to stow the rifle when he spotted Theresa's cousin's old Camry parked at the far side of the garage. She'd left it with them while she was on a trip to Costa Rica because she didn't want to leave it on the street in front of her apartment. An older Toyota was a much better choice for his mission than the flashy Bentley. It wouldn't draw unwanted attention to him. The Bentley caught everyone's eye, including cops, and he didn't need that kind of scrutiny now. Another benefit to taking the Toyota was the fact it wasn't registered in his name, so if the cops should run the plates, his name wouldn't come up.

Fitch closed the trunk of the Bentley and moved to the driver's side of the Toyota. He opened the unlocked door and found the keys in the center console where he'd been told they would be. He inserted the ignition key to check the fuel level and found it was almost full. That should be more than enough to get to San Diego and back. He knew the Camry had a seventeen-gallon tank and got about twenty-nine miles to the gallon on the highway. But to be safe, he grabbed the five-gallon gas can he kept under the workbench for emergencies and topped off the tank. You never could tell what unexpected thing might happen to eat up more gas: like accidents, road construction, detours, and the need to take a longer way back to L.A. It was better to be safe than sorry.

Fitch loaded the rifle in the trunk and put his backpack on the front passenger seat. He made another trip inside the house to see if any cops were still at the Lawrence house. There was a lot of yellow crime scene tape around the property, but he didn't see any police. And there were no cars in sight other than Jillian's.

As he was walking back to the garage, Fitch remembered he'd left Trudy's cell phone lying on the kitchen counter. He wanted to be able to monitor any calls she might receive, so he detoured to the kitchen and picked up the phone before heading back to the car. Who knows? Maybe he'd get more information about Davidson and his whereabouts.

In the driver's seat with his seatbelt securely fastened, Fitch started the engine and let it idle for a bit since it hadn't been run for several days. He unzipped the backpack, pulled out the whiskey, unscrewed the top, and took a big hit. He immediately began to relax and feel his confidence building as the warm liquid river worked its way down his throat to his stomach. Bringing the bottle was definitely a good idea.

Fitch turned on the radio and fiddled with the dial until he found a hard-driving heavy metal station. The scream of the guitars and pounding of the drums jacked his adrenaline level to the max. He cranked the volume up high, pushed the button on the garage door opener, and shouted, "Ready or not, San Diego ... here I come."

45

At 12:40 p.m. Sunday afternoon, Detective Banning was back at his desk going over his notes about the Lawrence murder when his partner rushed up slightly out of breath, and said, "Did you hear about Fitch, the Lawrence woman's neighbor?"

Looking up from a particularly gruesome photo of Mrs. Lawrence that had just been dropped on his desk, Banning responded, "No. What's up?"

"An APB was issued for him about five minutes ago. He's wanted for questioning in the disappearance of Trudy Greene. Apparently a homeless guy says he may have seen Fitch take her yesterday morning from the place where she works. At least the description he gave of the woman fits Greene's missing person profile that came out earlier today. And the time he claims he saw the woman taken matches the time Greene was last seen by her roommate."

"Bobby, I think we should pay Mr. Fitch a visit and see what we can find out. Something's up with that guy. I can feel it. I planned to talk with him again anyway, so we may as well do it sooner than later."

Banning closed the Lawrence file and locked it in his desk. He stood, arching his back to work out the kink that had developed from falling asleep in his lounger the previous night. He grabbed his jacket from the hook on the wall next to his desk and followed his partner to the car.

It was a short drive to Fitch's home. Within ten minutes, Banning was taking the off-ramp and turning east onto Mulholland Drive. The homes and views on both sides of the road were impressive. A slight burst of air escaped Banning's nose in a silent laugh as he looked at his partner and said, "Amazing to me that the horror we witnessed this morning exists in the midst of what seems so perfect."

"Yeah. You just never know what goes on behind closed doors."

Banning turned the car into Fitch's driveway and stopped at the gate. He lowered his window and pushed the CALL button on the code box. After thirty seconds there was no response, so he pushed it again. Another thirty seconds and still nothing. He pushed it again.

When he got no answer on the third try, Banning backed the car out of the driveway and drove next door to the Lawrence property. He still had the gate code from his earlier visit. As he punched it in, he told his partner about the gate connecting the two properties that he'd used when he initially contacted Fitch. He visually scanned what he could see of Fitch's property as he rolled down the drive and parked behind Jillian's Mercedes. Banning and Daniels got out and walked down the side yard to the gate. The wall, bushes, and trees obscured much of the view toward the Fitch compound, and what the detectives could see revealed no trace of human activity.

Standing at the gate, they had a clear view of the side of Fitch's house and a good part of the front, back, and side yard. It was quiet. There was no sign of Fitch or any movement inside the house. Banning opened the gate, and he and Daniels walked down the gravel path to Fitch's front door.

Banning pushed the button and the door chime sounded. There was no response and no sound indicating activity inside. Banning pushed the button again but got no reply. On the third attempt, he banged on the door and identified himself. "Police. Open up." When that produced only more silence, the officers split up, each walking around the house in a different direction while peeking in the windows as they walked.

When they met at the back of the house, Banning asked, "Anything?"

"No, not a thing. There doesn't appear to be anybody inside. I couldn't see into the garage because there aren't any windows, and the door is solid wood. If he's driving, someone is sure to spot his Bentley. They're kind of hard to miss."

"True. I didn't see anything either. We're gonna need a subpoena to get in and look around. If Fitch took that girl, she could be inside, or there may at least be something indicating what he did with her."

Banning pulled out his cell phone and said, "McKinley's the duty judge today, isn't he?"

"Yeah, today's his day."

Banning punched in Judge McKinley's number, and while it was ringing, said, "Great. He's a little more lenient with probable cause than some. We should be OK with the eyewitness statement about seeing Fitch take Ms. Greene, but you never know. The fact she's reported as missing will help too."

The judge answered, and after exchanging brief pleasantries, Banning told him where they were, what he and Daniels were doing, and gave a verbal affidavit of the facts supporting probable cause so the judge could issue a search warrant. Fortunately, the judge believed sufficient probable cause existed in this case to issue the warrant, and he said, given the circumstances, he would issue it to include forced entry if that became necessary. He told Banning it should be ready in about ten minutes and to have someone come by to pick it up. Banning thanked him and hung up.

As soon as the call to the judge disconnected, Banning dialed the station and asked to speak with Officer Ryan. Ryan was new to the department, having just graduated from the Academy two months before. He was a friendly, eager-to-learn, hard-working young man. Banning liked him and wanted to give him as much experience as he could. He gave Ryan instructions about what to do and the addresses for Judge McKinley's office and Fitch's house. He told Ryan he would wait with Daniels at the house in case Fitch showed up.

The detectives stood in front of Fitch's house making small talk and occasionally ringing the bell. If Fitch *was* inside, he may have been in some part of the house where he couldn't hear their prior attempts to get his attention.

Officer Ryan pulled into the Lawrence's drive-way and parked behind Banning's car twenty-five minutes after the detective had called him. He walked down the Lawrence's side yard, through the gate, up the gravel path in Fitch's garden, and handed Banning the warrant. Banning asked him to stay in case they needed backup. Excited to be included, Ryan smiled and said, "Yes, sir."

Banning rang the bell several more times and got no response. He banged on the door and again announced, "Police. We have a warrant to search the premises. Open up now or we'll break the door."

Still not receiving a reply, the officers drew their guns as Banning took a step back and gave the door a hard kick. A loud cracking sound could be heard as the door frame began to splinter, but the door didn't open. Banning gave the door another hard kick with everything he had, breaking off pieces of the frame as the door burst open. Banning was the first through the door with Daniels and Ryan right behind him.

The minute they were inside, Banning yelled, "Police. We have a search warrant. Come out now." Total silence. The place was deathly quiet. He continued in a softer than normal voice, "I'll take the downstairs. You two check upstairs."

Banning went from room to room with his 9mm gripped in both hands and held at the *low ready* in front of him. Daniels and Ryan went up the stairs, guns drawn, their eyes searching the visible area above.

When Banning reached the garage door off the kitchen, he stood to the side, turned the handle, and pushed it open. The garage was dark except for the little light coming from inside the house. He couldn't see much in the darkness, so he reached his hand around the door and felt for the light switch. He turned on the light and immediately saw the Bentley and a newer model Lexus parked next to it. The 1LUCKY1 license plate confirmed it was Fitch's Bentley. The space next to the Lexus was empty. Banning slowly entered the garage, sweeping the interior with his eyes as he worked his way to the driver's side of the Lexus. The door was unlocked, so he opened it and popped open the glove box to see if he could find the vehicle registration card. He found the card and saw the car was registered to Theresa Fitch. He knew she was Fitch's wife from his earlier conversation with the man.

Banning walked to the passenger side of the Lexus and did a visual of the empty space next to it. There didn't seem to be anything unusual at that end of the garage. He did notice a small spot of oil on the floor where you'd expect to see one if a car with an oil leak was driven into the garage and parked. He knelt down, touched the spot with his index finger, and rubbed the dirty-brown liquid between his finger and thumb. The stain was fairly fresh. It was wet and hadn't yet completely evaporated or soaked into the concrete floor.

Banning knew a car had recently been parked in that third space. He looked under both the Bentley and Lexus but saw no evidence of an oil leak, confirming that a different car had been parked at that location in the recent past. He wondered if Fitch was out there somewhere driving it—perhaps with

Trudy Greene. No sooner had the thought crossed his mind than he heard Daniels shout, "Chase, get in here. We found her."

Banning bolted past the Lexus and the Bentley, through the door, and back into the kitchen. He headed to the open door on the other side of the kitchen where he saw Ryan disappear down some stairs. The stench that hit him when he reached the doorway told him Trudy had been left unattended for a while. He could tell it was a wine cellar—and a very elaborate one at that—but it wasn't until he was half way down the stairs that he saw Trudy chained to the support post. Daniels and Ryan were kneeling beside her, working to set her free. Daniels was trying to gently remove the tape from her face and hair while Ryan untied her hands. Trudy was shaking and sobbing uncontrollably. Tears cascaded down her cheeks.

Standing at the bottom of the stairs, Banning could see the chain pinning Trudy to the post was secured with a padlock. He spotted a key placed at eye level on one of the shelves near the stairs. It fit the lock, and in a moment, Trudy was free for the first time in over twenty-eight hours. She threw her arms around Detective Daniels and held him in a vice grip, whispering, "thank you, thank you, thank you," over and over again in between sobs. Daniels was her connection to safety and freedom. She was afraid to let him go for fear the dream would evaporate.

Trudy slowly began to regain her composure and removed her arms from around the detective. She was embarrassed that she'd soiled herself and asked if it would be alright if she cleaned up a bit before they questioned her. Given the circumstances, Banning told her that would be fine and led her back up the stairs to a guest bathroom down the hall. He found a plastic garbage bag for her soiled clothes and said he had a pair of old jeans in the trunk of the car she could wear. He handed Ryan the keys to the car, and while Trudy showered, Ryan went to the car and retrieved the jeans. Soft crying could be heard coming from the shower.

Clean and refreshed, Trudy pulled on the too-large jeans and fastened the belt in the last eyehole before rejoining the officers. Banning asked if she knew where Fitch was. She said she didn't: although she thought he'd left the house about forty-five minutes ago based on the last time he'd opened the cellar door. The detective asked if she remembered seeing a third vehicle in the garage parked next to the Lexus. Trudy said she thought she recalled seeing another car but couldn't remember anything about it. She was so terrified when Fitch dragged her out of his car. Everything happened so fast. Banning told her he understood and not to worry about it.

Trudy sat in the living room with Ryan while Banning and Daniels scoured the house for any clue as to where Fitch had gone, or to the identity of the third car. Although their search turned up nothing on either, the detectives were disturbed by the fact the gun cabinet in the office was open—and one of the gun slots was empty. Had there been a gun in the empty space? And if so, what kind of weapon was it, and where was it now? Banning asked Trudy if Fitch took a gun with him when he left, but she had no idea since she didn't actually see Fitch the last time he opened the cellar door. Finding nothing more, Banning told Ryan to stay at the property for the duration of his shift in case Fitch should return, and assured him he'd be relieved by other officers. Banning then called the station and requested that Ryan's partner drive out to the house as back up.

The detectives escorted Trudy to their car so they could take her home where she'd be more comfortable for further questioning. As they drove down Mulholland, Trudy told the detectives she was concerned for her friend Tom Davidson. She explained her connection to Tom, that he was the lawyer at the Johnson firm handling the Lawrence matter, and that Fitch knew about her conversation with him. She had told Tom about the plan she overheard being discussed between Fitch and Senator Johnson. She said Fitch was really mad that Tom was aware of their plan.

Banning asked Trudy if she knew how to contact Davidson, and she said his information was stored in her cell phone contact list. Unfortunately, she didn't have her phone with her and thought Fitch may have taken it with him. But she remembered Tom's number because it was almost the same as hers, except for the area code and last two digits. Banning pulled the car to the shoulder of the road, pulled out his cell phone, and dialed the number Trudy gave him.

On the third ring, Banning heard, "Hello."

"Is this Tom Davidson?"

"Yes."

"Tom, this is Detective Banning with the LAPD. I got your number from Trudy Greene. She's with me now."

"Oh, thank God. I was worried about her and have been trying to contact her since yesterday. What's going on? How is she?"

"She's fine, Tom. A little shaken up, but fine. She's been held captive by Adrian Fitch since yesterday, but we have her now and she's doing well. She's worried about you, Tom, because Fitch knows about her conversation with you concerning the campaign contribution scam involving him and Senator Johnson."

After a slight pause, Tom said, "Then it's really true?"

"Unfortunately, yes. Listen, Tom. I hate to tell you this, but Mrs. Lawrence is dead."

Tom whispered, "Oh my God."

"She was found this morning shot in her home. I suspect Fitch had something to do with it given his involvement in her case and the fact he kidnapped Trudy after she contacted you." Hearing only silence on the other end of the line, Banning continued, "Tom we're concerned for your safety. Fitch has disappeared and may have a gun. We don't know where he is or how he's traveling since he didn't take his own car. It's possible he may be coming to San Diego for you since you know about his scheme with the Senator. We just don't know for sure."

Concerned for Trudy, Tom asked, "You'll protect Trudy?"

"Yes, of course. We'll have an officer with her until Fitch is caught. You're our primary concern right now. Tom, I want you to go someplace safe for a while. Get out of your house and don't go to the office until this blows over. Do you have family or a friend where you can stay?"

Sounding a bit dazed, Tom said, "Yeah. I'll find someplace to go."

"Good. Contact me when you get situated and let me know where you're staying. And Tom, don't call Trudy's cell or answer any calls coming from her phone. She doesn't have it, and we think Fitch may have taken it."

"OK. Thanks."

Banning disconnected the call, put his cell in his shirt pocket, and resumed the drive to Trudy's.

Tom sat staring at the wall with his cell phone still pressed to his ear, trying to assimilate what he'd just been told.

46

It was 12:50 p.m. Sunday afternoon. Fitch was about to enter the on-ramp from Mulholland Drive to the I-405 freeway south to San Diego when he noticed a black Ford Crown Victoria. It sported a large spotlight attached to the driver's side pillar above the side view mirror. He knew immediately it was a cop car. A second glance revealed a familiar face. It was that Detective Banning at the wheel with some other bozo riding shotgun. Fitch snapped his head to the right to avoid being seen. He checked his rearview mirror as he continued down the freeway on-ramp but didn't get any indication he'd been spotted. He wondered what the hell those cops were doing headed toward his place. He hoped they were just checking something back at the Lawrence house.

With the radio blaring, Fitch hit the gas and sped down the on-ramp onto the slow lane of I-405 south. It was Sunday, so traffic was light at that time of day. He accelerated and quickly merged into the fast lane. It dawned on him the accident that started this whole chain of events had happened just about where he was at that very moment. In fact, he noticed some damage to the center divider and wondered if that was the spot. His wonder was confirmed by what appeared to be a large burn area on the concrete in the three left lanes of the freeway. He glanced at the speedometer and saw he was doing eighty miles an hour. That would not do. He couldn't afford to get pulled over now: especially since he was driving a car that wasn't registered to him. He checked in his right side-view mirror, and seeing no cars close to him, pulled into the number two lane, slowing to the sixty-five mile per hour speed limit. He'd get to San Diego. He just had to be patient.

Seeing the spot where so many lives had been shattered was very unnerving. Fitch felt a shudder pass through his body, and his hands began to shake. He clenched his fists around the steering wheel to stop the trembling. What was happening to him? This wasn't the Adrian Fitch he'd created and knew so well. That Adrian Fitch was a solid pillar of ice and steel. The Adrian Fitch who could unnerve secretaries—and senators—with just a look or the inflection of his voice. No, this was not that Adrian Fitch.

He slammed his right fist down on the steering wheel, and screamed, "God dammit stop it," while Slayer's diabolical "Angel of Death" drowned out his words and caused the entire interior of the Toyota to vibrate. The violent impact sent a sharp pain shooting through his hand, bringing a sort of relief from the confusion he was feeling.

He needed a drink, bad. Fitch reached over with his still throbbing hand, unzipped the backpack on the seat next to him, and pulled out the pint of Jack Daniels Gentleman Jack. One of his cheap, sycophantic employees had given it to him for Christmas a few years ago. Not the stuff he was used to drinking, but what the hell, it would do under the circumstances. He unscrewed the cap, checked the rearview mirror for traffic—especially cop-type traffic—and seeing none close by, lifted the liquid confidence-builder to his lips and took a couple of big slugs. The familiar burning sensation worked its way down to his stomach and instantly brought a veil of calm over the unbalanced Fitch: allowing the confident, controlling ice master to again take charge.

Within three or four minutes, Fitch passed the world-famous Getty Museum and began to sense something was not right. The ice man was beginning to melt. The Fitch persona was slowly fading away. He could feel a knot starting to form in his gut. The knot tightened as his inner core began to shudder: just a little at first, but the shudders rapidly increased in both frequency and intensity. He reached for his buddy Jack and checked the rearview mirror. In the two minutes it took him to get to the Sunset Boulevard underpass, he managed to belt down another shot of his good friend, remembering to check for cars before each hoist of the bottle. No question the liquor helped to calm him, but the calm seemed to dissipate much faster than usual. Fitch began talking to himself, mumbling really, about things apparently only he could understand. His concentration wavered, and he couldn't get a picture out of his mind—the expression on Jillian Lawrence's face after he shot her in the chest and watched her slowly die. His mind zoomed in on her trembling lips as she struggled to tell him something just before dying. He wondered what she was trying to say. Then, out of nowhere, Jillian's mouth blew open to an inhuman dimension and spewed blood into Fitch's face as she moan-screamed, "I'll get you, Fitch."

Fitch snapped back to reality and caught himself drifting into the fast lane. He quickly pulled the wheel to the right, causing the car to fishtail, but he managed to get it back into his lane without hitting another car. The driver in the number three lane hit the brakes to avoid a collision and was almost rear-ended by a city bus. The driver behind him laid on the horn. Fitch looked in the rearview mirror just in time to see a twenty-something, gang banger-looking man with a shaved head present him with a wildly waving middle digit. The movement of the man's lips clearly indicated his physical gesturing was being verbally enhanced with a screamed, "Asshole."

Adrian Fitch was one of those rare people who contracted schizophrenia after the age of forty-five. In fact, he first became aware something was not quite right just two years ago when—while driving home from a particularly stressful day at work—he glanced out the driver's side window of his car and saw a large African elephant running down the street next to him. An emaciated-looking black man was sitting on its back, wielding a wooden shield in his left hand and waving an ominous-looking spear in his right. Fitch stared at the unusual sight for several seconds, until his car's right wheels went off the road and onto the grass shoulder. He turned his attention forward just in time to narrowly miss a pair of mailboxes and get back onto the road. When he looked back out his side window, the elephant and rider were gone. He checked his rearview mirror, but the beast had disappeared. Fitch spent the rest of the drive home with a frown creasing his forehead and wondering what the hell an elephant would be doing in his neighborhood. When he got home, he asked Theresa if she'd seen an elephant in the street. Thinking he was just being silly, she continued rolling out the pie dough she was preparing and said, "Yes. In fact, there were four of them in the yard earlier." Fitch gave her a quizzical look and continued to his study. They never spoke of the incident again.

A couple of weeks after the elephant episode, Fitch was telling Theresa about an opera that was coming to town when he suddenly stopped in mid-sentence and just stared at her. After a moment, Theresa raised her shoulders with her palms turned up and said, "What?" His only response was that the thought had just left his mind. Theresa chalked it up to the typical forgetfulness we all experience on occasion, but Fitch sensed it was more than that. When he later saw a large python disappear into an electrical outlet in the master bathroom, Fitch, unbeknown to Theresa, sought professional help. That's when he got the schizophrenia diagnosis.

Fitch was prescribed Clozaril, instructed to take it once a day, and told to avoid alcohol and drugs. He never told Theresa or anyone else about the diagnosis or the prescription. He kept the medication locked in his study desk drawer and took it religiously, first thing every day. The drug seemed to work pretty well in spite of the fact he hadn't stopped drinking. He had, however, gained ten pounds, his cholesterol level shot up, and on two or three occasions after consuming too much booze, he did see strange things no one else could see. At least he was pretty certain they couldn't see them.

Fitch's heavy drinking over the past two days, and the fact he'd stopped taking his medication, was starting to take its toll. He passed Wilshire Boulevard, Santa Monica Boulevard, and the I-10 freeway without further incident. The whiskey seemed to be doing its job, and he felt the calmest he'd been all day. But something in the rearview mirror caught his attention as he approached the Marina Del Rey turnoff. He looked in the mirror again. *Damn.* The elephant tamer was sitting in the back seat staring at him with a shit-eating grin spread from ear to ear. He had a toucan perched on his head as a headdress, was holding an angry cobra near Fitch's head, and appeared to be mouthing, "You die. You die."

This time, Fitch had the good sense to glance forward to make sure he stayed in his lane. When he looked back again, the man and beasts were gone. Beads of sweat broke out on his forehead as he tried to comprehend what he just saw. Part of him didn't think it was real, but another part was very worried there were things in the back seat intending to harm him. He reached into his backpack and removed his travel companion, Jack. By the time he reached the I-105 freeway, he'd knocked back another shot of the amber-colored calming-juice, and it seemed to be working, at least he didn't see any more weird creatures in the back seat.

The heavy metal sounds blasting from the radio helped keep Fitch awake, distracted from the evil around him, and focused on his purpose for the drive down south. The ride was relatively uneventful until he was passing through Long Beach. Without warning, the heavy metal music stopped, and static pulsed from the radio. Suddenly, a demonic-sounding voice pierced the static and slowly repeated, "Fitch ... you ... will ... die. Fitch ... you ... will ... die."

He switched off the radio, but that made it even worse. The same voice continued louder and louder while repeating, "Fitch, you know what you've done. You won't get away with it. Remember, Jillian ... Fitch, you know what you've done. You won't get away with it. Remember, Jillian ..."

Fitch rocked back and forth, vice-gripping the steering wheel in his hands and screaming at the top of his lungs, "Shut. The. Hell. Up." It worked. The voice stopped, and the car was silent except for the hum of the engine and whir of the tires.

A family of four passed him in the fast lane. Mom, dad, and both kids stared at him slack-jawed and wore quizzical expressions bordering on fear. Fitch gave them an odd smile. When mom and dad turned away, he stuck his tongue out at the kids and made a weird face. The kids obviously commented about what he was doing because mom glanced back in his direction. Fitch quickly retracted his tongue and turned his gaze forward.

He managed to keep the voices silenced and the back-seat visitors at bay by taking a little hit of Jack every ten miles or so. He took small sips—just enough to wet his tongue—because he didn't want to get so drunk that he couldn't finish his business in San Diego. He tuned in a classical station and was starting to enjoy the drive. He thought he had everything well under control as he noticed the sign indicating Costa Mesa was just three miles ahead. He'd be in San Diego in a little over an hour. Then it happened.

Fitch was driving with his left hand and conducting an imaginary orchestra with his right while the station played a beautiful piece featuring a violin solo. He loved to hear violins. He looked to his right to cue the imaginary cello section, when a SUV pulled past him in the slow lane with something on the roof. He looked closer, trying to make it out—and there she was: Jillian Lawrence. Sitting on the luggage rack, wearing blood-soaked clothes, hair whipping around her face in the wind, and playing a violin. Her bow and finger movements seemed to mimic the tune the orchestra was playing. Fitch blinked and she was gone, replaced by the skinny African dude holding Fitch's bloody, severed head in his hand and wagging his index finger back and forth. Fitch let out a shrill cry and was barely able to keep the Toyota from swerving wildly into the next lane. When he looked back, there was no Jillian and no African dude. In fact, there was no SUV.

The whiskey bottle found its way to Fitch's lips and remained there while the equivalent of a full shot worked its way down his throat. No sooner had he put the cap back on Jack than the orchestra abruptly quit playing, and a professional-sounding announcer came on and said, "Fitch, you know what you have to do. The devil lives in the left eye of both Senator Johnson and that sniveling lawyer, Tom Davidson. You must kill them both to save yourself and all of humanity. It is up to you Adrian Fitch. You, and you alone."

The announcer stopped talking, and the orchestra resumed playing right where it left off. Fitch's pupils narrowed, and his eye twitched. The announcer was right. The Senator and Davidson were evil and had to be eliminated. He, Fitch, was the one chosen to save the world from Satan, and he would not let the world down.

A freeway sign indicated the Harbor Drive exit in Costa Mesa was one mile ahead. Fitch checked the lane to his right, and seeing no cars close, moved into the number three lane. He checked traffic again, and seeing nothing within fifty yards, shifted all the way over to the Harbor Drive exit lane. Taking the off-ramp, he drove west on Harbor, keeping his eyes peeled for a Target Store, mini-mart, or any establishment that would sell the items he wanted. For some unknown reason, Fitch felt compelled to disguise himself. Perhaps so the devil wouldn't recognize him when he came to remove His Evilness from this earthly plane and save the world from his destructive powers.

Less than a mile from the freeway exit, Fitch saw a sign that read LIQUOR–GROCERIES–LOTTO and pulled into a parking spot in front of the store. He looked around to make sure he wasn't being watched and chugged half a bottle of Tasmanian Rain water before getting out of the car. The infrared beam was broken as he entered the store and set off the ding-dong bell announcing his presence. The only clerk he could see didn't even look up when he entered. He was at the cash register busily texting someone—probably the girl with whom he hoped to fornicate later that evening. Fitch was glad to not be seen.

The place had the usual assortment of stuff found in every other store of its kind—gum, candy bars, cereal, tape, tampons—and the three things Fitch needed—scissors, razor, and shave cream. He surreptitiously gathered each item while making sure he wasn't observed—well maybe by the security cameras, but not by the clerk. He didn't care about the cameras. No one would think to look for him here. Confident he hadn't been seen, Fitch headed to the men's restroom, and once inside, locked the door behind him. It was like so many other restrooms in that kind of mom-and-pop place. It smelled of urine, the floor was wet and littered with toilet paper, and a few wads of once-wet toilet paper still clung to the ceiling where some smart-ass kid thought it would be cool to leave his mark. Another person's attempt at restroom humor was visible on the toilet seat cover dispenser. There, in front of the instructions on how to remove a toilet seat cover—FIRST PULL UP, THEN PULL DOWN—were the words HOW TO JACK OFF. That one actually brought a smile to Fitch's face.

He walked across the damp floor to the sink and set his supplies on the bent and rusted metal shelf which management had so graciously attached to the wall above the sink. He admired himself in the mirror and considered the importance of his mission. He would not fail. With that, he removed the scissors from the cardboard and plastic packaging and began cutting his hair. He cut from front to back, first on the top, then the sides, and finally the back. He stuffed the cut hair in the trash can under the paper towel dispenser. Fitch then covered his head with shaving cream and opened the pack of razors. He shaved the remaining hair he was able to see right down to bare skin. The back was the hardest to reach, but he did the best he could without help.

When he'd finished shaving, Fitch washed his head with warm water, dried it with paper towels, and threw the scissors, razors, and shaving cream can into the trash. He looked at himself in the mirror. It wasn't a perfect job, but what could you expect under the circumstances? There were several wisps of hair still protruding from his scalp, and a few spots were bleeding from having been nicked by the razor. Still, the shave altered his appearance enough, so hopefully, the devil wouldn't recognize him. He peed—kind of like an animal leaving its mark—then exited the restroom.

The same clerk was now busy re-stocking the cigarette case on the wall behind the cash register and didn't even look back as Fitch left the store and walked to his car. He thought how easy it would be to rip that place off. Then realized, he just did.

When he got back in the car, Fitch looked in the rearview mirror and noticed a couple of places on his head were still oozing blood. He found a fast food-type napkin in the glove box and used it to tamp the blood dry. Although there were spots of dried blood still dotting his head, Fitch managed to get the bleeding stopped before starting the car and continuing his mission.

Back on the I-405 heading south, he stayed in the far-right lane and almost immediately caught the I-73 toll road. The toll road would cut time off his journey to San Diego. When he reached the turnoff for the toll booth, Fitch just kept driving. He'd never stopped to pay the toll on any of his many trips down the I-73, and so far, had never been caught. Why start now?

He maintained his strategy of taking a little sip of Jack every so often: it seemed to be keeping weird visions at bay. He saw the emaciated African a couple of times hitchhiking on the side of the road, but he just kept driving, telling himself the guy wasn't real.

As he continued through Camp Pendleton, the deep-voiced announcer came back on the turned-off radio and praised Fitch for his bravery and willingness to confront—and eliminate—the sources of evil and suffering in the world. This time, the voice didn't startle Fitch: it just stroked his ego and bolstered his confidence.

Fitch passed Oceanside, Carlsbad, and Del Mar. Then, there it was, the sign welcoming him to San Diego. He'd made it. He slapped his hand down on the center console. *Devil look out. Fitch is about.*

47

At 2:42 p.m. Sunday afternoon, Tom began to pull himself together and out of the fog that had enshrouded him since the call from Detective Banning. This was serious stuff. He had to do something. You don't get a call from a police detective telling you your life may be in danger and just ignore it. But what should he do? Ben was out of town for a few days visiting relatives back East, and Tom didn't really have anyone else he could turn to: except, maybe Jan. The thought of crashing at her place until this thing blew over was a very appealing prospect. But he didn't know how Jan would feel about it. He was attracted to *her*, but was she attracted to *him*? He kind of thought so but wasn't too certain given the extent of their relationship up to now: if you could even call it a relationship after a dinner on the beach, drinks at Jax, and a few casual dates. Tom got the feeling Jan didn't mind being around him on the occasions they had been together, either for work or the handful of times outside of work. He had to get away from his apartment for a day or two—the detective made that clear—so he might as well muster his courage and ask her if she'd put him up on her couch. Resolved, and excited by the possibility of spending time with Jan,

Tom pulled out his cell and pushed the CALL button next to Jan's name.

That terrific voice—sounding happy to get the call—answered with, "Hey, Tom. Long time no talk. I'm glad you called. What's up?"

Encouraged by the enthusiasm in her voice, Tom said, "A lot is up. An unbelievably scary amount is up."

"Tom, what is it?"

"You're not going to believe it, but I just got a call from a detective in L.A. who told me Fitch kidnapped my friend, Trudy. You know, the one who told me about Fitch's plan with Senator Johnson."

"Oh my God. Do they know where she is?"

"Yeah, they found her tied up in Fitch's house. She's with the detectives now."

"Is she OK?"

"I think so. They're taking her home as we speak, but there's more. They found Jillian Lawrence in her home this morning—dead. And they think Fitch may have had something to do with it."

Tom heard a gasp on the other end of the phone, followed by silence, and then the sound of quiet tears. He didn't say anything, giving Jan a moment to process what he'd just told her. Then, through sobs, Jan said, "Tom ... that's terrible. She was ... such a nice, gracious lady. Oh ... her poor kids. First they lose their father ... and now their mother ... and in such horrible ways." Tom remained silent as a lump formed in his throat, and Jan continued, "Tom, are you alright?"

"Yeah. I'm OK. But the detective told me not to go to the office, and that I shouldn't stay in my apartment until Fitch is caught. They don't know where he is and said he may have a gun."

"Tom, get out of your place right away."

"That's actually why I'm—"

"Come stay with me, Tom. You'll be safe here. Just get out of there right now and come over. You can stay as long as you like."

"Wow. Thank you, Jan. I really appreciate it. I don't think Fitch has any idea where I live, but you never know."

"Just hurry up and get over here."

"OK. I'll pack a few things and be right there." Tom disconnected the call and was overcome by conflicting emotions. He was so sad for Jillian and Trudy, so happy Trudy was safe, so scared by the prospect of Fitch coming for him, and so thrilled to be staying with Jan.

Tom pulled his suitcase from the back of his closet and put in enough clothes for three or four days. He found his Dopp Kit in the bottom drawer of his dresser and filled it with the toiletries he'd need: toothbrush, toothpaste, floss, hairbrush, deodorant, and shaver. He made a final sweep of the apartment before grabbing his suitcase, toiletry bag, and keys and heading out the door.

48

Fitch pulled off the freeway onto the Sea World Drive exit and turned right, heading west. He turned again at the first light where a sign pointed toward Fiesta Island. A gravel parking lot was located next to the water where a narrow isthmus crossed Mission Bay and connected Fiesta Island to the mainland. He pulled into a parking spot that was partially shaded by some low palm trees. His bladder was killing him after consuming so much liquid and not making a pit stop since leaving Costa Mesa over an hour and a half ago. The clock on the dash read 4:01 p.m. Fitch looked around and saw the car next to him was empty, and he didn't see anyone in the lot other than a couple loading beach cruisers in the back of a pickup truck at the far end. He got out, and standing next to the driver's door, pissed like the proverbial race horse. When he finished, he shook the last couple of drops from his manhood as high-pitched giggles erupted from behind him. He looked around as two little girls, each with a hand covering her mouth, ran away, presumably to nearby parents. Fitch checked in both directions but didn't see any adults in the area. He wondered if the girls were normal humans, or if they could instantly vanish like the skinny guy and elephant?

Fitch got back in the car and lowered the windows to take advantage of the breeze coming off the bay. His stomach gurgled from the alcohol gnawing at his gut, reminding him he hadn't eaten in a while. He unzipped the backpack and took out the almonds, apricots, and cookies. His stomach felt much better after he munched some of the almonds, half the apricots, and a half-dozen chocolate chip cookies. He returned the uneaten items to his backpack, zipped it up, and grabbed the Jack Daniels. He unscrewed the cap and slowly sipped the last of the whiskey while watching two seagulls on the far bank fighting over what looked like a piece of bagel. It amazed him what some critters fight over.

It was still too light outside to hunt down the Senator. The peaceful view, full stomach, effects of alcohol, and a warm breeze made a nap sound like the perfect way to kill some time. Fitch found the seatback release, lifted the lever, and reclined his seat as far as it would go. He was in a deep sleep within a matter of minutes.

The dreams were vivid, confusing, and sometimes terrifying. Fitch first saw himself at his current age wearing diapers and a blue baby bonnet while sucking on a pacifier in his parent's bedroom at his boyhood home. His mother sat in her rocker at the far end of the room wearing a wedding gown with a veil covering her face and her left breast exposed. Fitch felt shock and shame. His mother kept motioning for him to come to her while holding her breast and telling him to suckle. For reasons he could not understand, he dropped to his hands and knees and began to crawl toward his mother. Every time he made a move, however, his mother retreated in the opposite direction by a distance equal to his advance. He crawled and crawled, faster and faster: then suddenly, a dense fog rolled in through an open window, and his mother disappeared. Fitch sat in the middle of the bedroom floor and cried.

In the next dream, he was at his office wearing a business suit and standing in front of his entire staff conducting a meeting of some sort. The staff didn't seem to be listening but were laughing hysterically and pointing at him. He looked down to see what they were pointing at and saw that his trousers were unzipped, and his penis, five times its normal size, was protruding in full view of everyone. He tried to cover himself, but no matter what he did, his penis remained erect and exposed to the masses. When he looked up, his staff had vanished, and he was standing alone and naked in the middle of the desert. He felt very confused and wondered what the dream meant.

The third and final dream he remembered was equally weird, but also very scary. He was floating on his back in Mission Bay, eyes closed and wearing sunglasses, with a dry martini resting on his chest. The water was very salty, and he could float without paddling or being supported in any way. He began to feel a light tapping on his chest and slowly opened his eyes. What he saw caused him to jerk his arms up toward his face, knocking the martini and his sunglasses into the water. Sitting on his stomach was a miniature, flaming-red Satan brandishing a spear that he kept stabbing into Fitch's chest while repeating in a demonic voice, "You will not destroy me. You will not destroy me." In his attempt to escape, Fitch flipped over and immediately sank to the bottom of the bay. He was running out of air and about to inhale a deep breath of salt water when a car door slammed, and he instantly woke up. He was covered in sweat and clawing the air in the front seat of his car.

Baffled by his bizarre dreams, Fitch felt great relief at finding himself still in the front seat of the car—and not on the bottom of Mission Bay. He took a moment to fully return to the present, then sat up, pulled on the seatback lever and returned the seat to its normal position. He saw the taillights of a car leaving the lot and realized he was the only one still there. It was 7:55 p.m. and would be dark in less than an hour. The sun painted a few wispy clouds pastel-pink as it raced over the ocean to meet the horizon. Part of him wanted to stay and enjoy the view, but the other part was starting to feel anxious to get on with the task at hand.

Fitch knew he would need his energy for what was to come, so he ate the apple, a couple handfuls of almonds, and more chocolate chip cookies. He picked up the whiskey bottle, saw it was empty, tossed it into the weeds in front of his car, and said, "Shit!"

49

Max drove straight home after hanging up on Fitch. He hurried into the house and went directly to his study without changing out of his tennis clothes or showering. Sandy heard him come in and slam the study door: something he'd never known the Senator to do. Senator Johnson was a pro at maintaining his composure. Sandy went to the study to check on Max. He opened the door and saw him in a very agitated state: rapidly shaking his right leg, drumming his fingers on the desk, and staring blankly at the ceiling.

Sandy cleared his throat, and asked, "Sir, are you OK?"

Hearing Sandy's voice startled him, and Max abruptly sat up and turned his head toward the sound. He looked at Sandy but said nothing, his leg still vigorously bouncing. Sandy knew something wasn't right, and again asked, "Sir, are you OK?"

Jolted from his murky thoughts, Max repressed his true feelings, and responded with, "Yeah. Sure. No, I'm fine, Sandy. Thanks."

Sandy knew Max was not fine and said, "May I get anything for you, Senator?" Sandy almost never referred to him as Senator when it was just the two of them. He'd been instructed early on to be less formal, and to call him Max. This, however, did not feel like a time to be less formal.

Max's expression was one of shock, fear, confusion—maybe all three—when he said, "No, Sandy. Thank you. I'd just like to be alone for a while."

Sandy gave a slight nod and left the room, closing the door behind him.

Max continued to bounce his leg and drum his fingers until it dawned on him that an ice-cold beer might be just the thing to help calm him down. Booze had always seemed to help in the past, or at least he thought it did. He got up and walked to the kitchen, oblivious to everything around him. He found a six-pack of Corona in the fridge, took one out, and opened it. He started back to the study but turned around and grabbed the rest of the six-pack and the opener. One would certainly not be enough, so why not bring them all and eliminate a bunch of trips to the kitchen?

Max returned to the study and continued to bounce his leg while drinking a Corona. He debated whether to call Brad but decided against it. Brad had enough to worry about right now without being dragged into this mess. Besides, how do you tell your son you've done something so wrong? He'd have to be told at some point, of course, but Max needed more time to figure out how to handle things.

He was finishing his third beer when he heard the squeak of Claire's tennis shoes on the hardwood floor outside his office, and a cheery voice call out, "Max, honey, I'm home. Are you busy? May I come in?"

Who was this woman with the bright-sounding voice calling him honey? It couldn't be Claire. Max hadn't heard her so upbeat and sounding so happy in years. She must not have had any more to drink after the mimosa. What else could it be?

Max didn't respond, but Claire opened the study door anyway and stepped in. She said, "How's the prep going for your meeting tomorrow?"

Max continued to stare out the window, and without turning around, said, "Uh … fine."

The smile on Claire's face faded at his indifference and the sight of the six-pack on his desk with three empty bottles sitting next to it. Here she was sober, in a great mood, and Max was in a funk. Would they ever get on the same page? Claire's voice lacked its earlier vibrancy when she said, "Oh, OK. I just wanted to remind you we're having dinner with Ted and Bonnie at five."

Max slammed his hand down on the desk as he whirled around in his chair to face Claire. In a voice fraught with frustration, he said, "Dammit, Claire. I don't have time for that."

The sudden crack of his hand against the desk caused Claire to jerk backward. She steadied herself with the door handle, her jaw slack. With surprise evident in her voice, she said, "Max, we have to go. We can't just cancel now. I talked with Bonnie from the club an hour ago. She's been working since early this morning preparing that French dish you like so much. And Ted bought a couple bottles of the Cabernet the two of you were talking about last time we were together."

Max was surprised by his violent reaction, and regaining a semblance of composure, said, "I'm sorry, Claire. You're right. We can't back out now."

In an attempt to mollify him, she said, "We can make it a short night and tell them you have to get back to prepare for your meeting tomorrow. We can be home before nine. Does leaving here around four forty-five work for you?"

"OK. Sure. I'll get ready in a bit."

Claire stepped out of the study and closed the door behind her. The furrows in her brow revealed real concern as she turned her head toward the door, then lowered her eyes. After a moment, she shook her head, relaxed her frown, and headed to the kitchen for a martini. She had a feeling she was going to need one.

Max remained in his study, bouncing his leg, and staring into space. He kept asking himself over and over again how he was going to handle this mess with Fitch. How had his lust for power gotten so out of control that he allowed himself to get involved with such a man? Why couldn't he leave well enough alone? He was a successful lawyer, well respected in the community, and on track for a federal judgeship. *Jesus. When did things change? Does being a State Senator mean that much to me?* After only a few months in office, he'd found himself thinking about the old Peggy Lee song, "Is That All There Is?" He should have followed the song's advice and just kept dancing as a lawyer, because it didn't take him long to figure out that being a State Senator was not that big a deal—or was it? Like most things in life, the challenge and excitement were in achieving your goal. Once you did, you'd fall into a routine and re-alize that perhaps you weren't going to change the world. Oh well, it was too late now. He had to deal with the situation at hand.

Max killed the last of the six-pack an hour after talking with Claire. He tossed the empties into the waste basket next to his desk and left the study to get ready for dinner. He didn't even feel buzzed. At exactly 4:45 p.m., Max and Claire walked out the front door on their way to dinner with Ted and Bonnie.

50

It was final prep time. Fitch picked up his cell from the center console and scrolled through his contacts until he found the Senator's address. He knew Max lived close by in Point Loma, so he entered the address into Google Maps and almost immediately got directions to his destination. It was time to scout out his prey. He started the car and pulled out of the gravel lot, heading west down Sea World Drive toward Point Loma.

Fitch was almost starting to feel sober after his long nap, scarfing down snacks, and not drinking alcohol for the past several hours. However, anxiety was building as he considered the significance of what he was about to do. He still had plenty of time before it was dark, so he turned onto Sunset Cliffs Boulevard in search of a mini-mart or liquor store where he could replenish his stock of liquid courage. He found one a few blocks down and pulled into the parking lot. He went in, grabbed another pint of Jack, and feeling the need for meat, picked up several sticks of beef jerky. The clerk kept staring at Fitch's head while ringing up the order. The patches of unshaved hair and dried blood were obvious. Fitch laid two twenties on the counter and walked away without waiting for his change. The clerk called after him, but he kept on walking, absorbed in thoughts about the mission ahead.

Back in the car, Fitch gobbled down all the jerky before removing the cap from his amber-colored traveling companion. He alternated between pulls of Jack and pieces of dried apricot while watching an odd assortment of people walking past the store. Purple Mohawks, ragged clothes, nose rings, tattoos galore—where did these people come from, and where were they going? He certainly didn't see those types in his neighborhood.

After three modest hits of whiskey, Fitch caught a glimpse of an old Ford pickup stopped at the light next to the store. It was an ordinary old truck, but it appeared that an elderly black man was lying in the bed of the truck and peeking over the side, right at Fitch. Could it be his African tormentor? He briefly turned his head away: when he looked back, the light had changed, and the truck was gone. Maybe—hopefully—it was just a big black dog on its way home from a run on the beach.

Fitch felt empowered by the booze. He decided it was time to scout out the Senator's home and wait for an opportunity to eliminate the politician from the list of those who could harm him. He screwed Jack's cap back on, started the engine, and pulled out onto Sunset Cliffs Boulevard as instructed by the map on his cell phone. He passed through Ocean Beach and continued west until a female voice advised him to turn left, and up into the hills of Point Loma. The drive took him through some pretty nice neighborhoods that were lined with beautiful ocean-view homes, but they were nothing

like the luxury pads where he lived. His neighborhood was one of a kind, just like him.

As he neared the top of the hill, the woman in
his cell phone told him he was approaching his destination. Two blocks later, the same voice told him
he had arrived at his destination on the right. Fitch
looked right and saw the Senator's address in gold
numbers attached to a column at the entrance to a
long, curved driveway. The house was nice: the
most impressive he'd seen so far in Point Loma.
There was no sign of the Senator, or anyone else for
that matter, and there were no cars in the driveway.
Fitch continued to slowly drive past: slow, but not
too slow. The last thing he wanted to do was draw
attention to himself. He went on by the house and
drove for another couple of blocks before turning
around to make another sweep.

On his second pass, Fitch noticed there were no
other homes within fifty yards on either side of the
Senator's residence. The place was fairly isolated
with a wooded area that wrapped all around the
property. The house was situated at the apex of a
slight rise, so a person standing in the street in front
of Max's place could not be seen by the neighbors.
That was perfect. Much less chance there would be
any witnesses.

Fitch noticed an added bonus in that there were
no houses immediately across the street from Max's:
just more wooded area that appeared to slope down
and away from Max's property. He continued down
the street, made a right turn at the first cross street,
and another right at the next street. More luck. At
the bottom of the wooded slope was a small kiddie

playground. It had a picnic table, a couple of benches, swings, a slide, seesaw, and human-powered merry-go-round. Great for the kids, but the best part for Fitch was the fact the park was empty at night, and it had a small parking lot hidden from the street by a bunch of shrubs and trees. He checked the slope leading up to the street in front of Max's house and saw it wasn't too steep. It also had a crude dirt trail leading to the top. Probably used by neighborhood kids for easy access to the park. That would make getting up and down the slope much easier.

Fitch pulled into the lot at 8:26 p.m. and parked as close as he could to the shrubs, so his car couldn't be seen from the street. Everything was turning out to be just perfect. He ate a few more almonds and cookies, then picked up the whiskey for some last-minute reinforcement before heading up the slope.

After downing the equivalent of a couple of shots of Jack, Fitch retrieved the box of 30.06 cartridges from his backpack, got out of the car, and opened the trunk. He picked up the rifle, loaded it with the maximum five rounds, then tossed the rest of the box in the trunk and locked it. He was about to start up the hill when he had a brilliant idea. In the movie *Rambo*, Stallone smeared his face with dirt, or whatever, to make himself less conspicuous. Fitch wanted to be as inconspicuous as possible too. The idea of looking like Rambo gave him a sense of bravado. If it was good enough for Rambo, it was good enough for him.

Fitch looked around and noticed a drinking fountain at the other end of the parking lot. He walked to the fountain, got his hands wet, and rubbed them in the dirt next to the fountain. He wiped his muddy fingers across his forehead, down both cheeks, and over the bridge of his nose. That should help him blend in with the surrounding woods and make it nearly impossible for anyone to see him, especially at night. He wiped the excess mud off on his pants, slung the rifle on his back, and sauntered toward the slope.

Fitch reached the top of the rise huffing and puffing from years of no exercise and too much booze. He looked left and right to find the best place to stake out—and eliminate—his prey. About twenty feet to the left of the trail, and with a straight shot to Max's front door, he saw a fallen palm tree about five feet down slope from the shoulder of the road. A perfect place to remain hidden from anyone passing by on the road, and to steady his rifle when the time came to do what he was there for. Rambo couldn't have done it any better.

Fitch walked to the tree and found an area where the ground was pretty level and covered with thick, soft weeds. Just the right spot to kick back and bide his time until his target appeared. He checked the time on his cell phone, holding it close to the ground and partially covering the face with his hand to block as much light as possible. It was 8:42 p.m., and still no sign of life at the Johnson residence. Not a problem. Fitch was a patient man and could wait as long as it took to get the job done. The Senator would show up sooner or later.

A jogger ran by with an unleashed Rottweiler in tow. Could this be the black thing he saw in the truck earlier? He rested the rifle on top of the log as the dog stopped following his master, and with nose to the ground, headed toward him. Fitch's right index finger was on the trigger, poised to take out the dog—and the jogger if necessary. Fortunately, the dog was well trained, and when the master called, "Mick, come," the dog lifted its head, stared momentarily into the pair of human eyes just a few feet away, and resumed following his human commander. Fitch let out the breath of air he'd been unconsciously holding while the hundred pounds of muscle checked him out.

Fitch was apparently more anxious than he realized, because the next time he checked his cell phone it was 8:46 p.m., only four minutes since he'd last looked. By 8:50 p.m., it was dark enough for the crickets, or tree frogs, or whatever they were to start their nightly ritual of trying to outsing each other to attract a mate. It seemed all species were alike when it came to sex. Who was the most intelligent? Who had the best voice or the coolest looks? And in the case of the human species, who had the most money? If you didn't fit the bill, you were in for long nights alone: punctuated by occasional visits from the Mercy Sisters. Fitch wondered if other species masturbated. He was pretty sure he'd seen monkeys do it in the zoo when he was a boy, although he didn't know what they were doing at the time. God knows it helped him through many lonely, female-less nights, and some afternoons too. Theresa was great in bed, especially when they first met, but she wasn't always available—or in the mood when he needed release.

Thoughts of sex and masturbation made him excited, and he wondered if a little self-pleasure might not help him relax now. After all, it was dark, he had time to kill, and he was in a pretty secluded spot. As he was reaching for the zipper on his pants, the sound of an approaching car engine snatched thoughts of sex right out of his head and turned his focus back to the reason he was in San Diego.

51

Max and Claire stepped onto Ted and Bonnie's front porch at 5:00 p.m. on the nose and rang the bell. Ted answered the door wearing his standard attire of baggy cargo shorts, T-shirt, and flip flops: his hair wildly askew as usual, a grin spreading from ear to ear, and waving a bottle of Gamay wine from the Beaujolais region of France. Sticking with the French theme for the evening, he greeted them with, "*Bienvenue, mes amis.* Welcome, my friends." He'd looked it up on the Google translator five minutes before they arrived. Seeing his friend brought a thin smile to Max's face: the first time he'd smiled since the mimosa with Claire that morning.

Max was uncharacteristically quiet and did his best to follow the chatter going on between Claire, Bonnie, and Ted. When asked if he was alright, he passed his placidity off on the fact he was concerned about his upcoming meeting with San Diego's business leaders. His hosts seemed to buy it, although they'd never known Max to be particularly concerned about meeting with anyone. After all, he was the consummate trial lawyer.

Bonnie's dinner was exquisite. She started with escargots baked in garlic and parsley butter and paired with the Beaujolais Ted was brandishing at the front door. Max was still so upset recalling his earlier conversation with Fitch that he barely tasted the snails. The rich food mixed with the acid in his stomach resulted in gurgling sounds that could be heard by everyone in the room.

The appetizer was followed by a very rich *soupe à l'oignon*, again paired with the Beaujolais. The combination of snails and onion soup was more than Max's nervous stomach could handle. He excused himself from the table and hurried into the guest bathroom where he proceeded to lose everything he'd just eaten. His stomach felt much better after purging the rich food. He took a moment to calm himself, rinsed his mouth, and went back to join the others. Thankfully, no one heard him barf and just assumed he'd visited *la toilette* at the behest of Mother Nature.

There was more casual conversation—without much contribution from Max—while they finished the Beaujolais and prepared for the main course. Carla Bruni whisper-sang French love ballads through the in-ceiling speakers as Bonnie presented a *blanquette de veau* with sides of French green beans and yellow squash, paired with a French Cabernet. Max was thankful the veal stew was blander than the first two courses.

After his third glass of wine, Max was beginning to shake off the thoughts of Fitch and participate more actively in the tennis club gossip and assorted meaningless conversation the others seemed to really enjoy. The wine made Bonnie a bit giddy, and she served dessert with a flourish: chocolate éclairs filled with real chocolate cream, not the vanilla custard used by most American bakeries and restaurants. Dessert was paired with a rich red port.

The éclairs were exquisite and the port a perfect complement. Max was doing pretty well, all things considered, until Ted expressed his sadness about what had happened to Max's client—or rather, the firm's client.

"What did you say?" asked Max, as his smile faded, fear crept into his eyes, and his complexion blanched.

"You know, the woman who was murdered in L.A., the doctor's wife. You told me your firm represented her."

Max's response was evasive. "I don't know what you're talking about."

"The neurosurgeon's wife. The guy who was killed by a semi-truck several months ago. I think her name is Lawrence. Jill Lawrence, or something like that. I saw it on the Internet news this morning. I'm sure you told me your firm represented her."

His face now the color of alabaster, and with a lump in his throat, Max continued to lie. "I really don't recall. I try not to get involved with firm business these days. Brad is handling everything. Maybe he knows. If what you're saying is true, that's terrible. I'll have to ask Brad about it." A sense of terror grabbed Max as his vision narrowed, and he again felt like he was going to vomit. He excused himself and went back into the bathroom. He didn't throw up but had an explosive case of diarrhea. Sweat was dripping from his forehead as he finished his business and tamped his face with a towel. He wondered why he'd said anything to Ted. But at the time, telling him seemed so innocuous. Now it was different. He didn't want anyone connecting him in any way with the Lawrence matter. And now he'd interjected Brad into the mess by saying he handled the firm's business. *Oh, God.* Max felt like his head was going to explode.

Max finally pulled it together enough to rejoin the others and immediately apologized, saying he didn't feel well and needed to get back home to prepare for his meeting in the morning. Ted and Bonnie expressed understanding and their hope that Max would feel better real soon. Max and Claire both raved about the meal, conveyed their regrets at having to leave when the party was just getting started, and were back in their car heading home at 8:40 p.m.

52

Fitch couldn't tell how far away the car was when he first heard it, or if it was even heading in his direction. It seemed to be coming from down the hill and to his left. As he strained to hear, the sound grew louder and louder. It was getting closer. *Could that be the Senator?* His question was answered in a matter of moments when an expensive-looking gray Mercedes passed in front of him and turned into Max's driveway. Fitch only got a quick glance into the front passenger-side window as the car went by. It looked like there was a woman passenger. Probably Max's wife.

Fitch felt his pulse quicken as a surge of adrenaline coursed through his body. His palms were damp, so he wiped his hands on his jeans and grabbed the gun: index finger on the trigger. He pressed the rifle against his cheek and looked through the scope, following the vehicle as it advanced up the driveway and came to a stop at the front of the house. He realized he'd been holding his breath since the car first appeared, so he took a couple of deep breaths and let them out slowly. It seemed to help him focus.

The Benz sat there with its engine turned off and no one getting out for what seemed like forever. After a few seconds, however, the passenger door opened, and an attractive woman stepped out. She had to be Max's wife. A moment later the driver's door opened, and a face familiar to Fitch emerged. It was the Senator. *Bingo.*

Fitch didn't fire because the driveway was dark, and Max was partially hidden by the fountain and surrounding shrubbery. The woman walked up the steps onto the porch and waited at the front door. Max walked around the back of the car, and just when Fitch thought he had a clear shot, the Senator disappeared behind the passenger side.

Fitch took his finger off the trigger and rotated his shoulders a couple of times to relieve the tension. When he looked back through the scope, Max was already on the porch and well-lit by the large chandelier hanging from the ceiling of the portico. He involuntarily licked his lips and increased the pressure on the trigger. He took a deep breath and was slowly letting it out to steady the shot when the woman stepped behind Max. She blocked Fitch's perfect view of his target—and the opportunity to take out his prey. *Dammit.*

Keeping the crosshairs of the scope centered on Max's general location, Fitch took another deep breath and slowly exhaled. Max got the key in the lock, opened the door, walked in ahead of his wife, and closed the door behind her. It all happened too fast for Fitch to get a clear shot. What luck. He rolled over onto his back with the rifle laid across his chest and silently cursed into the night sky. *Shit. Now what?* He had to act before the Senator had any more time to think about his predicament and do something stupid—like go to the cops.

Fitch needed time to think and formulate a plan B. He also needed something to both calm his nerves and boost his courage to complete the mission. Staring through the branches of the trees, he remembered his good friend Jack: the perfect friend for the job.

Fitch rolled back onto his stomach and pushed himself up onto his knees. He steadied himself by placing the rifle butt on the ground and leaning his weight against it. He looked to his left and right to make sure the coast was clear before putting his weight on the rifle and pushing himself into a standing position. There didn't seem to be anyone about, so Fitch walked to the trail and jump-walked down the path to the playground parking lot below.

There were no other cars in the lot, and his visual sweep of the area established there were no other people in the park. Fitch opened the front passenger door of the car and got the bottle of whiskey out of his backpack. He shut the door, walked to the front of the car, and sat on the hood. He opened the bottle and took a good long swallow. He instantly felt the familiar, warm, calming sensation begin to work its way down his throat and into his stomach. He had to figure out how to get to Max without drawing attention to himself.

Fitch was raising the bottle for another belt when car lights shined on the road next to the park. He dropped to his knees as a car came into view and stopped at the park entrance. His heart was pounding as he crawled into the bushes, dragging the bottle and rifle with him. The car suddenly accelerated and drove on past the park and out of sight. Lucky for Fitch, and lucky for whoever was in the car, they decided to move on. Probably some lovers looking for a place to get it on and deciding Fitch's car was one too many for the privacy they wanted.

Sitting in the bushes, his heart rate slowly returning to normal, Fitch again removed the cap and hoisted the whiskey to his mouth. But before taking another drink, he realized he was already buzzed and might fail in his mission if he lost control. He thought his best option was to go back up the hill and walk around Max's property to see if he could get a clean shot. The fact there were no houses close by, and a wooded area surrounded the property, should provide him an opportunity to do reconnaissance without being seen. He twisted the cap on Jack before getting back on his feet and walking to the passenger side of the car. Fitch put the whiskey in the pack and opted for bottled water instead to stay hydrated.

As he closed the car door and turned to go back up the hill, he heard a sharp whistle off to his left. He swung his body and the rifle in the direction of the sound but didn't see anyone. Then suddenly a glowing red Satan appeared sitting cross-legged on top of the jungle gym. He was staring straight at Fitch with eyes that seemed to be on fire. Fitch let out a sharp yelp as he stumbled backward a couple of steps. The thing had thick curving horns on top of its head and a long, pointed tail that hung halfway to the ground. Fitch raised the rifle to shoot but instantly thought better of it. The sound of gun fire would surely bring cops to the park. He blinked once, and the demon was gone. The jungle gym was again just a dark skeleton silhouetted against the distant lights of the city.

Unnerved and bemused by what he'd seen, Fitch slung the rifle over his shoulder and hurriedly turned back toward the hill. Before he could take a step, a loud crashing sound came from the far end of the park, again breaking the stillness of the night. He whirled to his right with rifle raised. Although he wasn't certain, it looked to him like the shape of a large elephant disappearing into the brush. He kept the rifle pointed in the direction of the sound, but when nothing happened after several seconds, he lowered the gun and ran as fast as he could to the trail leading up the hill.

53

Max turned the deadbolt to secure the front door and started to walk to the study. With a gesture long absent from their relationship, Claire intertwined the fingers of her left hand with those of Max's right. She gave a slight tug to stop him and turn him toward her. The move surprised him, and he wasn't exactly sure how to react. Claire looked him directly in the eye, and with genuine emotion and concern for her husband, she said, "Max. Something is bothering you. I can tell. You're not yourself. Talk to me. Let me know what's going on. I'm your wife, and I do love you, in spite of the troubles we've had lately."

Max stared at his wife without speaking, immobilized by fear over his involvement with Fitch, and caught off guard by Claire's unexpected tenderness and real compassion. Overcome by emotion, and feeling extremely vulnerable, a tear formed in the corner of Max's eye. Claire saw it and immediately pulled him to her. Wrapping her arms around his neck and pressing her cheek to his, she whispered, "Oh, Maxie. What is it? Let me help you."

The strong, confident, always-in-control lawyer and Senator broke down at the feeling of Claire's warm embrace and her expression of love for him. No longer able to suppress the stress that had been building in him since the call from Fitch, his sobs came in short, quick breaths. His shoulders began to shake, and tears flowed freely down his face onto Claire's neck. "Claire. Oh God, Claire. I've made a terrible, terrible mistake." His quiet sobs evolved into a vociferous outburst of fear-laced emotion.

Claire had never seen Max show any vulnerability. He had been the strong one ever since they first met when he was in law school. The sudden realization Max wasn't invincible took her by surprise. Claire gathered her strength, slipped her arm around his waist, and steered him toward the study. "Max, whatever it is, I'm here for you. Let's sit down and talk about it."

They sat in silence holding hands on the sofa while Max regained his composure. Claire stared at the vase of fresh flowers on the desk and occasionally squeezed his hand in response to his gradually diminishing sobs. Claire turned her head to look at Max, when she sensed calm had returned, and said, "Max, talk to me."

Max pinched the bridge of his nose between his thumb and index finger and slowly shook his head. His voice sounded flat and dead when he finally said, "This is such a mess. I don't know where to begin."

"Why don't you start at the beginning?" Claire's voice was filled with tenderness but tinged with fear as to what he might say next. She pulled his hand into her lap and cupped it in both of hers as a knot formed in her stomach.

Max told her about Fitch, how he met him, and their plan to funnel money into his campaign in violation of the campaign contribution laws. Claire listened without speaking, her heart pounding, as she unconsciously rubbed the back of Max's hand. When he stopped talking, Claire asked, "Is Brad involved in this?"

"No. No. Absolutely not. He doesn't know anything about it. I would never involve him in anything like this."

Relieved, Claire let out a sigh and said, "Oh, thank goodness. Max, you've done nothing wrong. Just back out of the deal and walk away. It's not too late. No one will ever know."

Max stiffened, then bowed his head and began to cry again. Claire slid over closer to her husband and put her head on his shoulder. To comfort him, she said, "Honey, it's going to be OK."

Max's voice was racked with pain, and his lower lip was trembling when he said, "Claire, there's more. Lots more." Claire's head jerked up, and the nearly-dissipated knot in her stomach returned with a vengeance.

Doing his best not to break down, Max said, "I got a call from Fitch on my way home from the club this morning. Apparently his secretary overheard him talking to me about the plan—so he kidnapped her."

"What!"

"That's what he said. I don't know anything more about it. He said he's holding her captive at his home.

"Oh, my God."

Max crossed his arms over his stomach, rocked back and forth, and began to convulse. The expression on Claire's face was a mixture of horror, shock, and fear as she witnessed a side of her husband she'd never known before. Max pulled it together just enough so that in between moments of immobilizing emotion, he said, "Claire ... Fitch killed Jillian Lawrence."

Claire sprang off the couch, and screamed, "No!"

Max put both hands over his face and cried uncontrollably. Between howls that sounded as if they came from a wounded animal, Max said, "He also told me his secretary called Tom Davidson. The lawyer handling Jillian Lawrence's case for us. He asked me to kill him."

Claire stopped pacing, whirled to face Max, and with a raised, tremulous voice, blurted out, "He what? What did you say?"

Trying his best to sound innocent, Max replied, "He asked me to get rid of Davidson. But Claire, I told him there was no way I would do such a thing. I told him I'd go to the police if he ever contacted me again, and I hung up on him."

For a moment they stared at one another—faces etched in anguish. Sitting back down next to her husband, Claire finally broke the silence and said, "Max, you've done nothing wrong. You didn't kidnap or kill anyone. You hung up on him when he asked you to kill Davidson. Max, you can walk away from this thing. This is Fitch's problem."

"Even so, the press will find out about my dealings with Fitch, and I'll be ruined. I'll lose the election, maybe even be disbarred, and at the very least, shamed forever."

Taking Max's hand in hers, and with as confident a sounding voice as she could muster, Claire said, "Max. To hell with it all. Just go to the police and tell them Fitch tried to bribe you. You didn't have anything to do with his decision to kidnap and murder."

"I'll lose it all."

"So what if you're no longer a Senator or a big-time lawyer? If worse comes to worst, we still have each other. That's huge. We have enough money to get by just fine. We'll cutback on our spending. Live a simpler life. We'll probably even be happier without all the struggle to impress and have more."

A surge of energy passed through Max as he hugged Claire with renewed conviction, and whispered, "Oh, Claire. I do love you. Thank you for understanding and believing in me."

Claire sat back, raised an eyebrow, and with the slightest trace of a smile on her face, said, "This calls for a toast to new beginnings. You wait right here while I run to the kitchen and get us a bottle of champagne." With that, she stood, gave a slight nod to Max, and headed to the kitchen.

Max watched her leave and then leaned back into the sofa as the dread and intense anxiety started to melt away.

54

Fitch stopped at the top of the hill just before the road and looked back to ensure he was not being followed by any demons—or elephants. Seeing nothing out of the ordinary, he paused for a moment to catch his breath. He looked left and right to make sure there were no pedestrians or cars heading his way. He took the rifle from over his shoulder, gripped it in his right hand, and stepped onto the road.

The front of Max's house was well-lit by the porch light and a plethora of accent lights scattered throughout the yard and bordering the driveway. Fitch decided the best way to conduct his surveillance was to walk through the wooded area surrounding the property and to stay clear of the manicured yard adjacent to the house. If he did get off a shot, he'd be much less likely to be spotted if he was hiding in the trees. He'd be able to get out of there and back to the car before anyone figured out his location.

Fitch walked down the middle of the road until he reached the edge of the wooded area. As he cut from the center of the road toward the trees, a car started to turn the corner at the intersection to his right. He ran into the woods and hid behind the first tree he found. He pressed his body up against it and tried to make himself as thin as possible. Luckily, he'd made it to cover before the sweep of the car's lights caught him. It passed him by without slowing. Fitch watched the tail lights until they disappeared over a slight rise about two blocks farther down the road. He relaxed his body, turned back into the woods, and as he walked, surveyed the side of the house for any sign of his quarry.

There were no lights on in any of the windows on that side of the house except for the second-floor window nearest the back yard. Fitch imagined he was a leopard stealthily creeping through the forest to get a better view into the lighted window. When he was directly across from the window, he looked up and saw an old black man wearing a white T-shirt and performing moves that looked like something Mr. Miyagi did in the movie *The Karate Kid*. Although he found it interesting, the man in the window was not the person Fitch was hoping to see.

He continued to sneak through the woods pretending he was an Indian sneaking up on a sleeping cowboy, carefully placing one foot in front of the other so as not to make a sound. Strange activity for a grown man, but it seemed to help him focus. He veered to his right to reconnoiter the back of the house but saw only one window illuminated: it appeared to be the kitchen. After looking through the window for a minute or so and seeing no activity, Fitch started to turn away. He'd taken only a couple of steps when he heard a twig snap. He froze in place and slowly turned his head in the direction of the sound. A large chocolate lab was standing about eight feet away, still as the night, and staring straight at him. Fitch flexed his hand around the rifle but realized he couldn't shoot without alerting the whole neighborhood to his presence. The staring match lasted for what seemed like an eternity, then abruptly ended when the dog, its curiosity sated, lumbered off in search of whatever dogs search for. Fitch let out a sigh of relief as he watched the animal disappear into the darkness.

He began to move on when his eye caught sight of a figure in the kitchen window. He stepped back a few feet and saw the same woman he'd seen enter the house with Max: now busy doing something in the kitchen. She had a bottle of what looked like champagne sitting on the counter and was washing a couple of flutes. It appeared she was preparing to celebrate. Fitch figured the second glass had to be for Max. He waited for a few seconds to see if Max would come to the kitchen. He didn't, so Fitch continued to circle the house.

When he reached the far side, he noticed another lighted window. The light spilling from this window revealed a well-manicured garden overflowing with roses of every color and variety. Pretty, but he wasn't on a garden tour. Fitch continued to look through the window as he moved forward. Suddenly, there he was—The Target. One of the two reasons he'd come to San Diego.

Max was sitting on a sofa with his hands clasped behind his head and staring at the ceiling. It didn't look like anyone else was in the room. He was probably waiting for his wife to bring in the champagne. Fitch couldn't imagine what Max could be celebrating after the news he'd given him that morning. Everything had turned to shit. It was no time to party.

Fitch knew he had to act fast. Max's wife, or whoever she was, would be coming back into the room soon. He looked around for a place to position the rifle while still having a clear view of the Senator. A four-foot high wall separated the woods from the garden area. It provided the perfect spot to support his weapon and give him a clean shot at his victim. Fitch moved up to the wall, set the barrel of the gun on top of it and dropped down on one knee. He quickly scanned the area to make sure there was no one else around and to scope out the fastest route out of the woods and back to his car. The trees to his right continued as far as he could see. The grove behind him was dense and continued for another twenty-five yards, with the nearest neighbor another fifteen yards beyond that. The road was farther away to his left with a clear path the whole way. A thick marine layer had come in from the Pacific, covering most of Point Loma, and making it that much easier for Fitch to do his business undetected.

He turned his attention back to the window and to the lone man who was visible from mid-torso up. He gripped the forestock of the rifle with his left hand, clicked the safety off with his right index finger, then moved it to the trigger. Fitch settled his cheek against the gun with his right eye peering through the scope. The cross hairs of the sight came to rest on Max's upper-left chest about eight inches from the top of his shoulder. Fitch's heart was pounding. He was holding his breath: a mistake which ultimately caused his aim to be off the mark. He rotated his shoulders one time, took another deep breath, let it out slowly, and pulled the trigger.

The roar from the rifle destroyed the silence of the night. The bullet crashed through the window and set off two neighborhood dogs. A startled owl took flight from somewhere in the woods. Fitch looked through the scope to take another shot, but the impact of the bullet had knocked Max out of Fitch's field of view. Fitch jumped to his feet, adrenaline surging through his veins, and ran for the road.

55

Claire was holding the bottle of champagne and reaching for the flutes when she heard the explosion of the rifle and the shattering glass. It sounded like it came from the study. She froze for an instant, processing what she'd heard, then dropped the bottle and screamed, "Max!" She ran to the study as the champagne exploded behind her and showered the kitchen with liquid and glass.

Sandy heard Claire's scream and stopped in mid-kata. He knew by the sound of her animal-like wail something was dreadfully wrong. Discarding his usual formality, Sandy raced out of his room wearing only boxers and a T-shirt.

Claire grabbed hold of the door frame to keep from falling as she bolted through the study door. The first thing she saw was the shattered window, followed immediately by the sight of her husband lying on his side on the sofa, feet dangling over the edge, and a large red stain where his back had rested only a moment earlier. She screamed, "Max! Oh God, Max!" as she ran to his side and clutched him in her arms.

Sandy entered the study right behind Claire and became immobilized at the sight. He just stood there shaking his head while uttering unintelligible noises that sounded like he was going to throw up. "Uhhh ... ahhh ... ohhh ... gaaa."

Rocking back and forth, clinging to her mortally wounded husband, Claire shrieked at Sandy, "Call nine-one-one."

The sound of Claire's voice jolted Sandy back into the moment. He darted to the desk and picked up the land line. He was shaking so violently he didn't get 911 correctly punched into the phone until the fourth try. On the second ring, he heard, "Nine-one-one, what is your emergency?"

In an urgency-laced cry, Sandy said, "Help! Please help!"

A very professional woman's voice responded with, "Sir, what is your emergency?"

Through his sobs, Sandy said, "He's been shot. Senator Johnson has been shot. We need an ambulance."

"Sir, what is your location?"

Sandy gave the operator the address and started to put the phone down when he heard, "Is the person who shot the Senator in the home?"

Sandy put the phone back to his ear, and in a shaky voice, said, "No. I think the shot came from outside. Hurry. Please, hurry."

The professional voice came back with, "Sir, an ambulance and the police are on their way. Don't hang up. Stay with me until they get there."

"Yes, ma'am."

"I'll let you know when they arrive so you can answer the door. Is the Senator breathing?"

Through his own gasps for breath, and other unintelligible sounds, Sandy said, "I don't know. I'm across the room. There's blood everywhere. Hurry. Please hurry. Oh, God, how could this happen?"

After what seemed like an eternity, but was only five minutes, the 911 operator said, "The police are at your door, Sir. Go ahead and let them in."

Sandy disconnected the call and dropped the phone. He glanced at Claire as he ran from the room and said, "They're here." He threw open the front door. Two paramedics, gear in hand, and a San Diego Police officer were waiting. Sandy stepped aside as they entered and said, "He's in the study. This way," as he ran back toward the study, motioning for them to follow.

When the paramedics got to Max, Claire was crying and telling him, "Hang in there, baby. I'm here," as she pressed a throw pillow against his wound to slow the bleeding. She didn't want to let go of her husband even though help had arrived. One of the paramedics firmly pried her away from Max so the other one could check to see if he was still breathing. Seeing a slight rise and fall of Max's chest, he began measures to stop the bleeding, treat for shock, and get the oxygen flowing.

Sandy stayed by Claire's side as the paramedics worked on Max and the police officer questioned them about what happened. Other sirens could be heard getting gradually louder as they approached the neighborhood. When he completed his questioning, the officer stepped aside and called a detective back at the station to convey the information he'd obtained. It was the same detective that had asked the officer to keep an eye on the Johnson residence after he'd received a call from Detective

Banning concerning the possibility Adrian Fitch was heading to San Diego to get Senator Johnson.

Several other police units had arrived and were parked on the street in front of the Johnson home. Red, white, and blue strobes lit up the neighborhood like a lurid nightclub, while small groups of curious neighbors began forming and speculating among themselves as to what happened. Police officers, including one K-9 unit, were searching the wooded area and the yard surrounding the house. Other officers were cruising the neighborhood for any sign of a suspect.

The paramedics strapped Max onto a gurney after they'd done everything they could to keep him alive at the scene. With an oxygen mask secured to his face, an IV drip attached to his arm, and his chest encased in bandages, the paramedics wheeled Max out of the study, through the front door, and into the back of the ambulance. Claire gave Sandy a big hug and squeezed his hand before getting in the ambulance with Max. The ambulance sped out of the driveway and into the street with its lights flashing. The siren was turned on about a block from the house. Claire held Max's hand and told him how much she loved him. The paramedic continued to monitor his vitals.

Max was still breathing, but barely. His heart was still beating, but very faint. Five minutes from the hospital, as cars pulled to the side of the road to let the ambulance pass, as his wife kissed him on the forehead, Max Johnson, successful lawyer, distinguished State Senator, died.

56

Fitch made it through the woods to the edge of the road panting like a winded horse. Out of the corner of his eye, he saw the porch light come on at the neighbor's house to his left as another high-pitched scream from the Johnson residence pierced the air, shattering the silence for a third time within a matter of seconds. He was far enough away that whoever was standing on the porch couldn't see him through the gloom and thick brush. Wearing the black shirt, dark blue jeans, black running shoes, and smearing dirt on his face a la Rambo was a brilliant idea and helped to keep him well camouflaged.

Fitch paused to make sure the road was deserted as several more dogs joined in the neighborhood alert chorus. Seeing that the coast was clear, he ran diagonally across the road to the trail leading down to the park. He hit the trail at full speed and half slid half fell to the parking lot at the bottom.

Before taking the last step to the gravel lot, Fitch put on the breaks—hard—and fell backward on his butt. The demon from the jungle gym was leaning against his car, laughing hysterically, and clapping his hands together. He looked straight at Fitch with his burning eyes, and in an unearthly voice, said, "One down. One to go." He pointed a finger right at Fitch, let out a loud howl, and vaporized into the dark.

Fitch scanned the park for any further sign of the fiend, and seeing none, pushed himself back to his feet and continued at a fast walk toward the car. His mind was completely jumbled by thoughts of what he'd done, and in extreme turmoil about what he'd just seen and heard. He wondered if anyone else heard the devil's words and raucous laughter. If so, people would figure out his location, and the park would be swarming with bodies at any moment.

He pulled open the driver's door and tossed the rifle onto the back seat just as a deep male voice yelled from the top of the hill. "Hey. You. Stop." Fitch was evidently not the only one to hear the satanic laughter. He jumped behind the wheel, started the engine, and tore out of the lot, throwing gravel and dust in his wake.

The man on the hill watched as the car sped out of the park. He didn't get a good look at the person or the car due to the thick foliage. Visibility was further hampered by the fact the single light in the parking lot burned out two or three months ago and hadn't been replaced. As the car passed under the street light at the far end of the park, however, he got enough of a view to see it was a dark color, either blue or green, and was an older model sedan like a Honda, Toyota, or maybe a Nissan. He pulled his cell phone out of his pocket and dialed 911 to pass on what he'd seen.

Fitch slowed down when he was out of the immediate neighborhood so as not to draw unwanted attention to himself. He was on an adrenaline high and needed to calm his nerves. He reached over, got his traveling companion out of the backpack, unscrewed the cap, and took a couple long gulps. The familiar warmth began to work its way through his body as his heart rate slowed.

About ten blocks from the park, Fitch heard more sirens and assumed they were headed to the Johnson residence. A minute later, a police car sped past him in the opposite direction with lights flashing and siren screaming. Fitch pulled over to the curb and stopped to let it pass. A few seconds later, an ambulance raced by in the same direction as the police car. Although he wanted to just keep going, Fitch again pulled to the curb to let it pass. This was no time to risk getting pulled over for a traffic violation: especially with a rifle and booze in the car—and his face smeared with mud.

Fitch accelerated and continued down the road after the ambulance passed. He needed to find a place to pull over, regroup, and plan his next move. Davidson still had to be eliminated before he could head back to L.A., take care of Trudy, and rethink his life. So far, everything seemed to be falling into place just as he'd planned. Fitch believed that by the time Theresa returned home all this mess would be behind him, and he'd come out of it unscathed.

Two more cop cars flew by him with sirens wailing and light bars ablaze: others could be heard approaching the scene in the distance. Fitch again moved on after making the obligatory curbside pause. A few blocks farther down the road, he turned onto a side street that ran through a peaceful residential neighborhood. A couple of blocks in, he found a dark, secluded section of the street and stopped the car under a large jacaranda tree.

Surrounded by quiet darkness, Fitch felt a heavy fatigue wash over him, spawned by the stress of the day. He thought about reclining his seat and catching a nap before finishing his San Diego errand but realized he couldn't waste precious time with sleep. There'd be plenty of time for that when his mission was accomplished. He felt ravenous after the energy he'd expended taking care of Max and took the last of the almonds, apricots, and snacks out of the backpack. The snacks were interspersed with sips of bottled water, and he almost began to feel normal.

Fitch rested his head on the seat back and closed his eyes for a moment. Within a minute or two, his bladder reminded him of its existence and the need to be relieved. He got out of the car, checked for little girls or other observers, and gave the jacaranda a good watering.

Back in the car, his mind turned to Davidson and how he was going to find him. He thought about going to the Johnson law firm in the morning and waiting for him in the parking lot. But it would be daylight, and other people were sure to be around. That was too risky, and he didn't want to wait that long. He needed to take care of Davidson in the dark, in a more secluded place. Then it dawned on him. He had Trudy's cell phone. Maybe, just maybe, Davidson had given her his address in one of his messages, or she had included it with his contact information.

Fitch felt around in the backpack until he found Trudy's phone. He turned it on, opened her contacts list, and pushed the button next to Davidson's name. *Bingo.* There it was. Davidson's home address along with his phone number. He punched the address into his cell, and a map with directions to Davidson's place popped up almost immediately. A smile cut Fitch's face. *Ya just gotta love technology.*

A renewed sense of energy pervaded Fitch's body and psyche as he started the car and pulled a quick U-turn to follow the directions on the map.

57

Sunday was warm and cloudless in San Diego as Tom started up his rust bucket and headed over to Jan's. He hoped to not only evade any potential threat from Fitch, but to spend some quality time with the woman he'd been fantasizing about for three-plus years. He worked his way over to Rosecrans Street and followed it toward the tip of Point Loma until he reached Nichols Street. He turned onto Nichols and made another turn half a block later into the driveway leading to Jan's condo complex. He found a spot marked VISITOR exactly where Jan said he would, and parked. Thankfully, the Bug didn't backfire when he shut the engine off.

It was 3:28 p.m. when Tom started up the walk to Jan's unit. The door was open, and Jan was standing on the threshold with her hair in a pony-tail, flashing that perfect smile, and wearing a spa-ghetti-strap T-shirt and skintight jeans. The sight of her made Tom pause—*God. Is she beautiful, or what?*

"Hi, Tom. I'm so glad you're here. I've been worried about you ever since you called."

Jan threw her arms around his neck and gave him a long, tight hug. Tom dropped his suit case, slipped his arms around her waist, and pressed her body against his. She melted in his embrace. "Yeah,

I'm really glad to be here too, Jan. Thanks for having me."

The hug ended, and Jan grabbed Tom's hand, leading him inside. "Come in. It's so good to see you." Tom reached down with his other hand, collected his suitcase, and followed his fantasy woman into her home.

The place was exactly as Tom imagined it would be, a vase of fresh flowers on the coffee table, another on the kitchen counter, and feminine touches everywhere. The condo even smelled feminine: like a mixture of lavender potpourri, Chanel perfume, and fresh-baked bread. There was something to be said for a woman's touch.

Tom carried his suitcase into the guest bedroom, then joined Jan in the kitchen. She was busy getting things out of the refrigerator, and asked, "You hungry?'

The thought of eating drew Tom's attention to his empty, gurgling stomach. "Yeah, I am actually. I've been so concerned for Trudy and distracted by the detective's phone call, I forgot to eat lunch."

"Well, how does a ham and turkey sandwich sound?"

In a feeble attempt at humor, Tom said, "I don't know. I've never heard one."

Jan dropped the bread she was holding, turned to Tom, and bursting with laugher, said, "Oh my God, that's great. You're a veritable comedian."

Tom grinned from ear to ear, and in a feigned, cocky-sounding voice, quipped, "I know. It's a gift. Been passed down through the family for generations. I'm just the latest in a long line of comics."

Regaining her composure, Jan finished preparing lunch: ham and turkey on rye with Dijon mustard, mayo, tomato, cucumber, lettuce, and slices of dill pickle on the side. They settled at the kitchen table and washed the sandwiches down with ice-cold Coronas and wedges of lime.

After lunch, they decided to go for a walk around the harbor. Jan slipped out of the sandals she was wearing, put on a pair of tennis shoes, and they headed out the door. They walked through a neighborhood of high-priced homes that backed up to the water along Kellogg's Beach, then passed by the San Diego Yacht Club, and onto Shelter Island. A gentle breeze was blowing in from the ocean, and white sails dotted the harbor as weekend sailors took advantage of the day. Half way through their walk, Tom reached over and took Jan's hand in his, hoping she wouldn't resist. She didn't.

They strolled on at a leisurely pace, talking about whatever came to mind, and getting to know one another: the same thing lovers of all ages have done since forever. By 7:35 p.m. they were back in Jan's condo, ensconced on the living room sofa, sharing a bottle of Merlot, and ready to watch *The Notebook*. It was a film Jan had seen several times but never grew tired of, and she always wound up needing to dab her eyes with tissue at the end.

They were holding hands part way through the movie, and when it was over, Tom had his arm around Jan, and she was resting her head on his shoulder. The closeness felt very comfortable, and right. As the credits rolled, they chatted briefly about the movie before both leaning in and experiencing their first kiss. It was warm, tender, and the perfect first kiss. As their lips came together for a second kiss, Tom suddenly stopped and said, "Damn!"

Wondering what had broken the moment, Jan asked, "What is it?"

"I left my cell phone back at my place. Detective Banning asked me to let him know as soon as I found somewhere to stay so the cops could locate me if necessary. I've got to run back and get it."

"I'll go with you."

"No. Stay here and be comfortable. My VW bomb is not the best ride. It's only nine forty-five. I'll grab my cell and be back in thirty minutes." With a faint smirk on his face and one raised eyebrow, Tom continued with, "Stay in the moment and we can pick up where we left off."

Jan pressed her face to his, softly licked his lips with her tongue, and smiled. "You got it."

Tom gave her one last kiss, stood, and walked to the door. As he was closing it behind him, Jan called out, "Be careful."

58

As he turned back onto the main drag heading out of Point Loma, Fitch lifted the bottle of Jack to his lips and found it empty. He apparently didn't get the top secured the last time he'd taken a drink, and the remaining contents had leaked out onto the passenger seat. As luck would have it, a large, green neon sign flashing LIQUOR appeared two blocks down with an arrow pointing to a white cinder block building bordered on three sides by a trash-strewn, gravel parking lot—unusual for typically well-manicured Point Loma. He parked in a spot near the entrance and entered the store. A Middle Eastern-looking man stood behind the cash register wearing a white linen turban and sporting a full salt-and-pepper beard.

Fitch found the Jack Daniels display near the back of the store, grabbed a pint, and walked to the register. He selected a pack of spearmint gum from the rack in front of the register and set it on the counter next to the whiskey. The clerk eyed him suspiciously, and in a deep, heavily accented, smoker's voice, asked, "Are you OK?"

Fitch looked up from getting money out of his wallet and said, "Yeah. Why?"

"I was just wondering. You have dirt smeared all over your face."

Having forgotten about the dirt, Fitch raised a hand to his cheek and said, "Oh, uh, I forgot. I was playing paintball with some buddies earlier."

The clerk took Fitch's money, and without counting back the change, laid some bills and a few coins in his hand, then closed the register. Fitch noticed the security camera pointing down at the front counter as he walked to the door and wondered if it was working. He didn't like the idea of being on camera, even though it probably didn't make any difference since the cops had no idea he was in San Diego, let alone responsible for Max Johnson's death. Nevertheless, he looked down at the floor as he exited, just in case there were other cameras watching him.

Fitch got back in the car and immediately opened the bottle. He took a long swig before carefully securing the cap and tucking the bottle back in the knapsack. He unwrapped the gum and popped a piece in his mouth before tossing the rest of the pack in the center console and driving out of the lot. Hopefully, the gum might mask the smell of alcohol on his breath in the unlikely event he was pulled over by the cops. There was nothing he could do about the wet seat except to keep the windows rolled down and the air circulating.

Fitch kept an eye on the GPS as the map and accompanying voice directed him east on Rosecrans, through the Point Loma business district, and on toward the destination address he'd entered for attorney Davidson. He passed the Old Town Trolley station and turned left to cross over the San Diego River to Linda Vista Road. He'd only gone a short distance up the road when the GPS lady told him he was approaching his destination on the left. Fitch slowed and turned onto a dead end-street that took him up a slight hill, ending in the parking lot of Davidson's apartment building. He backed into an isolated spot that was overhung by trees and as far away from the lights of the building as he could get. He cut the engine, turned off the headlights, and sat surveying the area. Almost all the parking spaces were filled, and light shone from most of the windows overlooking the lot. It was Sunday night, and most people had wrapped up their weekend fun. They were at home relaxing and getting ready to start a new work week.

Fitch checked the address in Trudy's contact list and saw that Davidson lived in Unit 15. He looked up and saw the number 15 affixed to a door in front of him and slightly to the right. That had to be the one. It was one of the few units devoid of light. He reached in the backpack, retrieved the .38, checked to make sure it was loaded, and set it on the center console. Touching the gun sent a chill through Fitch's body, so he brought out his faithful friend Jack to help boost his resolve.

After a couple swallows of whiskey, Fitch looked left and right to make sure the coast was clear and got out of the car. He slipped the revolver in his front pocket and walked to the far end of the building, checking each apartment as he went. When he reached the last parking spot, he moved closer to the building and again scoped out each unit as he returned to the car. The blinds were partially open at Unit 15, so Fitch slowed his pace and glanced into the unit. He didn't see any light in the unit except for a red glow that appeared to be the digital readout of an alarm clock.

He got back in his car, disappointed he hadn't found Davidson, but confident he'd appear in time. And when he did, Big Daddy Fitch would be waiting. He took another sip of whiskey and was tempted to turn the radio on and blast heavy metal to get himself pumped up. The temptation passed, however, as he realized the loud, pulsing beat of the music would probably draw unwanted scrutiny. Instead, he reclined the front seat a bit and leaned back while keeping his eyes glued to Unit 15.

Fitch noticed a young couple in their twenties walking in front of the apartments in the direction of Unit 15. He sat up, wondering if the young man was Davidson. They walked past Unit 15, got into a small pickup truck, and drove off. Fitch turned the radio on to a heavy metal station, adjusted the volume so as not to attract attention, and leaned back in the seat. The music would help to keep his energy up even if the volume was low.

A few minutes later, car lights briefly flashed across Fitch's windshield as a car drove up the hill and turned into the lot. Fitch slid farther down in the seat to avoid being seen: his eyes glued to the approaching vehicle. The car, a beat-up old VW Bug, slowed and made a turn into Space 15. Fitch felt his muscles tighten as his heart rate elevated and his breathing became more pronounced. A young man got out, walked to Unit 15, and went in. A light flicked on, throwing a bright, white shaft through the opening in the blinds and onto the sidewalk in front of the unit. Fitch sat there, motionless as a cat about to pounce, contemplating his next move. He wondered if he should approach now or wait until later when most people would be sleeping, and he could catch Davidson zonked out. Later there would be less chance of people driving in and out of the lot. But what if Davidson decided to leave and drive off? Fitch didn't believe that would be a problem because he was sure he could take Davidson out before he got in his car.

Fitch decided to bide his time and strike at a more opportune moment. After all, his prey was trapped. He relaxed his muscles, reached for his friend Jack, turned the music up a touch, and leaned back in the seat: all the while keeping his eyes on Unit 15.

59

Tom turned on the lamp next to the sofa before heading to the refrigerator to grab the rest of the Gatorade that was left after his run on Saturday. He took a couple of swallows, put the bottle back in the refrigerator, and walked into the bedroom to get his cell phone. He switched on the bedroom light and immediately saw his phone wasn't on the dresser where he usually kept it. It wasn't on the bed, the night stand, or anywhere on the floor. He even checked under the bed. No phone. Tom thought for a moment, then remembered he'd been in the walk-in closet to get his suitcase and some clothes. He walked into the closet and found the phone on the bottom shelf where he'd left it when he got his suitcase.

Tom sat on the edge of the bed, turned on the phone, and located the detective's number. He almost didn't make the call when he realized it was already after 10:00 p.m., and the detective was probably off duty. But the detective had specifically requested Tom give him a call when he'd relocated, and given the seriousness of the situation, would most likely want Tom to call no matter what the hour. Tom tapped the detective's number and sat looking around the room to see if there was anything else he might want to take back to Jan's.

His call was picked up on the fifth ring, and Tom could hear sitar music playing on the other end of the line. A man's voice answered with, "Banning."

"Detective, it's Tom Davidson in San Diego. Sorry to call so late, but you asked me to contact you when I found a place to stay."

"It's OK, Tom. I'm glad you called. Where are you?"

"I'm at my place right now. I came back to get my phone."

"Listen, Tom, get out of there right now and go back to the place where you'll be staying. I got a call from my counterpart in San Diego about thirty minutes ago. Senator Johnson has been shot."

"Oh my God."

"We're pretty sure it was Fitch. And Tom, Trudy said she put your contact information on her phone. So if Fitch has it—and we're almost certain he does—he can find out where you live."

Tom stood up and started turning off the lights in his apartment as he gave Banning Jan's name, address, and cell number. He turned off the light next to the sofa and told Banning he was walking out the door and should be back at Jan's in about fifteen minutes. They both hung up as Tom opened the door to his apartment and stepped outside.

There was a chill in the air Tom hadn't noticed earlier. He stood scanning the parking lot as a quiver ran through his body. Not noticing anything out of the ordinary, Tom turned and walked toward his car. What he did not notice, however, was the man who stepped out of the dark-colored Toyota parked under the overhanging trees on the other side of the lot.

Tom made it to his car, opened the door, and was about to get in when he felt a hard object press into his lower back, and a rasping voice said, "Don't turn around." Tom was pretty sure the hard object was a gun and sucked in a short breath as he felt his knees weaken.

The object was jabbed harder into Tom's back as the gravelly voice, almost a whisper now, said, "We're going back to your apartment. Do you understand?" The strong smell of alcohol pervaded Tom's nostrils as he rapidly nodded that he did. A hand grabbed Tom's shoulder and turned him toward the building as he heard the command, "Move."

Tom walked toward the sidewalk running along the front of the apartments. He stepped over a cement curb that had been placed in front of each parking space to prevent cars from driving into the building. By the time he'd taken two more steps, Tom heard a dull thud behind him as Fitch's foot hit the cement curb. Fitch tripped and smashed into Tom's back. Tom lurched forward but stayed on his feet. He turned just in time to see Fitch land face first on the sidewalk: the gun he'd been holding flew free and skidded about ten feet away.

Tom wasted no time in deciding what to do. He turned and ran as fast as he could toward the gravel road at the far end of the parking lot. Residents used the road to leave his complex and access the main street. When he reached the gravel, Tom glanced over his shoulder and saw Fitch had retrieved his weapon and was starting after him. Seeing Fitch in pursuit provided Tom with even more adrenaline, and a surge of energy. His already fast pace quickened considerably.

Fortunately for Tom, Fitch turned his ankle when he fell and was only able to execute a hobbling run. That gave Tom a decided advantage. He had to keep a sizable distance between himself and Fitch, however, because the revolver gave Fitch a considerable advantage of *his* own.

Tom ran up the main street to the stairs leading up the hill to the University of San Diego campus. He took the stairs three at a time and found himself on the road running behind the law school. This was familiar territory to him. He'd gone up and down those stairs many times during his three years at USD. He looked left and right, trying to figure out his best move, as he heard Fitch starting to make his way up the stairs. The campus police offices were to his left, so he headed in that direction. When he reached the security building, Tom tried the door, but it was locked. He pounded on the door but got no response. It was summer, so the campus security force was at a minimum. There was most likely only one officer on duty at that time on a Sunday night. He or she was probably making their routine hourly circuit through the campus.

Tom frantically looked around for the best escape route. Knowing Fitch would soon be right behind him on the road he'd just run down, Tom decided to head toward the greenbelt that passed through the center of campus. Perhaps he'd see the security officer making rounds. Tom sprinted through the grassy area between the security building and the science building. He banged his shin on a wooden stake that had been driven into the ground to support a newly-planted tree. Although he hit the stake at a full-out run, he barely felt it. The fear-induced adrenaline surge kept the pain to a minimum.

Tom made it to the end of the lawn and pressed himself into a recessed area at the front of the science building. The stone surface of the building's facade was cool and felt good against his sweating back. He looked up and down the street, but there wasn't a single person in sight. *Did everyone really stay in their rooms on Sunday night?* He peeked around the corner of the building and saw Fitch standing in the road in front of the campus security offices, looking up and down the street. He must have seen Tom stop there.

Tom took a deep breath as he tried to decide his next move. He couldn't run to his right. That would put him in the open area between the buildings, and in clear view of Fitch. His best option was to keep moving to his left. As he scanned that way, he saw The Immaculata across the greenbelt and half a block down. It was a very large, beautiful church, and the most impressive architectural feature on the whole campus. A church seemed like the kind of place he needed right now. He looked up and saw the large statue of Our Lady of the Immaculate Conception mounted on top of the massive dome covering the far end of the church. Although he wasn't Catholic, he said a silent prayer as he made a dash across the open area toward the front door of the church. *Dear God, please, let the door be open. And please let there be someone inside who can help me.* Tom reached the massive bronze door at the entrance to the church and pulled on the handle. The door swung open and he rushed inside. *Thank you, God.*

On the other side of the greenbelt, Fitch was standing at the corner of the science building scanning for his prey. As he looked across at the church, he saw a familiar figure slip inside the front door and disappear.

The large door closed quietly behind Tom as he stood in the vestibule searching the dark to see if anyone else was in the church. His soft "Hello" echoed throughout the vast marble and glass interior. The gospel side wall of the nave was intermittently dotted with faint, multi-colored patterns as ambient light passed through the stained-glass Stations of the Cross located high above the side chapels on the epistle side of the church. The only other light came from the red sanctuary lamp hanging above the center of the altar and a couple dozen votive candles burning in the south transept. The place was deathly quiet.

Tom slowly walked down the center aisle of the nave, checking each side chapel on his left and right as he made his way toward the sanctuary. His tennis shoes squeaked on the marble floor as he walked: the sound magnified by the vast emptiness. When he reached the crossing, he checked the north and south transepts for any sign of life. Perhaps someone was in prayer and didn't hear him call out when he entered. No one. He was alone.

Tom passed over the crossing and went up the steps of the chancel leading to the high altar. His cell phone rang just as he reached the altar. The sound seemed to scream in the emptiness as the shrill ring ricocheted off the ceiling and walls, making him jump. He pushed the button to silence the ring as he pulled the phone from his pocket. Seeing Jan's name on the screen, and in a voice barely above a whisper, Tom said, "Hi."

Jan's cheery voice responded with, "Tom, where are you? I've been worried. I thought you'd be back by now. I ran out to get another bottle of wine, and I'm about eight blocks from your place."

Continuing in a whisper, Tom said, "I'm in The Immaculata on campus. Fitch is after me. He's got a gun and—" Tom heard someone at the front door of the church and immediately disconnected the call. He froze, staring at the door. When it began to open, he grabbed a large bronze candlestick from the altar, ran to the pulpit, and hid in the open space beneath it. He clutched the candlestick to his chest and felt his heart pounding. He slowly poked his head around the side of the pulpit and saw Fitch's dark form standing in the vestibule, gun clutched in his hand, and his head turning from side to side in search of his victim. Tom reached in his pocket and turned his phone off in case Jan called back.

Fitch moved down the aisle, scanning left and right for any sign of Davidson. With each step, his shoes made a screech that bounced around the dark void, sounding like the cry of a distant eagle circling high above a doomed rabbit. When he reached the crossing, the flames of the votive candles suddenly caught his eye. Startled, Fitch's head snapped to the right and he pointed the .38 into the south transept. There, standing on his head in the center of the transept was the glowing red Satan that had been following Fitch all day. Seeing the sinister apparition, Fitch recoiled violently, involuntarily squeezing the trigger on the revolver. The roar of the small weapon sounded like a canon inside the vast, empty church. Tom jerked backward, banging the candle stick against the side of the pulpit. He froze, but it was too late. Fitch heard the thud of bronze against wood and spun to his left with his gun pointed at the pulpit. After a moment, he let out a soft chuckle, and in a diabolical voice, said, "Well, well, well. Mr. Davidson, I presume. Looks like we meet again."

USD campus police officer Clarice Riley was making her rounds and patrolling past the front of The Immaculata when she heard a gunshot from inside the church. Having served two tours of duty in Iraq before retiring and joining the campus police force, there was no doubt in her mind about the origin of that sound. She drew her 9mm service pistol from its holster and quickly made her way to the front door of the church.

Fitch stood at the top of the crossing, and yelled, "Come out now, Davidson. Keep your hands above your head. And don't make me ask you again."

Terrified and shaking violently, Tom crawled from the security of the pulpit. He stood facing Fitch with his hands in the air. He assumed this was where he was going to die.

Fitch lowered his voice, but in hate-filled tones said, "So, Davidson, you thought you were going to take me down? Well, guess what," then yelling again, he shrieked, "You're not." He raised the .38 revolver and pointed it directly at Tom's head. With unexpected calm, he said, "Good bye, Mr. Davidson."

At that moment, the front door to the church flew open. Officer Riley stepped through, and yelled, "Drop the gun!"

Fitch wheeled toward the door with his gun pointed right at Officer Riley—a fatal mistake.

In the time it takes to blink, Officer Riley fired four shots: only one missed its mark. One bullet hit Fitch in the upper abdomen, another pierced his lung, and the last one entered his head through the left eye. Fitch continued to stand for a moment then released his grip on the .38 as his legs buckled and he collapsed to his knees. His life had ended by the time he did a face plant on the marble steps of the chancel.

Officer Riley moved quickly up the nave, keeping her gun pointed at Fitch until she reached his body and confirmed he was dead. She looked at Tom who was still standing with his hands above his head, and asked, "Are you OK?"

As emotion swept over him, Tom dropped his arms to his sides and in a shaky voice, replied, "Yes." He slumped to his knees, and placing his hands flat on the floor with his head bowed, began to weep.

Distant sirens could be heard as the front door of the church opened, and Jan's form appeared silhouetted against the ambient light of the distant city. The pistol she was permitted to carry, and always kept in her car, was gripped in her right hand. She could see in the dim light cast by the sanctuary lamp that Tom was down on the floor. As she ran up the nave, she cried, "Tom! Tom, are you alright?"

Tom looked up and couldn't believe what he was seeing. There she was—the woman he'd been crazy about ever since first laying eyes on her, and only a block from this very spot. He sat up as Jan dropped down next to him and grasped him tightly in her arms. They rocked back and forth holding one another: tears of joy and released emotion flowing down their cheeks. Jan cupped Tom's face in her hands, and as their eyes locked, said in a trembling voice, "Oh, Tom. I was so worried." She pulled him toward her, and their lips met in a soft, deep kiss as uniformed officers rushed through the front door and took control of the scene.

FREE COPY OF THE VISITOR

Visit <u>www.stephenrossauthor.com</u> for a FREE copy of my suspense/thriller short story "THE VISITOR" and Notice of New Books/Sales

~THE VISITOR SYNOPSIS~

The morning broke like every other in the small Midwestern town of Porterville: quiet and peaceful. It's a farming community where church basement potlucks and Sunday drives in the country are the main sources of entertainment. Nothing much ever happened there until the arrival of the visitor.

Eighty-six-year-old resident Ima Plummer could not have imagined how her day would end when she awoke that fateful Wednesday.

You won't want to stop reading.

ABOUT THE AUTHOR

Stephen Ross practiced law until retiring in 2017.
His first novella, MEMOIR FROM HELL, received
the 2019 Reader Views Reviewers Choice Award
and the 2019 Independent Author Network Book
of the Year Finalist Award. It was praised by Reader
Views as "realistic and genuine ... the ending is
dramatic and haunting," and by author Anthony
Avina as "an emotionally charged novel that needs
to be read." Stephen's other work includes, POW-
ER LUST, a legal and political thriller set in California, and a supernatural thriller, THE VISITOR.
Born in Iowa and raised in Nebraska, Stephen now
lives in San Diego, California. When he's not writing, he enjoys reading, hiking, camping, and movies.
He can be reached via his website at
www.stephenrossauthor.com on Facebook at
www.facebook.com/stephenrosswriter, on
LinkedIn at www.linkedin.com/in/stephen-ross-

639114105,   and   on   Twitter   at
www.twitter.com/stephenross48.

ALSO BY STEPHEN ROSS